LOST GIRL LAKE

A COZY MYSTERY

C.K. CRIGGER

CITY LIGHTS
PRESS
— LAS VEGAS —

Lost Girl Lake: A Cozy Mystery
C.K. Crigger

Paperback Edition
© Copyright 2018 C.K. Crigger

City Lights Press
An Imprint of Wolfpack Publishing
6032 Wheat Penny Avenue
Las Vegas, NV 89122

ISBN: 978-1-64119-192-0

LOST GIRL LAKE

CHAPTER 1

"Hey you! You work here or what?"

Truth Diamond snapped upright. Since she was bent almost double cleaning crud from beneath the fish-gutting station at the time, her head whacked the under-edge of the counter a dizzying blow. As if that weren't enough, an errant fish hook snagged in her thumb.

Blood gushed, bright red and profuse.

"Hey, you," the gravelly voice came again, "can I get some service over here?"

Wincing, Truth removed the hook and turned to face her customer. Middle-aged, burgundy-red faced and loud.

"Good morning, sir." She pasted a smile on her face. "Be right with—"

"Today," he interrupted.

He didn't seem to notice the blood dripping from her thumb. Wrapping a corner of her white linen apron around the injured appendage, she applied pressure.

A typical Monday, she sighed, rolling her eyes. On a cheery

note, get the bad stuff over early and the rest of the day should be a breeze.

And at least her tetanus shot was up to date.

~

"I WISH," Truth exhaled a gusty, irritated breath. "people like him would stay away from my resort."

It was a rhetorical remark, aimed at the tiny Pomeranian panting in the shade beside her. Not unnaturally, the dog made no reply, although judging by those little-pricked ears Truth thought she could if she wanted. And have plenty to say, too.

Truth spiked a drooping lock of platinum blonde hair from behind her ear with a fishy-smelling hand, scowling at the man's back as he hiked the cedar bark trail from the store up to the car park. He'd just paid a week's rent on a campsite, money always being welcome. But what a jerk.

Swooping in from the bluff on the other side of the Golden West Resort's bay, a gull circled over their heads, its raucous, complaining cry an example of what had roused her temper. The man's voice had a great deal in common with the bird's.

"Why," she went on, "does there have to be a jerk like him show up every week? And why does he always have to arrive first thing in the morning? Correction. First thing *Monday* morning, the very day Jason and Becca are likely to be late?" Her mouth pursed. "Just like they are today."

Jason and Becca Keene, teenage siblings, worked for her, when they bothered to show up.

The Pomeranian yawned.

As a businesswoman, Truth had no choice other than do as the man had requested. Oops. Another correction. Demanded. From where she stood at the end of the dock, she could see the empty space where he wanted to park his trailer. Sometime during the night, the battered pickup and scrubby camper previously occupying the plot had gone. Pulled out without notice and left a big pile of trash for her to dispose of. Several other good spaces were scattered around the resort. This guy could've parked his trailer in any one of them without fuss, but no. He had to have this particular one. And he wanted the trash picked up *pronto.*

She sighed. Why, just once, couldn't somebody choose a day other than when she was cleaning the fish-gutting station to be rude and annoying? The chore tended to provoke her irritability factor under the best of circumstances, especially since Jason should be doing it.

"Come on, pooch," she told the dog, resigning herself to the inevitable. "I suppose we'll have to jump to it. Customer service and all that jazz. It's what earns our dinner, after all."

The Pomeranian got up, shook out her creamy blonde fur —the shade an almost exact match for her mistress's hair—and pranced at Truth's side into the Golden West Resort store.

By the time Truth came out with a new pair of rubber gloves shielding her injured thumb and a package of stout garbage bags, the new tenant was already see-sawing his trailer back and forth in an attempt to position it on the site. Collecting a rake from the storage shed, she put her paraphernalia in a wheelbarrow and trundled toward him. He didn't, she noted, smiling evilly, seem very experienced at parking the twenty-seven-footer.

His frustration wasn't being helped by the woman with him. She'd taken a position outside the viewing area of the big SUV's rearview mirrors and was screeching conflicting instructions. A lipstick-stained cigarette drooped from her lips. The diamond in her wedding ring, which must've been at least four carats, flashed like sunlight off an Alaskan glacier.

It was just an impression, but Truth couldn't see the woman

being real cooperative about using the "butt cans" set prominently at every site. Setting Razz atop the load in the wheelbarrow for safety, she took a shortcut and steered across the park-like grass to the scene of confusion.

"Sir," Truth called, giving the distracted driver a wide berth. "Sir, if you'd steer your Suburban in the opposite direction you want the trailer to go, I promise it'll put you in the correct position. And back in slowly, please. You're getting a bit close to the motorhome on your right."

"I've been trying to tell him that," the wife huffed, earning herself a glare from her husband. "But will he listen to me? Of course not." She polluted the air with a lung-emptying final drag before dropping her cigarette on the ground and shredding it beneath a foot clad in high-heeled sandals. Her toenails, to Truth's amusement, were painted glistening black with a red heart in the center of each. Spoiling the stylish treatment, the back of her legs, starting at the knees, bulged with varicose veins in dire need of repair.

Unable to think of a diplomatic comment, Truth dodged around the trailer now headed right for her. Parking her wheelbarrow behind a sturdy tree in case the driver became even wilder, she started raking up trash. Razz jumped from her perch, weaving between Truth's feet as though guiding the business.

A grinding sound drew her attention from the job. The woman screeched again, loud, piercing, and vituperative. On the chance the husband had run over his wife, Truth glanced their way. He hadn't, but he had managed to catch the bottom of the trailer's door atop one of the stumps dotting the space. He got out of the Suburban leaving the door open, motor running, warning bell dinging, and tromped around to check the damage.

"Fer Pete's sake, Larry," the Mrs. squawked, "look what

you've done. Thirty-six thousand dollars for this stupid trailer and you have to run it over a stump first time out. Now what are you going to do, huh? Pull it off there and you'll lose the damn door."

From his expression, Larry knew what he wanted to do, but it wasn't legal, and he had a witness. "Shut your face, woman," he said. "If you'd stayed outta the way and kept your trap shut I'd've done fine."

He may have had a point, Truth conceded. Hiding her grin with iffy success, she tried to act as though she were both blind and deaf as she hurried through the raking. Jason's job, she noted again with some rancor.

Razz had no such constraints. She danced over to the action, yapping advice. Truth thought the dog was telling them both to desist before they disturbed the rest of the resort's customers, and ordinarily she would've agreed, but it was already too late. The couple's dilemma had drawn an audience.

Digbee Madden, one of her regulars, stomped up from the lake where he'd been fishing to watch the show, leaving his grandson, Pratt, on the dock. Pratt, she noticed, didn't bother to look up.

"Lady," Digbee said, staring at the woman's garish toenails with a reproving scowl, "give the man a break, why don't you? And be quiet. You're so loud you'll scare the fish."

The missus, who'd already lit another cigarette and flipped a still-burning match to the ground, sneered at him. "Know what you can do, don't you?" she said to him, and then to Razz, "Shut up, you stupid little rat, before I drop kick you into the lake."

Digbee turned scarlet as a poppy while Truth's amusement evaporated like spit on a hot sidewalk. Insult the clientele, would she? *Call Razz names and make threats, would she?*

Shifting uncomfortably, Larry kept his attention on the

stuck trailer as if pure desire might give it an extra half-inch lift. The couple from the endangered motorhome in the adjacent parking spot joined him.

Gritting her teeth, Truth ceased her work and leaned on the rake, the better to listen. Naturally friendly people, Ken and Mandi, the motorhome's owners, had been coming here weekends since fishing season started a couple months ago. They glanced at each other. Mandi nodded.

"I used to own a twenty-seven-footer before I bought the motorhome," Ken informed Larry, his expression commiserating. "Had a heck of a time parking it at first. Could probably give you a couple pointers if you wanted."

Figuring he was setting himself up for a snub, Truth appreciated his offer even if Larry didn't. But Larry surprised her.

"I'll give you fifty bucks to park it for me." He looked grateful. "Then maybe the old lady'll button her lip."

"Who you callin' an old lady?" His wife looked daggers sharp enough to slice liver at him. His liver.

"You, Fran, you. You're an old lady, like it or not!"

"Phooey with paying some busybody." His wife could've blistered paint with her fiery glare. "Get outta the way, both of you. I'll do it myself." She lunged toward the Suburban.

"Oh, be quiet, Fran. You can't even drive the truck."

Ken, fortunately, intervened. "Won't take a dime. RVers help each other out. It's the rule of the road."

Truth caught Mandi's eye roll, although she didn't think anyone else noticed.

"Are you sure you can do it without tearing off the door?" Mandi looked a little doubtful.

Ken grinned. "Guess we'll find out, won't we?" His stride jaunty, he slid onto the Suburban's driver's seat and put the automatic transmission into reverse. A tiny scraping sound warned him to shift to drive, and so he rocked the SUV back and forth a few times until the trailer door came free of the stump. Damage free, too.

Seeing all was well in hand as the men congratulated each other, Truth resumed her raking, hurrying to clear the space before Ken backed the trailer in. Consequently, Razz had to bark twice before Truth paid attention.

"What?" She nudged the dog with her rake. "Move, Razz. You're in the way."

Razz's sharp, piping yap became more insistent. Truth looked over to see the Pomeranian standing over an oddly shaped, blackened object. Even at a distance she could smell its ripe stench.

"It'll mean a bath if you touch that," she warned the tiny dog. Razz, notoriously, was not fond of bathing. Truth swept the stinking thing toward her debris pile with the rake. Only then did she recognize the object, or think she did, and at a second horrified glance, her stomach turned over.

"Stop," she hollered at Ken, who even now was easing the trailer into position to hook up to the space's electrical outlet.

He braked and stuck his head out of the Suburban. "Is something wrong, Truth?"

"Hurry it up," Fran snapped. "I need to use the bathroom."

"C'mon, miss," said the miserable Larry, whose vacation seemed already doomed. "I paid for the space. Let us in. You can finish raking later."

Truth, almost oblivious to anything they said, beckoned Digbee to her. The old man moseyed over, scowling as he went past Fran.

Digbee had been a patron of the Golden West Resort for a few dozen years longer than Truth had been alive. A fixture, who rented the best space in the resort by the year, only leaving when he went south for three months during the winter. This summer, his grandson Pratt, a man of some mystery, accompanied him.

Although just shy of becoming an octogenarian, Digbee's powers of observation had not deserted him, which was why Truth needed him now.

"What's the matter, sis?" He adjusted the bill of his Mariners cap against the sunlight as he peered at her.

Turning away from Larry and his wife, Truth, wordless, pointed at the object on the ground. Razz, still on guard, swished her fluffy tail. "Is . . . is that what I think it is?"

Digbee bent and poked a toe at it. When he raised up, his faded hazel eyes had widened. "It is if you think it's some-body's hand."

Truth gulped. "Oh, man," she moaned. "Shi . . . Cracker-doodles!"

The old man nodded agreement and stirred himself to kick through the other junk on the ground.

She noticed he avoided touching the hand. "What are you doing?"

"Looking for the rest of the body."

Behind them, a piercing shriek split the soft summer morning as Fran, charging forward complaining as she came, spotted Razz's prey. At the noise, gulls flew into the sky. Razz turned, yapped once reprovingly, then growled a warning.

Truth couldn't have agreed more.

CHAPTER 2

"Hush," Truth hissed at the screaming woman. She stuck a finger in her offended right ear to save some part of her hearing.

Fran teetered backward a step. Her mouth hung open, but at least the sound stopped. "What did you say?"

"I said hush." Truth gestured toward a four-seat swing set occupied by a trio of wide-eyed five and six-year-olds who, with uncanny osmosis had already figured out a crisis was at hand. One of them, a girl, pointed at the adults.

Truth's lips tightened. "As you can see, children are playing on the swings. I won't have them frightened by a lot of hysterical screaming." Never mind that she felt like indulging in a few squeaks herself.

The older woman's nostrils flared. "Larry," she said to her husband, her voice as raw as one of the dockside gulls, "did you hear what this little rip just said to me? She told me to shut up. What're you going to do about it?"

"She said 'hush,' Fran. And she's right."

Fran's eyes bulged; her face turned a queer puce color. It

must've been sheer surprise that kept her new outburst at a more reasonable decibel level.

Like a shadow, Digbee appeared at Truth's side and gave her a little nudge. "Think you'd better take advantage of the lull and call the cops."

Truth nodded. "I'll use the phone inside the store. Can you keep these people from tracking all over the place?" Her hands flailed as though fighting cobwebs. "I suppose there must be evidence or something, if I haven't already destroyed it."

"I'll manage," Digbee said. "Hang in there, Truth. Don't panic. Doesn't look like there's any great urgency about this." A wave indicated the mysterious object. "This didn't just happen today, or even yesterday or the day before, if I'm any judge. And now it ain't going anywhere."

Taking a deep breath, she eased it back out and felt a shade better. "You're right. It's just—" Whatever she'd meant to say lost, she cast a hesitant look at Sam, one of the bystanders, who came forward to join them at a gesture from his friend Digbee. Sam, at about three-quarters of Digbee's age, hunkered down, making a closer inspection of the hand.

Glancing at Mandi, Truth saw the other woman had turned a peculiar shade of greenish white yet couldn't seem to turn away. Then there was Ken, coming forward to slide his arm around his wife's shoulders, whereupon she gazed at him as if asking, "How'd this happen?"

Just what Truth wanted to know.

Next in line-of-sight were the intractable Fran and brow-beaten Larry. Then the three little kids, all too aware of something secret going on, and trotting toward them with all due speed. Her customers. Some of them her friends. It was her duty to protect them all. *Crackerdoodles!*

"I'll be right here, but you'd better hurry," Digbee said to her, then shifted his attention to Mandi. "Think you can head off those kids?"

Mandi blinked. "Yes. Of course."

Scooping Razz up and carrying the dog like a football beneath her arm, Truth headed off to the store. Restraining herself from racing across the grassy park, she settled instead into a fast, purposeful walk.

Hurry, like Digbee said, but she didn't want to be so obvious as to alarm everyone at the resort. The peaceful vacation atmosphere would change anyway once the police arrived. She shuddered, imagining all her customers packing up and demanding their money back on the way out. Especially those with families. Could she blame them?

The landline phone inside the store was the resort's only reliable source of communication, cell phone service being intermittent in the bowl-like bay. To make a wireless call you had to do one of two things. Either you climbed to the bluffs circling Lost Girl Lake, or you took a boat to the lake's center where you could sometimes latch onto a signal. She wasn't prepared to take either of those options.

To her dismay, she found Mrs. Thompson from lot seventeen waiting outside the store as she hastened up.

"You're late," Mrs. Thompson called, puffing. With eagerness or the stress of overweight?

"Sorry," Truth said. The store was locked tight since Truth's teenaged hired help had yet to appear. Renewed irritation scratched like an inner itch. Why couldn't those kids be on time once in a while? Today was already almost more than she could handle alone. She was too busy to take Becca's place behind the counter, or to sub for Jason renting out fishing boats from the dock.

If the cops didn't shut down her business.

Mrs. Thompson tapped the man's watch strapped to a

meaty wrist. "I've been waiting a full four minutes, my dear, which is terribly unfair of you since the smell of your baking has been tempting me for hours. Is it cinnamon rolls this morning, or does my nose deceive me?"

Said nose, a button nearly lost in Mrs. Thompson's roly-poly face, sniffed the air. The elderly lady had forgotten to comb her hair this morning and shorn white locks stuck out here and there in rooster tails. She wore a set of sweats straining around her bulges, and bunny bedroom slippers, all of which had seen better days.

"Your nose is correct." Truth gritted her teeth and tried to contain her impatience. "I've made my special walnut sticky buns."

She set Razz down, bid the dog a stern, "Stay," and fished the door key out of her cut-off's pocket. Inserting the key in the lock, she twisted it hard left before reversing to the right. The store had just celebrated its one hundred and fifteenth birthday and the door and lock were original to the building. Usually, she took a perverse pleasure in its ancient eccentricities. Today, they were simply more nuisances to deal with.

"I noticed that lovely boy, Ken, helping the new fellow with his trailer," Mrs. Thompson chatted on. "What a silly one he is. I heard that woman yelling, too. Some people just have no class at all, do they, dear? Gives you an idea of why they're called 'trailer trash.'"

Opening her mouth to say she didn't think that particular saying quite appropriate for the situation, Truth changed her mind. Initiating further conversation was *not* the way to go. Mrs. Thompson did love to gossip and if encouraged, thought nothing of talking away the whole morning. Truth had been caught in the old lady's trap more than once.

"Yes. Excuse me." Feeling as if she were wading through chest-deep water, Truth brushed past the woman. Leaving her at the counter, she crossed the worn, uneven floor planks and headed through a door into the kitchen. Razz frisked ahead of her.

"Half a dozen, Mrs. Thompson?" she called out.

"Better make it a full dozen, dear. I never know when some of the grandchildren will show up."

A phone extension hung on the wall beside the sink. Truth turned on the tap and, under cover of the gushing water, punched in 911, giving information in a low voice. The dispatcher, telling her to speak up, asked twice for the resort location, twice again for the nature of her emergency, until Truth wanted to scream.

The whole process seemed to take hours. Truth's sense of both urgency and annoyance grew.

"Deputy Ortiz knows us," she said. "Send him."

"Deputy Ortiz may not be available," the dispatcher, a woman with a snippy voice, countered. "I'll send whoever is nearest to you. Meanwhile, keep everyone away from the scene."

"That's what we're doing." She hung up, hardly reassured. Whoever is nearest the resort. Did that mean the dog catcher? And when? Today or tomorrow or—?

A picture of that twisted little hand, tendons shrunken, fingers blackened and curled, filled her mind as she lathered and rinsed her own hands, and donned plastic gloves. Concentrating on placing a rack full of rolls into a Styrofoam container, she looked up to find Mrs. T standing in the doorway, almost drooling at the sight of the soft, walnut-caramel topped rolls.

Even so, the woman wasn't completely overwhelmed. She studied Truth with a worried expression. "I heard you on the phone. Did you say something about needing a deputy, dear? What's wrong?"

Truth shook the gloves from her hands. *Hands. Two of them. Who, out there, was minus one?* "I'm afraid you heard correctly, Mrs. Thompson. Razz has found a . . . uh . . . an object the police need to see. Nothing to be concerned about."

Sometimes she didn't quite live up to the meaning of her name.

She needn't have bothered with evasion. Mrs. Thompson paid, then snapped the container open and extracted one of the gooey cinnamon rolls. "Yum." Her teeth closed on the treat. A beatific smile expressed delight. "I wish you had a bakery in town, dear. But then, I'd just be that much fatter. Well, must go. Toot-a-loo."

Clutching her purchase to her ample breasts, she stuffed the rest of the roll in her mouth and headed across the park to her motorhome, an older, though well-kept thirty-two-footer.

Even if her grandchildren did show up, Truth doubted there'd be any sweet rolls left for them.

Her call made, and the customer cared for, duty demanded she get back and let Digbee off the hook. It took unfair advantage to set him the task of guarding the hand, even though she figured his stomach was nowhere near as delicate as her own. The mere thought . . . erk.

Shutting Razz in the enclosed backyard where she'd be safe and out of the way, Truth relocked the store. Hurrying back to the campsite, Truth saw Mandi had delivered the little ones to their parents' camps, and now she and Ken sat under the canopy of their motorhome, watching from a distance. Somehow, they had persuaded Larry and Fran to join them, and glasses of what looked like iced tea were on a little redwood table. Larry's trailer, still partially blocking the narrow road leading to the other campsites, was no immediate cause for concern.

Bless Mandi and Ken. Customers—no, *friends*—like these made Truth's job so much easier.

She was almost to where Digbee and Sam, like a pair of Roman Centurions, stood guarding the dog's find against curious onlookers, when a tan Chevy Suburban embellished with the Washington State Fish, and Wildlife logo drove through the arched gate.

Help had arrived in the form of Hunter Blaine. Her heart gave a little anticipatory jump.

Following Hunter into the parking lot was an old Suzuki Samurai with a cut-down top and giant tires. Jason Keene sat behind the wheel. Becca, his sister, sat in the passenger seat hanging onto the roll bar with both hands. The Samurai squealed to a halt a scant six inches from Hunter's bumper.

Truth's employees, finally making an appearance. Her mouth tightened. Too bad Consuelo and Eddie Morales, her other set of part-time workers hadn't been on the schedule today. They always showed up on time.

The girl piled out, her long, dark brown hair twisted in knots from the wind. She glared at her brother. Spying Hunter, she batted eyes decked out in plum-colored eye shadow and enough mascara for three women at him and waved a languid hand to Digbee.

Truth, hurrying toward them, might as well be invisible.

"Hi, Officer Blaine," Becca cooed to Hunter before announcing, "I am never riding in this miserable darn dune buggy ever again. Look at my hair! Look at my clothes, covered in dust. There's a perfectly good road, but did my idiot brother think to use it? Nooo. We had to drive across every rock and creek and buffalo patty in the whole country."

One thing you could say about Becca—she was never at a loss for words.

"Sorry we're late," she added as Truth joined the group. "It's all Jason's fault."

Jason curled his upper lip at his sister and said, "How many times do I have to tell you? It's not a dune buggy; it's a rock crawler."

"Whatever." Becca shrugged.

Hunter, eyeing the mussed hair and nubile young body clad in skimpy shorts and even skimpier cami, acknowledged the girl with a little finger wave. "Is that thing even legal?" he asked Jason, his deep blue eyes glinting.

Before Jason could get started on his favorite subject, Truth interrupted. "Do you kids want your pay docked a half-hour, or do you want to stay late this afternoon?" Yeah, she was feeling a bit testy.

"Sorry, Truth. Stay late," Jason said over the top of Becca's, "Pay docked."

Truth figured they could work it out between themselves if they ever stopped bickering for long enough. She was just glad neither kid sensed the tension in the air or noticed the stiff way Digbee and Sam stood in the middle of a camping lot.

"Becca," she said, "three people are waiting outside the store. Please go open up right away. The cinnamon rolls are $10.00 a dozen." Her attention shifted to Jason. "As for you, somebody left a bunch of fish guts and a disgusting mishmash of worms and marshmallows in the bottom of number nine boat. It needs cleaning before we can rent it again."

"Yes, ma'am. Right away, ma'am." Touching fingers to forehead, Jason hunched his shoulders at being assigned this unpleasant task and departed at a trot.

"Sorry," Becca said again as she took the key Truth offered. She crossed her heart as Digbee begged her to save a dozen rolls for him. Turning to Hunter, she pouted her glossy lips and smiled coyly. "Want me to save anything for you, Hunter? Anything at all?"

Truth wanted to fire her on the spot, stopped only by her need of the girl's help. Hunter shook his blond head and winked at the girl.

With her young assistants dispersed to their appointed tasks, she took a deep breath and let her attention wander. Its course led straight to Hunter who, she acknowledged, made the butterflies nesting in her tummy lift off even under circumstances like these. Disgusting! She was as bad as Becca.

Officer Blaine straightened from his languid pose and fixed his disapproving gaze on her. "Why are you so angry with those kids, Truth? What's going on?"

"Angry? Who says I'm angry? But I pay them actual money to work for me. I get annoyed when they're always late."

"You didn't sound annoyed. You sounded downright mad."

"Hmph." Looking past Hunter's shoulders, she saw Digbee gesturing at her. "Hurry it up," he seemed to be saying, and she nodded.

"What are you doing here two days in a row, anyway?" she asked Hunter as she moved toward the campsite where the hand lay exposed. "You were here yesterday harassing my dock fishermen. Don't you have other lakes to patrol?"

Hunter moved along with her. "My presence might have something to do with a certain call to 911 asking for the first available officer. That would be me."

"I wanted a real cop," she said without thinking.

Hunter missed a step, his expression turning chilly.

"I'm cop enough for you. So, what's your problem, Ms. Diamond? Somebody steal a boat? Rob the store? Lose a kid?" Then he shook his head and answered his last question. "Not a lost kid or you'd have the whole resort in an uproar."

Truth, glancing over at Digbee, saw him waggle his

eyebrows. Officer Blaine wasn't one of the old man's favorite people, for reasons he'd never explained to her. She inhaled, breathing pine-scented air deep into her lungs before letting it go.

"Not a whole lost kid, anyway." The retort sharpened. "Just part of one."

Blaine's eyebrows drew together. "What are you talking about?"

"I can't even tell you. Razz—my dog—found something you have to see." She jerked her head. "Over there. Mr. Madden is standing guard over it. We didn't want any of the kids getting too close."

Blaine followed her the dozen or so steps to where Digbee and Sam stood trying to look as if they were merely chatting and enjoying the fine summer day.

Sure. Smack dab in the middle of an empty lot and back of an unparked, unattended trailer blocking the access road.

Digbee winked at her and stepped aside for the Fish and Wildlife man, gesturing with his arm like a magician's assistant introducing a new trick.

Hunter Blaine gazed down a moment before, using his toe, he flipped the hand over, some of the char from the fire in which it had been immersed coming off on his shoe. He stared down with a sick look on his face.

After that, events picked up their pace. Hunter called dispatch on his radio, which had the effect of prodding local law officials. Within ten minutes Truth heard sirens blazing out on the secondary road leading to the Golden West, announcing the imminent arrival of the cops—real ones.

Apparently, Officer Hunter Blaine had a better way with dispatchers than she did.

CHAPTER 3

"Hey!" A bare-chested man Truth didn't recognize—but since he yelled from within Dottie Amholt's trailer he probably numbered among her many boyfriends—poked his head around the screen door. "Are those cops coming here?"

"I'm afraid so." Truth blinked as he ducked back inside. She suspected Dottie's 'friends' weren't always on the up and up, but they at least stayed out of sight—for the most part.

The siren's wail drew most everyone within earshot from their various trailers, campers, motorhomes or, in a few instances, tents. Truth thought it must even be pulling boats in off the lake as the racket bounced off the rock bluffs like they were part of an echo chamber. To her surprise, even Digbee's grandson, the quiet and withdrawn Pratt Madden, reeled in his fishing line and hiked the path from the dock to stand beside his grandfather. His eyes were hidden behind mirrored sunglasses, but a slight tightening of his mouth showed reaction as he spotted the hand.

All in all, quite a crowd gathered to stare at Deputy Ortiz, his brown skin flushed a vivid maroon, as he stepped from the patrol car. The passenger door opened as well, revealing another man. He wore dress pants, a wilted white shirt, and a scowl, all accessorized by an automatic pistol in a shoulder holster. His attitude said he was the one in charge and nobody'd better forget it.

Hunter Blaine went to greet Ortiz, drawing the scowling man's disapproval down on his blond head.

"Detective Gunderson," the man introduced himself, loudly enough for everyone to hear. "You the one radioed in?"

"Yep. Got something here you'd better take a look at." Hunter drew the detective and Officer Ortiz over to where Truth, Digbee, Sam, and Pratt huddled around the hand in a protective wall. "These folks have made a kind of, um . . . grisly . . . discovery."

Truth sought to clarify Hunter's somewhat underwhelming explanation. "My dog discovered it actually, though I can't imagine where it came from in the first place. There's been no—"

Detective Gunderson cut her off by snapping his fingers. "Stop. If I need anything from you, I'll ask. Let me get a handle on this. Well, Blaine, where is this so-called *thing*?"

Much affronted, Truth gaped at him.

Hunter pointed down at their feet. "Right here."

Fingers curled, the hand lay palm up. The charred flesh, burned entirely through in one place, showed gray bone and blackened tendon. It reeked of rotted meat.

Truth's second look showed more sickening details than the first. The lone cup of coffee in her stomach eddied once again, and she swallowed as if a glob of fish guts was caught in her throat. Behind her, someone who hadn't previously seen the discovery gasped.

Gunderson, much as Digbee, and then Hunter had done earlier, poked at the object with his shoe. "What is it?"

"A hand." Truth burst out. "A human hand." Was the man blind as well as insufferably rude?

Gunderson snorted. "A hand, eh? Burned badly enough it's hard to tell exactly what it is. I wouldn't worry too much, ma'am. I'd say you folks are scaring yourselves for nothing. This is hunting country, isn't it? I expect we'll find this thing is a bear paw. They look just like people paws, or so I'm told. Takes an expert to tell the difference."

Truth shot a glance at Hunter, whose face had gone almost as red as Ortiz's. How could Gunderson have forgotten Hunter *was* an expert. Or had he forgotten? A peek at his smug face indicated not. She expected the Wildlife officer to defend himself, but that took the quiet, seldom-heard voice of Pratt Madden.

"First time I've ever seen a bear wearing nail polish and a ring," he observed, deadpan.

Gunderson's head jerked up. "Who said that?"

"I did." Pratt separated himself from his grandfather and Sam. He took off his sunglasses and tucked them in his shirt pocket.

"Who're you? What's your business here?"

Truth drew breath to utter explanations, or introductions, or something, but Digbee gripped her arm, stilling the impulse. Pratt was well able to speak for himself. Which he did, cool as the ice melting in Mandi's tea.

"My name is Pratt Madden. My business here is my own."

Seeing he was carrying a fishing pole with a silver and green lure sparkling where it hooked into one of the pole's eyes, Truth believed his business should be self-evident.

"I ask the questions, you answer them," Gunderson said. "That's the way this works."

Pratt shrugged. "Ask a question that makes sense and I'll

consider it." He turned away as if to return to the dock and his solitary fishing.

"Hold it, smart ass." Gunderson stepped in front of him and fixed Pratt with a steely gaze. "If this . . . thing . . . is what you say it is, I'll be making a list of every person here. You, mister, are heading up my list."

Something—a flash of dark eyes, or a twitch of jaw muscles—flickered in Pratt's lean face. Truth figured she wasn't the only one who noticed his reaction as Digbee's fingers on her arm tightened to the point of pain.

"Better have a good reason," Pratt said, as if it didn't matter much.

"Oh, I'll find a reason, all right." Gunderson touched the gun in his shoulder holster. "And it starts with your attitude." He turned to Deputy Ortiz who, having shared coffee at the resort cafe with Pratt Madden on occasion, looked embarrassed and miserable.

"Rodriguez," Gunderson continued, "get this man's particulars and run a background check on him. If anything *is* wrong here, I'll want to talk to him again. First, do the same for everybody else in this . . . " His gaze swept the resort, lingering a moment on the store's sagging roof. ". . . place. And see if any records are kept of previous customers. I'll want their names, too."

"My name is Ortiz," the deputy said, his voice soft and almost inaudible. "Deputy Joseph Ortiz."

Gunderson hadn't the grace to apologize. "I don't give a hoot if it's Barney Rubble. Just do what I tell you to do."

Truth'd had enough. "I don't know what's making you so obnoxious, Detective Gunderson, but there's no excuse for being rude. I'm certain everyone here is willing to cooperate. That's why I called. But—"

Gunderson snapped his fingers. "I'll get around to you soon

enough. You can say your piece then. In the meantime, stay back. I need to keep the facts clear in my mind. Now, who found the hand? And where?"

Chest heaving like a steam-powered engine, Truth was already deep in the mental composition of a letter to his superior. "As I tried to tell you, my dog found it mixed up with some trash I cleaned out of this site when the previous camper left."

"And?" Gunderson's fingers flexed.

"And what? That's all I know."

"Come now. You must've noticed more than that. That the camper?" Gunderson started toward Fran and Larry's trailer, thereby setting off a collective gasp. Larry's face turned a bright red as he jumped to stand protectively in front of his rig. Fran just looked belligerent.

"No, no, Detective Gunderson," Truth protested, trying to head him off. She didn't want Fran to explode, after all. And cause even more body parts? Not on your life! "These people just arrived. They haven't even gotten parked yet."

"And I don't want to park," Fran said. "I want to leave. Now." She turned to her husband. "Larry—"

Pratt twisted his left foot into the ground, but his aside to Ortiz remained cool. "Got some little girls staying here, Joe. Wouldn't want you to overlook them. And Truth's dog. The dog was first on the scene. Don't know how much sense you'll get out of her."

If glares came equipped with blades, Gunderson's would've sliced and diced Pratt. Truth wondered, especially in view of Pratt's general reticence, why he was egging on the surly detective. Although she must admit she enjoyed his refusal to buckle under to the officer's bad temper. If only she had as much nerve.

Deputy Ortiz, covering a twitch of his lips, shook his head

as if warning Pratt to silence. "I'll put in a call for a search party first thing, then get right on it," he told Gunderson. Suiting action to words, he set off for the cruiser.

"Search party?" Gunderson's scowl grew.

"To find the rest of the body," Ortiz said over his shoulder.

Gunderson glanced around as a tiny sound escaped Truth. "Yeah. Right. But bring me an evidence kit first," he ordered. "And a camera."

Gunderson snapped a few photos, but the physical act of inserting the hand into a plain, brown paper bag fell to Hunter Blaine. Gunderson, along with Truth, Pratt, and every other camper near enough to do so, watched as the Fish and Wildlife officer, with the aid of a stick, scooted the object into the sack. Carefully, he taped the bag closed and wrote on the outside. Ortiz was in the cruiser again, speaking into the radio.

"I want this site gone over with a fine-tooth comb," Gunderson told Hunter. "And it looks like you're elected. Be quick about it so I can cancel the search. I'm guessing we'll find the rest of the body buried under the fire pit. Blaine, you borrow a shovel from the resort and get busy digging." Prepared to supervise, he perched on the stump Larry and Fran's trailer had been stuck on a mere half-hour ago.

Truth hoped the sap had been stirred up enough to gunk Gunderson's fat heinie with pitch. She nearly laughed out loud when Hunter made a big show of eyeing the Fish and Wildlife patch on his sleeve.

"Seems you've claimed the crime site, detective," he said with an ironic arch of one eyebrow. "Which means it's your shovel work."

Gunderson opened his mouth. Closed it again—and torched Hunter with a scathing look.

"No," Truth broke in, which earned questioning glances

from both Hunter and Pratt. "Nobody needs to dig in the fire pit."

Gunderson got back in form and snapped his fingers. "They do if I say they do."

What did he think she was, a dog in obedience training? She ignored the fingers. "You won't find a body buried there."

"And how would you know that, Ms. Diamond?"

"Because, as anyone can see, the bricks around the pit haven't been disturbed in months. Besides, this is one of our most open campsites, right on the path to the showers and restrooms. I hardly think—"

The fingers snapped.

"I hardly think anyone would chance burying a body in this particular fire pit," Truth's voice rose as she soldiered on. "Plus, there's been someone parked here every minute for the last three weeks." She turned to Blaine. "Hunter? I remember you ran a check on those guys' fishing licenses. Since they kept on fishing, I assume they were okay. Not the kind of people to bury bodies in my fire pit, anyway, since they stayed their full time—" She thought a moment. "And a day extra, for which they owe me."

Hunter smiled at her and nodded. "You're right, Truth. Their fishing licenses were in order."

"Maybe so, maybe no." Gunderson conceded the earth around the fire pit appeared undisturbed. "This hand might be older than three weeks. The coroner's office can tell."

"I think the medical examiner will tell you it's fresher than that." Hunter handed the filled and notated evidence bag to Gunderson.

"And you know that how?" Gunderson demanded.

"The flesh around the bit of arm bone. It's not burned like the fingers and palm, and the state of decomposition isn't all that far along."

"Bones buried a long time turn color. These haven't," Pratt added.

This earned him another of Gunderson's glares from under lowered brows. "What makes you the expert, hot shot?"

Pratt shrugged. "Lots of bones in Afghanistan, detective. Old ones, new ones, burned and buried ones."

Digbee, standing beside Truth, let out a slow breath and stared at the ground. He'd mentioned once that Pratt had left a part of himself there. Gunderson, for a change, refrained from remarking.

Caught up by the quiet horror she sensed behind Pratt's words, a cloud-light touch on her shoulder made Truth flinch. Turning, she found Dottie Amholt, her wide, sad eyes fixed on Pratt.

"Hello, Dottie." Truth tried to sound as if she weren't surprised to see the woman. "What can I do for you?" Dottie usually didn't get up before noon, yet here she was, dressed in respectable shorts and a t-shirt, her face scrubbed free of makeup, her brown hair done up in a long ponytail.

Dottie addressed Truth, although her message seemed meant for Detective Gunderson. "We seen the cops here," she said. "Then Mandi told me about you finding a . . . a piece of a body. And now, the detective. I mean—" Her gaze flicked once to Gunderson. "About where the hand came from. I think a coyote dragged it into camp. Me and my boyfriend came back from town late the night before last and we seen—"

"Yeah, yeah." Gunderson snapped his fingers.

Did he mean speak—or be silent? Truth wondered.

"Well, this coyote ran right in front of us," Dottie continued after a moment. "Darren had to stomp on the brakes really hard to avoid it."

"So?" Gunderson's impatience almost shook the air.

"The coyote had something in its mouth. When our brakes

squealed, it dropped whatever it was and took off." She glanced at Hunter and finished, "Dropped it right about here, I mean, just before it ran into the trees behind this campsite."

"So that's what made the holes in what's left of the skin," Hunter said. "Marks from the coyote's teeth. Makes sense." He eyed Gunderson. "This is good information, detective. Coyotes don't range too far from their dens, so the body is probably somewhere fairly close. She shouldn't be hard to find."

"Well, for . . ." Gunderson huffed until he was short of breath. "Why didn't you say so right away? Garcia," he bellowed without looking around for Ortiz, "put a call in for a cadaver dog. Looks like we'll have to traipse around this bit of heaven looking for body parts."

Ortiz, coming up behind Gunderson, made a throat-cutting gesture the detective failed to see. "Already done," he said. "The dog'll be here in about an hour."

Gunderson stared out over the brown bluffs overhanging the lake and, behind him, at the scabland hills dotted with basalt boulders and blue bunch grass. Timber only grew in any amount around the lake itself. "This is rattlesnake country, isn't it?" he asked.

"It is. Better find yourself some boots." Straight-faced, Pratt delivered the sage bit of advice.

"Thanks, Dottie," Truth thought to say before the other woman went over to Pratt and whispered something to him. His dark eyes softened, a smile touched his mouth, and he nodded. Curiosity aroused, Truth wondered what Dottie had said that amused him?

Why had he never smiled at her like that?

ORTIZ'S ESTIMATE of the search team's arrival was a little off.

More like two hours went by before a mud-splattered Ford F-250 drove up and parked in the shade of the huge old ponderosa pines bordering the resort parking lot. The driver of the truck, a lean man wearing hiking boots and a Boston Red Sox cap over his longish gray hair, went around to lift the canopy. A couple of hounds hung their heads over the tailgate.

The arrival of the search dogs brought the resort staff and patrons away from their scattered pursuits yet again. That included Truth, who'd been keeping an eye peeled for him. She stuck the gallon of potato salad she was making back in the refrigerator and, snatching Razz up under her arm, ran to the car park to watch.

Digbee emerged from his fifth-wheel to join her, as did Mandi and Ken. Fran and Larry peered from the window of their half-parked trailer, sipping something tall and cold and probably alcoholic, even if the sun wasn't yet over the yardarm.

Even Mrs. Thompson, rumpled and sleepy-eyed, waddled down from her motorhome to watch the dogs.

Pratt, to Truth's disappointment, was nowhere to be seen. She hadn't the nerve to ask Digbee about him.

"Where do you want us to start, Ortiz?" the cadaver dog guy yelled to the deputy over the dogs' eager howls. Ignoring Gunderson, he gave an abrupt nod to Hunter Blaine as the dogs, a blue tick, and a black-and-tan barely out of his puppy stage, jumped from the truck.

Ortiz waved him over to the campsite. "When'd you get another dog, Jack?"

"Training the pup for a man in Stevens County." The cadaver dog man was sparing of speech. Not so the dogs. Noses close to the ground, they caught a whiff from the paper bag, taking the scent. Immediately, they began baying and pulling at their leashes.

Meanwhile, Razz, although firmly controlled in Truth's

arms, raised a ruckus of her own upon the strange dogs' intrusion into her territory, making her displeasure known by her Pomeranian yap.

The hounds, tending to business, ignored the tiny dog. Hiding a wry smile, the whole process reminded Truth of Gunderson's attempt to take control of the search, and the way the dog handler brushed him off when the detective started issuing orders.

"Ortiz knows the drill," he said, eyeing Gunderson's shoes and shaking his head in disapproval. "You aren't dressed for tromping over this country, detective. Besides, you'd just get in the dogs' way. I'll take 'em out by myself. Ortiz and Blaine can follow us—if they can keep up. Anybody else will just confuse the scent trail."

"You'd better be right." It was easy to tell Gunderson, while relieved he wouldn't have to walk, didn't like taking orders, or even suggestions, from a civilian. "But watch your mutts. I don't want any damn dogs messing with my evidence."

"Mutts? Look, mister, if you don't trust me to know my business, I'll be happy to pack up my animals and leave." The dog guy spat on the ground at Gunderson's feet. "County'll owe me for my time and expense coming out here."

Truth saw Digbee hiding a grin under the guise of scratching his nose.

"No, no," Gunderson backpedaled, "You're here. You're on the job. Just watch it."

"Yeah, I'll watch it, all right. Which shakes both ways, mister." The handler played out the leashes in a signal to his dogs, the blue tick baying a deep, chest-rattling cry. Both dogs accelerated into a quick trot, ears almost dragging the ground as they searched out the scent. The man trotted too, keeping pace. Within seconds all three plunged into the trees beyond the campsite. A minute later, with the man being towed by two eager dogs, they all disappeared over the ridge in the direction of Truth's buffalo ranch.

"Well." Gunderson glared at Ortiz and Blaine. "What're you waiting for? Get going. Don't let that guy out of your sight."

The two officers set off jogging. Gunderson looked at his watch, then at Truth. "Believe I'll have a cup of coffee while I wait. And maybe one of those buffalo burgers you got advertised. I've never had buffalo. Gotta see if it's any good."

Truth, feeling too antsy to sit still, stared at him. A burger? She hadn't even started the grill yet. "How can you think of eating? What about the woman—girl—whoever she is?"

"What about her?"

"Well . . . I don't know. I'm sure the dogs will find the person the hand belongs to, but what about an ambulance? Shouldn't you hurry? Shouldn't there be—"

"What for?"

"What do you mean 'what for?' To take care of her, of course."

Digbee intervened. "Not much point in an ambulance, Truth. Or much hurry, either. The only thing they're apt to need is a hearse."

CHAPTER 4

PRATT MADDEN CAST HIS LINE SOARING A GOOD HUNDRED FEET out over the lake, lure glittering in the sun before it splashed into the still water. He propped the fishing pole over the edge of his tackle box, unconcerned that the line floated on top of the water and leaned against the bench's seat back. His objective here wasn't to catch fish. He could care less about the trout inhabiting the depths of Lost Girl Lake. The aim was to rest his mind and let the peace of the bucolic setting restore him.

Yeah, and keep his eyes open, senses alert, and never let down his guard.

The last couple years had been rough. First the stint in Afghanistan, the wounds, then the segue directly into this present enterprise. And that led to this latest problem, with the end nowhere in sight.

Closing his eyes to the giddy whirl of gulls in the cerulean blue sky, he welcomed the sun beating down on his face.

Right at this moment, he was glad he'd yielded to his Granddad's invitation to spend a couple weeks at the Golden West resort. Digbee Madden could be persuasive, not above playing the pathetic old man card. As Digbee said, "Even a man with a job like yours is entitled to a few days off every once in a while." Not that Pratt was ever truly off the clock.

What his granddad didn't know was that the invitation fell into place like it'd been ordained, a lucky convergence with his plans. Pratt would've been his guest, welcome or not.

He blinked his eyes open.

His granddad, upon occasion, could be a real piece of work. Take his insistence on Pratt's visit, for instance. Pratt had a notion his granddad was trying to set him up with the owner of the Golden West, only without Truth Diamond being in on the joke. Anyway, he hadn't had any trouble avoiding her. She worked too hard, too many hours, to have much time or energy for anything else.

He could relate. Why else was *he* here?

A corner of his mouth crooked up. Nope, Granddad was in line for a disappointment if he hoped Pratt and Truth would get together. Pratt noticed, even if the old man did put on blinders, the way she eyed the fish cop when he showed up to check her patron's licenses, as Hunter Blaine managed to do a couple of times a week. Excessive oversight, if you asked him.

A tug on the line rattled his fishing pole against the metal tackle box. Pratt grabbed the pole, set the hook, and reeled in a nice ten-inch trout. Smiling, he gently detached the fish and slid it back into the lake. Granddad hadn't caught on yet, but Pratt used barbless hooks and practiced catch-and-release. He wasn't much of a fish eater, lake trout least of all.

He was halfway into another cast when a woman's scream echoed from bluff-to-bluff across the bay. An explosion of birds sailed overhead, squawking alarm. His arm jerked.

"What the—" Pratt's lure plunked into the water a mere twenty feet from the dock. Leaping to his feet, he dropped the pole and cocked his head, listening. Seconds ticked by. After a while, when the scream was not repeated, his muscles relaxed, and he sat back down on the bench.

Jumpy. Yeah, he had a problem, all right. He had to remind himself every sudden noise didn't mean danger. Sound carried in a place like this. A woman's cry might mean nothing more than a hooked finger or an aversion to fish guts.

Like Truth Diamond's nose took on a kind of wrinkled, pinched look every time she came near the gutting station. Pratt's mouth twitched into a grin. Not that he'd ever heard her scream, but still. Easy to see why she hired Jason Keene and Eddie Morales to do the dirty work.

Picking up his discarded pole, he started reeling in his line, only for the mechanism to come to a hard stop. "Just great." His line had formed a massive hairball, kinked into knots.

Sighing, he opened his tackle box and prepared to perform surgery. At least he didn't have to catch any more fish. He could just sit here in the peaceful sunlight with the soothing lap of water against the dock's underpinnings, and wile away the morning.

Barely aware of cars and fisherman coming or going, he was ten minutes into the disentanglement procedure when a siren's quickly approaching wail reached his ears. His head snapped up. A dust cloud marked the progress of a car speeding toward the resort.

"Coming here," he muttered. Apparently, the scream he'd heard hadn't been because of a pile of fish guts. Faint excitement stirred as he tried his reel again. The recalcitrant line wound onto the spool and, gathering his gear, he settled sunglasses over his eyes and headed up the steps.

Not too fast. Don't want to look anxious, just curious.

He found almost the whole resort population gathered in a semi-circle at the first campsite. He went to stand at the edge of the little crowd.

His granddad, spotting him, motioned him over, whispering an explanation of sorts that Pratt didn't quite grasp. Something about Truth and her little mutt. He got it about the hand, though. An anomaly showing up where it had no business. And he got Truth's shaken horror, too.

Sheltered by the mirrored sunglasses, he studied the group gathered around the camping space. His alarm meter stirred, soaring up the scale.

The siren faded as the county sheriff's department cruiser came to a halt. Deputy Joseph Ortiz, whom Pratt had met in passing and with whom he was on easy terms, got out. The passenger car door slammed open, discharging another man. According to the man's body language, Pratt assessed him as trouble.

"Detective Gunderson," the man announced.

Hunter Blaine, already on scene, stepped forward to greet the detective.

An hour later Pratt made an excuse to his granddad and drove east toward Spokane. At last, movement on the case to report. It wasn't much, a woman's charred hand, but something, call it a sixth sense, told Pratt this was the break he'd been waiting for.

CHAPTER 5

ABOUT FOUR IN THE AFTERNOON, TRUTH SPIED THE DOGS AND their handler walking down the middle of the road, making their way back to the resort. The hounds' tongues lolled from the sides of their mouths; the black and tan pup limped on a hind leg.

Jack, the dog handler, looked as worn as his canines. Upon reaching the car park, he let down the tailgate of his pickup and drew out two big stainless steel bowls, filling them with water from a cooler. He set the bowls on the ground and stood back for his dogs to drink.

"Oh, poor things," Truth told Razz who sat on her haunches and growled. They were on the store's front porch where Truth was deadheading overflowing petunia baskets. "Don't you give them a hard time, missy. They've been working."

Abandoning her gardening chores, Truth hurried across the grassy picnic area toward them, Razz prancing beside her. "Did you find her?" she demanded as she drew near.

"Not a sign. Dogs lost the scent over by a pond." The handler dug a dripping bottle of iced tea out of the cooler and twisted off the cap, draining the contents in a single tilt. "Where's the detective? I suppose I'd better report." He tossed the empty into the back of the truck and found another full one.

"I don't know where he is," Truth said. "He left about noon without saying anything to any of us here. I think he'd been talking to Deputy Ortiz. Didn't he tell you?"

"He never caught up." The handler grimaced. "Ortiz is a good cop, but he's too fat. He couldn't keep up with my grandma, let alone me and the dogs. As far as the other guy, the game warden, well, maybe he was just trying to keep the deputy from having a heart attack." He tossed another empty into the pickup bed as the black and tan hound raised his leg on a rear tire. "Suppose I'll have to wait for the deputy to get back before I can go home," he groused. "Hope it don't take him the rest of the day."

Truth, warned by a little "whuff" from Razz, peered into the distance. "I don't think it'll be that long. They're on their way."

The handler, squinting at the deputies ambling along a half-mile or so out, spat into the dirt beside his truck. "No faster than they move, looks like you got time to build me a nice, juicy buffalo burger, rare."

Having already been left holding the bag for one of those today, Truth said, "I'll be happy to. They're $10.00 and include a scoop of potato salad and a pickle."

"Sold," he said and urged his dogs into their crates under the pickup canopy where they curled up and closed their eyes. Parked under the big shade trees, it was cool there, and he left the canopy open to catch the breeze.

Razz, ears pricked in what may have been disdain, watched, spinning to follow Truth as she headed back to the kitchen. Shaping a thick patty of buffalo meat, she slapped it on the grill where it sizzled enticingly.

The handler, who told her to call him Jack, judged the deputies' speed right on the nose. Truth had just set a laden plate, heavy on the pickles, in front of him when Deputy Ortiz and Hunter Blaine walked in. Sweat rolled down Ortiz's red face, the armpits and back of his shirt wet. Hunter, not quite in such dire straits, nevertheless flopped down on a stool at the counter beside the dog handler and panted, "Water, Truth, before I die. And I'll have one of what he's having, please." He pointed at Jack's plate.

Ortiz took the other side. "Ditto for me. Man alive, I'm dry enough my mama could grind my bones into flour for a tortilla."

"Ick." Truth broke into a smile. "Not in my café." She went into the kitchen where she formed more meat patties and set them to grilling. Inside a few minutes, the sleigh bells on the door chimed three or four more times, a summons for a subdued Becca to return to waitress duty from the kitchen where she'd been helping Truth prep tomorrow's menu. But when the burgers were done, Truth, not wanting to miss a word of any information they might let drop, brought the food out to Ortiz and Hunter.

Hers wasn't the only curiosity running rampant. The latest customers turned out to be Digbee and Sam, Mandi and Ken, and strangely enough, the newcomer, Larry. They ordered coffee, iced tea, and in Larry's case, a beer.

"So, did you find any more of the girl?" Larry asked Ortiz. "Any spare body parts?"

Ortiz, burger halfway to his mouth, shot Larry a quelling look. "No."

"What are you going to do now?" Mandi asked, eyes wide and her voice quivering.

Ortiz sighed and set his burger down. "Call out County Search and Rescue. If Ms. Amholt is right about what she saw, and a coyote dragged the hand in from somewhere else, we're apt to need a horse patrol, too, so we can cover more ground. And maybe the Eagle Scouts will lend a hand."

Hunter, swallowing a huge bite before speaking, nodded. "A coyote doesn't usually wander far from its den. This time of year, there may be pups to consider. I'm thinking the body won't be all that hard to find."

"Hard enough if my dogs couldn't scent her," Jack said, firing up in defense of his trackers.

"Nobody is faulting your dogs." Hunter held up two fingers in a peace sign. "I just meant it's hard telling which direction the coyote came from. We had a little windstorm out here last night, and scent doesn't hang in the air all that long. Now, if it'd been dragging the whole body—" Grimacing, he cut off his comment, looking guilty.

Digbee nodded. "This is rough terrain, too. Truth, is this all your land hereabouts, or is some of it Bureau of Land Management? Do you know where the coyotes den up?"

Truth wiped her hands on a dish towel and answered his questions in order. "This end of the lake is mine, along with three hundred acres pasture land. I also own one hundred and sixty acres at the other end. In between is BLM. That rocky hillside east of here is where the coyote's den. Out in the middle of the buffalo pasture."

Ortiz swallowed coffee. "We'll try there first, then. Sorry, Truth. There'll be people all over your property."

"I don't care as long as you don't leave the gates open," Truth said. "I just want this poor girl found. But don't turn the scouts loose on foot in the pasture, Joe. Buffalo are not the friendliest creatures in the world. The horse patrol will work better."

"Are you going to lead the search party, Hunter?" Ken asked.

Hunter shrugged. "Guess that's up to Gunderson. Where is he, Truth? Why'd he take off?"

She tossed her head. "I have no idea where he is. His phone rang, he answered, stuffed the last three bites of his burger in his mouth, and ran out to his car—without paying."

Ortiz studied his potato salad, picking out a chunk of egg to eat next. "Leaving me stranded." His expression turned glum.

Not that he remained stranded long. Using the radio in Hunter's rig, Ortiz called his dispatcher and, whether he spoke to Gunderson or someone higher up, before another hour passed, pickups and horse trailers began pulling into the car park and blocking the roads. Two or three of the resort's campers asked for and got permission to leave. The rest couldn't have been driven away by Indiana Jones and his bullwhip.

Much to Razz's displeasure, Truth shut the dog up in the backyard once again. Always fascinated by horses and in an attempt to announce dominion over them, Razz barked incessantly. In the quiet, Becca and Jason, having made up their half-hour tardy penalty, climbed into the Samurai. The sensibility of the vehicle proved itself as, to avoid blocking traffic, Jason drove the rock crawler over a high bank and cut across the country for home, dust roiling up behind its wide tires.

"I'll saddle up Uncle Harry," he told Ortiz before he left— Uncle Harry being his horse, not a relative— "and come back to join the search. I know this country like the back of my hand."

Which he did, Truth assured Ortiz. And inside the hour, which was as long as it took to organize the mélange of horses, riders, and a van load of Eagle Scouts, Jason was back, enthusiasm unimpaired, riding a bay horse and leading a sorrel. She was surprised to see Hunter Blaine mounting the sorrel in a fashion indicating horses were not his forte. As if by magic, the staging area cleared, leaving Ortiz alone in a county car monitoring the radio.

The Golden West campers returned to their various sites, or alternatively, gathered in quiet groups to talk. The store and café emptied. Another trailer pulled out, the camper not even asking for a refund for the six days remaining on his rent. Nothing Truth said swayed the man's mind against leaving.

"Can you assure me there isn't a serial killer on the loose?" He squinted at her through alcohol induced red eyes.

A good many answers flashed through her mind. *We found a hand, not a whole body,* for instance. And, *out of 5000 parts, a hand is only one,* like maybe it was a spare. *We don't know she's dead,* was another, even though the police seemed to consider it a foregone conclusion. For that matter, so did she.

"No," she said. "But there's no reason to think there is, either." The logic did nothing to dissuade him.

Digbee Madden and his pal Sam strolled away from the staging area. Soon she saw them with their fishing gear headed for the far dock and their evening quest for rainbow trout. Apparently, it took more than finding an errant human hand to sidetrack these passionate fishermen. And thank goodness for that. They provided excellent role models for some of the other fishermen and women.

Pratt Madden, back at the resort after being gone most of the day, climbed in his pick-up instead of joining the hunt and, after stopping to speak briefly to Ortiz, headed up the hill toward town once more.

Out on the lake, a breeze kicked up choppy waves. Gulls glided overhead, screaming as though angry and, for the first time since morning, Truth found herself alone. She went out back to rescue Razz, grown hoarse from a round of non-stop barking.

~

ONLY A FINGER of light remained in the sky when the searchers began straggling back to the headquarters Gunderson had set up in the Golden West's car park. Back from wherever he'd spent the afternoon, and looking more untidy than ever, even at a distance Truth knew he was reading Ortiz some kind of riot act.

Having kept an eye peeled for the searchers, Truth strolled out to the staging area to learn whatever there was to learn with Razz prancing beside her. She headed over to Jason first. Her employee wouldn't dare keep any news from her.

Jason, dismounted and standing under one of the tall yard lights with Uncle Harry's head hanging over his shoulder, jumped when she spoke to him from behind. "Did you find her?"

"Jeez, Truth, don't sneak up on a guy like that."

Uncle Harry, mane flying, flipped his head around as though agreeing with his rider, which made Razz growl.

"Well, did you?" She was pretty sure she knew the answer. There was no sense of a job well done going the rounds. Men and animals just looked tired, thirsty, and frustrated.

"Nope. Officer Ortiz called us in. It's getting too dark to see. He said we might miss something or screw up evidence bumbling around tonight." His brow puckered. "I'll probably have to miss work tomorrow. We gotta find this woman. Hope you don't mind."

"No problem. She's priority." Not that she'd tell him so, but she was actually proud of him.

Hunter Blaine, still astride Jason's other horse, rode over and stopped beside them. He hefted a leg stiff as a tree branch over the horse's back and thumped to the ground, expelling a held breath. "I hate riding," he muttered, "and I hate horses. And all this effort for nothing."

Truth gave the horse a pat and smothered a smile. Not at the nothing part, but because of his pained condition. "Jason told me. No luck, huh?"

He shook his head, kind of like Uncle Harry. "Lot of country to cover. We'll find her tomorrow for sure."

"If she's even here." Her attention drawn to the car where Ortiz and Gunderson were, to put it nicely, conversing, Truth rolled her eyes. "What's Gunderson complaining about now?"

"Thinks we should get some heavy-duty flashlights and head out immediately. He doesn't like the delay."

"Who does?" Truth sure didn't. The resort ran on a thin profit margin to begin with. If the camping spaces weren't full every day, the line narrowed even more. And families weren't going to enjoy camping where a body part had been found. One cancellation had been phoned in already, from a woman who'd heard about the search on the early news.

"Not a good idea," Hunter said. "People can get hurt, stumbling around in the dark."

"You're right, Hunter. I should've thought of that."

Gunderson's yell interrupted them. "Blaine, get your rear over here. I need you."

Hunter Blaine's eyebrows twitched—more of that pained reaction, although Truth guessed it was Gunderson's fault this time, and not the horse. He handed the sorrel's reins over to Jason. "Thanks for the loan of the horse, Jason. You better get home before full dark. Tomorrow's apt to be another full day."

"I'll be here at daylight." Jason latched a lead line to the sorrel's bridle and mounted Uncle Harry.

Truth put her hand against the horse's shoulder. "I'll call your mom and tell her you're on your way." She couldn't help worrying about the boy heading off across country alone during this kind of situation.

Jason started to protest, then nodded his head. Gigging Uncle Harry, he rode into the dusk, Razz scooting neatly out of reach of the horses' hooves. By the time Truth turned back to Hunter, she had found him already crossing the lot to join the group of men around Gunderson.

Picking up Razz and tucking the dog under her arm, Truth ambled toward them. The Golden West was her property, her home. She had a right to know what was going on. Nevertheless, instead of walking across the crunchy gravel, she kept to the grass where her footsteps were noiseless. She stopped behind the patrol car where the men had gathered under the yard light. She wasn't alone. Pratt Madden, almost invisible, sat atop a picnic table a few yards away, shadowed by a big fir.

She hadn't known he'd returned.

Gunderson was leaning over what appeared to be a large map spread over the hood of the cruiser's hood. Uniformed men were talking among themselves while he jabbed a fingernail onto the map hard enough to tear the paper.

Hunter Blaine shook his head at something Gunderson said. Apparent disagreement, as the detective's face turned red and the game wardens grew stiff and cold. Ortiz stood, his back propped against the side of the car, dark eyes flicking from one man to another.

"I'm telling you, Blaine, I want a boat, two boats, here first thing in the morning. We're gonna start dragging the lake." Gunderson's voice was aggressive.

"Dragging a lake as deep as Lost Girl is a dicey proposition," Hunter argued. "Haven't you heard how it got its name?"

"No, and I don't care."

"Lost Girl got its name," Hunter forged on with his little tale, "because of three Indian sisters who went out in their canoe to fish in a deep hole up at the other end of the lake. They never came home, and their bodies were never found."

"Yeah? So why isn't it named Three Sisters then?" The question was almost belligerent.

Hunter sighed. "Not to mention nobody *drags* lakes anymore." he went on. "You ever heard of sonar? Which is, by the way, expensive. I say we see if we can find the body on land first and save the lake as a last resort. Then, if this woman is in the lake, chances are she'll have come to the surface by herself."

Other men muttered agreement. So, did Truth.

The sound of a woman's voice brought Gunderson's glare around to her. "What are you doing here?"

His tone raised her hackles. Razz's, too, since the dog rumbled her dislike. "This happens to be my home, in case you've forgotten," Truth said. "It's my land, my lake and my livelihood that's being threatened. I have a right to know what's going on. You should listen to Officer Blaine. He is an expert, after all, and he's right about the way bodies rise. There've been a few drownings here over the years, aside from the lost girls. Enough to prove the case." That would've sounded better if her voice hadn't shaken there at the end, she thought.

Gunderson didn't appear impressed.

"I'm running this investigation, Ms. Diamond. You interfere with me and you'll see what rights you have." He glanced at Ortiz. "You did say this woman's name is Diamond, didn't you?"

Ortiz's brows drew together. He nodded.

"I'm right here," Truth said. "You can ask me face-to-face. There's no excuse for being rude, Detective Gunderson. I do have rights, and one of them is the right to common courtesy from law enforcement. I intend on reporting your lack of professionalism to the sheriff in the morning."

Gunderson's face got even redder. "Get this woman out of here before I run her in," he told one of the uniforms, who, feet dragging, inched forward.

Razz had begun growling like she thought she was a pit bull, ready to go for the cop's throat.

Truth didn't budge as she snuggled Razz closer. "Furthermore," she continued, "one of my complaints to the sheriff will refer to the way you walked off this afternoon without paying for your meal."

Behind the detective, Hunter's cheeks bulged as he smothered laughter. Someone else, less controlled, tittered like a little girl. Ortiz looked away into the night.

Gunderson touched the pistol at his hip as if his greatest wish was to pull it on her. "County's running a tab," he said.

"Really?" Truth countered. "First I've heard of it. I don't give credit. To anybody." A buzzing sounded in her ears like a teakettle set to whistle.

Pratt, just in time, she thought later, materialized out of the shadows. "C'mon, Ms. Diamond," he urged, turning her away. "This looks like a battle you'd be better off avoiding." He glanced at Gunderson. "Tonight, anyway. Tell it to the sheriff tomorrow after you've had a chance to sleep on it."

She shook with anger. And with weariness—it had been a long, long day. A fearful day. Add a whole lot of other emotions to the list, including wonder that Pratt had actually spoken to her beyond a polite good morning or while placing an order in the cafe. Then she became aware of something else.

He was shaking too.

Only not for the same reason.

Oh, no indeed.

He was silently laughing his extremely attractive behind off.

CHAPTER 6

"What," Truth gritted from between clamped teeth, "is so gosh-darn funny?"

"You are." An unexpected dimple in Pratt Madden's cheek flexed. "He is. Gunderson's expression? Priceless. Wish I had a picture of you accusing him of not paying for his meal."

Truth didn't see anything funny about Gunderson. Nothing at all. "Nothing accusing about it. Just saying what he did."

Pratt's laughter died. "And now everyone knows. Be prepared, Ms. Diamond. I doubt you've made a friend there."

She shrugged. "Friends like him I can do without."

"Ump." His grunt could've meant anything.

"And you might as well call me Truth," she continued. "Your grandfather does. So does everyone who pulls in here if they stay more than a day."

"I noticed."

Oh, had he? And what did that mean?

She'd left the lights on at the store when she saw the search party come in and gone to meet them. A yellow glow shone through the wide front windows onto the porch as they climbed the three low steps onto it. She set Razz down.

The dog scampered about, head up sniffing myriad odors wafting around the park. Dinnertime. After an exciting day, people were cooking late suppers, some over campfires. The fishing docks were empty, boats back in their assigned slips. The afternoon heat was gone. Chilled, Truth could've used a sweater.

Pratt, his dark eyes serious, waited as she jiggled the key in the door's lock and shook his head. "I know Gunderson is a snaggle-toothed wolverine, but you shouldn't provoke him. The sooner he clears this case, the sooner he's out of your hair. Annoying or not, he's in charge of the investigation. Take my word for it. It's always best to stay on the good side of the local constabulary."

His advice irked Truth. What made him an expert, anyway? "And some people wonder why this county is always calling for more police oversight! He's a perfect example of the need. But I suppose you're right. Not that you've been taking your own advice. He didn't appreciate your comments this morning, either. It sounded to me like you were baiting him."

"Maybe a little. But I . . ." His mouth twisted, and he fell silent.

After a while, Truth asked, "You what?"

"I don't have anything at stake as far as Gunderson is concerned. You do."

She didn't think that's what he'd been going to say, even if he was right about who held the higher stakes. But Truth, who'd been paying close attention to Pratt this morning, couldn't help thinking there was something else, something deeper, behind his taunting the detective. Something almost competitive.

"Who do you suppose she is?" she asked. "This woman

without a hand. Neither Gunderson nor Ortiz has told us one darn thing."

The question of the woman's identity had nagged her all day. And why had her hand turned up at the Golden West Resort?

"Someone—a mother maybe—must be wondering where her child has gone," she went on. "We know she's young, because of the nail polish and the ring. The hand bones are small and smooth, almost child-sized." Truth shivered again "But where do you suppose she came from? Why would anyone chop off . . . " She faltered to a stop.

Pratt stared up at the sky where a white moon was beginning a timed race across the sky. "I can't say. You might ask Gunderson, although I doubt forensics has come back on the hand. Until it does, there's not much he can tell anybody."

"Or maybe Joe Ortiz—"

"He'll talk only when or if Gunderson clears the message."

Razz returned from a sashay under a lilac bush overhanging the corner of the porch, and scratched at the door, wanting in. Truth figured she should go in, too. She had prep to do for tomorrow's baking, and another potato salad to make. The influx of posse members had totally depleted her supply. And yet she was too unsettled. Too worried. And, in a strange way, enjoying this one-on-one time with the elusive Pratt Madden, even if the subject of their conversation was a charred hand.

"I hope they find the girl tomorrow," she said, fretting once again. "It isn't right for anyone to lie out there where the coyotes and birds—" She couldn't finish the thought.

"No," Pratt said. "It isn't."

Hurrying footsteps stirring the wood chip footpath to the store caught their attention. Razz gave a little yip of welcome as Mandi Henning trotted toward them. "Oh, good, Truth," she called as she neared. "I've caught you." She glanced at Pratt. "Hi, Mr. Madden."

He nodded. "Pratt."

"Pratt," Mandi repeated obediently. She laughed through a grimace. "Truth, the stupidest thing! I ran out of coffee if you can imagine. Is the store open? Ken will have withdrawal symptoms for sure if he doesn't have his coffee first thing in the morning."

Her words were frantic, but she wore the good-natured smile of someone able to avoid a total meltdown if her wishes weren't met. Truth had no intention of disappointing her. Not after the way Mandi and Ken had helped with Fran and Larry this morning.

"The store *was* closed," she pushed the door ajar and held it wide, "but for you, it's open again. Go on in," she invited the other woman before turning back to Pratt. "Thank you for rescuing me from Detective Gunderson. I guess it is unwise of me to tangle with him."

Back to his normal reticence, Pratt just nodded. Reaching down, he picked up Razz, who'd been standing up scratching at his shin, and handed her to Truth. Then, silent as a silhouette, he retreated down the path toward his grandfather's fifth-wheel.

Truth, frowning, followed Mandi into the store. Pratt Madden was a strange one. Silent and brooding one minute—or for days on end, as seen since he arrived at the resort—laughing and easy the next, like he'd been just now until Mandi showed up. She wished she could spend more time with him, find out what made him tick. Her old friend, Digbee's grandson, intrigued her.

Mandi had already buzzed down the store's food aisle and found a small can of coffee. Shaking it overhead like a hard-won trophy, she brought it over to the cash register. "What are you baking for tomorrow morning?" She smiled at Truth, handing over a ten-dollar bill. "I'm telling you, those sticky buns this morning were to die for. I could eat them every day."

"Glad you liked them, although they're a little too labor intensive to make very often." Truth handed out change. "They always go over big with the fishermen, too. I'm making huckleberry scones for the morning. I'll serve them slathered with jam and fresh clotted cream."

"Yummy. Sounds delish—and very British." Mandi pocketed her change and picked up her coffee but hesitated before leaving. "I saw you talking to Detective Gunderson a few minutes ago. Did he have anything new to say? What are his plans? Have they found who the hand belongs to?"

Truth closed the old-fashioned cash register. "He ran me off. Said I had no business sitting in on his meeting." Her anger flared anew, a struggle to tamp down. "But I heard enough to learn that if they don't find the body with a land search, using sonar on the lake may be their next move. If they do, I might as well shut the resort down for the season."

"Oh, don't shut down." Mandi looked startled. "I think you'll find most people have short memories." She grinned impishly. "Especially fishermen. Just look at the way their visual impression skews when a fish jumps off their line."

Truth dredged up a chuckle. "Hmm. You could be right. And those in trailers or motorhomes probably won't be so fussed. But tent campers aren't going to like sleeping in the open with . . ." She stopped. Idiot! What was she doing, running her mouth and almost saying "with a murderer on the loose?"

"Does what happened make you nervous, Truth?" Frowning, Mandi fumbled with her coffee can. "I mean, every campsite has at least two people, so no one is alone. Except you."

"I have Razz." At the sound of her name, the Pomeranian licked Truth's chin.

Mandi pursed her lips. "Face it, Truth, as fierce and loyal as she is, Razz might not be the best guard dog in the world." She gave a theatrical shudder. "If I were you, I'd stay inside after dark. Lock your doors and close your windows. It'll make you feel safer. I'm glad I have Ken to hold me. Try not to think about this business." Her eyes glinted. "Just don't open up for anyone at night that you don't know. Or—"

Anyone you do know seemed implied.

The hair on Truth's bare arms stood at attention. "Are you trying to frighten me, Mandi? Because if you are, you're doing a good job."

"I'm sorry." Mandi's mouth turned down. "No, I don't want to scare you. I'm just saying maybe you should practice a little caution until this business is cleared up."

"Yeah, well, I've got a business to run. If the night bell rings, I'm the one who answers it. No choice."

Suddenly, Mandi waved a hand in the air as though erasing a blackboard. "Don't mind me, Truth. Forget everything I said. Ask Ken; he'll tell you my imagination is prone to running away with me. He says I watch too much TV. I'm sure there's nothing for any of us to worry about. As Dottie said, a coyote dragged the hand in. Heaven only knows where it actually came from. What if it's hospital waste that somehow fell off the truck on the way to the Seattle disposal site? Problem gone. In fact, that's probably the answer, and I'll mention it to the detective in the morning."

A tremendous sense of relief swept over Truth, leaving her shaken. Of course. Why hadn't this occurred to anyone else? But even as she said, "Thank you, Mandi! That's a much more comforting concept," and smiled until her mouth felt stretched, she knew the idea didn't make sense. She was sure it couldn't be that easy. Besides, a voice inside her head kept whispering something about the ring. *What about the little silvery ring welded to the finger bones?*

She surfaced to find Mandi thanking her for staying open to sell her the coffee, and saying she'd see her tomorrow and to sleep well and not to worry. In the rush of words, the opportunity to mention the ring was lost. Even so, as Truth made a quick call to Sandra Keene about Jason being on his way home, and prepped the kitchen for the morning breakfast rush, a vision of the ring continued to haunt her. She skimmed the thickened skin of clotted cream off the pan and put it in a big covered bowl, and sifted dry ingredients together for the scones, but she couldn't help worrying.

As convenient—more—as comforting as Mandi's solution regarding the hand's origins seemed at the time, it made no sense. Only when Truth finally shut off the kitchen light and went upstairs to relax under her shower's warm rain, did she realize Pratt, when she'd asked about the girl—the who, the where, the why— had said he couldn't say. He hadn't said he didn't know.

CHAPTER 7

"So." Special Agent-in-Charge Frank Ernhardt sprawled behind his cluttered desk with his ankles crossed, his swivel chair tilted back as far as it would go. "You got any evidence this is the break we've been looking for, or do we chalk this up to a gut reaction?"

"If you can wrestle the forensic report on the hand away from the county medical examiner, I think we'll finally have something solid to go on." FBI agent Pratt Madden leaned against the wall beside Ernhardt's office door, looking for all the world like he couldn't wait to escape the confines of the artificially cooled room. Which, he had to admit, was true. He'd regarded closed-in buildings and their rabbit warren rooms with intense distrust since his last tour of duty in Afghanistan.

"Be better if we had the whole body," Ernhardt said.

"Tell me something I don't know. People are out looking. Sheriff's office, Fish and Wildlife, cadaver dogs. Even a troop of boy scouts."

Ernhardt shook his head in disgust. "Mucking around like a

herd of elephants, I suppose, not that there's much choice. What about the resort?"

"What about it?"

"Are the people who own the place involved?" Ernhardt scowled as if he suspected Pratt of holding out on him. "Are they a front? C'mon, Madden. When we started this operation, it was because of you saying the Golden West was an ideal spot for their headquarters. An area without a big stationary population, but a lot of people coming and going for apparently legitimate reasons. That it has good access to the Canadian border as well as a straight shot to the coast. And, you have a ready-made in, what with your grandfather."

"More to it than my wild guess and you know it. Credit is due to a sharp-witted cleaning person at the rest area for turning in a diary in need of translation. One thing led to another." As it always did, eventually, in his line of work.

"But so far you've got nothing conclusive."

Pratt pushed away from the wall, dropped into the chair opposite Ernhardt, and forced himself to relax. "No. Not yet. I haven't changed my mind about the locale, but I doubt the resort owner is involved."

"Because?" Ernhardt's already squinty eyes narrowed.

"Because the single woman who owns the resort works from daylight to dark. From my observation, I can't see when she'd have time to transport illegal aliens or run a human trafficking ring, busy as she is. The resort has been in her family for a hundred years or so. And she's not the type."

Ernhardt snorted. "You know better than that. Anybody is the type if enough money is up for grabs."

Anger zinged through Pratt, although he said coolly and with a slight smile, "Even you, Frank?"

The quip earned him a sharp look. "Watch your step, Madden."

Pratt shrugged, unrepentant. "I've watched her, night after night. She doesn't leave her house. Others staying there do. Night fishermen, a couple guys tomcatting around. And I find the elderly often take walks at night. My grandfather says that's common. Pain gets them up and walking relieves it." His mouth pursed thoughtfully. "They generally stay on the paths. That said, I'm still convinced someone around there holds the key. I just haven't got a line on who, whether it's one of the regulars or one of the drop-ins."

"What does your grandfather say about that?" At Pratt's look of surprise, Ernhardt expanded on the question. "He's your excuse for sticking around a dead-end hole like the Golden West, isn't he? And the one who clued you there might be some funny business going on?"

"He is. I don't think he'd like you referring to his favorite fishing site as a dead-end hole, though."

"I tell it like it is." Ernhardt looked smug. "So? What does he have to say?"

Pratt ticked items off on his fingers. "Digbee talks to me about hearing people sneaking around during the night. People out walking off their pain. He sees boats on the lake that are being launched without using the resort's facilities. And he speaks of more transient campers showing up than he's ever seen before. He's gotten nervous about Ms. Diamond being by herself, especially at night."

"Has your grandfather asked the lady proprietor what she thinks?"

"He has."

"And?"

"She laughs and says it's about time business picked up. But Digbee is under the impression she's a little worried, too. She seems a bit strung out. His words."

Ernhardt didn't look impressed. "Doesn't sound especially

worrisome to me. Isn't that what any business person wants?" His lips pursed. "I drove out and stopped by there one day, you know. Couldn't even get a decent adult beverage. All the place sold was bottled beer and iced tea. Plain old tea." It was as if he'd been insulted. "And it smelled of fish."

"It's a family resort on a small lake. People fish. What do you expect? And since when did you become so elitist you can't drink a common beer? And I hear Ms. Diamond sells a pretty good local hard cider." Pratt's eyebrows rose.

"Elitist? Not me. I'm particular, is all. I like my comforts and as far as I'm concerned, the Golden West doesn't meet my standards. Cider!" He snorted. "I'm partial to a quiet bar with plenty of Johnny Walker Red for sale. I like padded chairs, soft music, and good conversation." He thought a moment. "Although I did have a pretty waitress—a friendly blonde with spiked hair. And the joint did actually stock Dr. Pepper."

The Dr. Pepper part was lost on Pratt. "The blonde is Truth Diamond. The owner."

Ernhardt arched a brow.

"Hard to miss the spiked hair," Pratt elaborated. Ernhardt was deliberately derogatory about the Golden West. And condescending toward Truth. As he frequently stated, Ernhardt, born and raised in Atlanta, didn't like the West in general and Washington state—aside from Seattle—in particular. Too big. Too open. Too in-betweeny. Just because. And he made no bones about wanting to go back east.

Pratt didn't see a thing wrong with avoiding crowds and, if one person didn't care for an out-of-the-way place like the Golden West with its old-timey atmosphere, plenty of people still did. Even if only secretly. He counted himself one of them.

Except he was working and his opinion of the area, the resort, or, for that matter, Truth Diamond, didn't figure into the equation.

Nor did Digbee's suspicions, recently roused by his long-term familiarity with the resort and its people. On their own, they would never have drawn Pratt or Ernhardt into the undercover exercise Pratt had undertaken. It took the serendipitous discovery in a rest area out along the Interstate to have done that.

Ernhardt gathered in his long legs and sat erect; a sure sign he was prepared to get down to business. "Tell me again what the diary revealed."

Pratt quelled his impatience with an effort. "You know our handwriting expert is willing to swear—in court if we ever bring charges—the writer is an ill-educated teenage girl. One kidnapped from Lithuania. Several pages are stained with water droplets that Mort says are tears. And, although there's more to the diary, the part that we're working from indicates the trafficking ring headquarters is nearby. Unfortunately for Truth Diamond, the Golden West's position puts it in the hub. This severed hand seems to prove it. We know it can't be a coincidence. We just need to keep working with what we've got."

"I agree with you." Ernhardt huffed out a breath. "Dig deeper, Madden. Dig faster. Funding for this enterprise is apt to get quashed, what with the budget cuts. I want . . . I need . . . progress."

"Getting closer." Pratt'd been kicking back long enough in Ernhardt's stuffy office for a headache to start. He got to his feet.

He couldn't help thinking this meeting had been a total waste of time.

CHAPTER 8

U<small>P AT DAYLIGHT AFTER A NIGHT OF ROLLING HER BED INTO A</small> muddle of wrinkled sheets, Truth threw on shorts and a tank top, washed her face and spiked her hair. Head clanging like somebody was shaping horseshoes inside it, she tossed down a couple crumbling aspirin long past their expiration date. She couldn't help wondering what new catastrophe was in store for today. Would it be worse to find the body, or worse if the searchers did not? This was the third day since finding the hand, and so far, nothing had turned up.

Accompanied by a rambunctious Razz, she hurried down the stairs to get the scones in the oven. She'd no more than wrapped the big white chef's apron around her middle than the first customer of the day arrived, a full hour ahead of regular opening time. He was still fumbling open his wallet when Ortiz drove in. After that, a regular parade of searchers, including a busload of Eagle Scouts, overran her parking lot with cars and horse trailers. The café filled with men in need of fortification before beginning the hunt. Truth dashed from kitchen to dining room like one demented in an attempt to satisfy everyone's needs.

To her surprise, the brouhaha in the parking lot did nothing to drive off the fishermen, in particular, a young guy already going soft around the middle. Openly curious, he delayed to watch the action.

"Yeah," he said as he forked over a twenty for his boat rental fee, "I saw on the news last night that something was going on out here. Missed what it was, though." Staring out the front window as the search parties organized into groups, he slathered on some expensive sunscreen.

His lack of information suited Truth just fine. She heard the question in his voice, one she was loathed to answer, so she didn't.

"On the news? Really?" she said as though surprised. "I never saw any of the station trucks out here." Like *that* meant anything. She truly hadn't though. But then, she'd been much too busy to watch TV last night. The reception wasn't good here anyway.

According to the fisherman, reporters had interviewed the sheriff's office spokeswoman in town, then the station ran a few seconds worth of footage taken at the resort on the opening day of last year's fishing season.

"Didn't figure it had anything to do with the resort or how good the fishing is." He shrugged. "So how is it this morning?"

The question stumped her. Darned if she knew. As far as she could tell, no one had been out yet this morning, even the regulars more concerned with the search for a dead woman.

"Great." She made it enthusiastic, maybe lying, maybe not, and not much caring which. "The rainbow are biting on worms and marshmallows." *Probably.* Hands hidden beneath her apron, she crossed her fingers.

With that, they went their separate ways: Truth to finish whipping up her scones and the fisherman to lug thirty pounds of equipment out onto the farthest dock, the one still under the shadow of the sun, where the rentals were tied up. Barely in time to save Truth's sanity, Becca arrived. She was riding the sorrel Hunter Blaine had borrowed yesterday, and promptly turned the horse over to a young deputy, flirting all the while. Truth couldn't help but admire—and maybe envy—the way a careless tilt of her head and a twitch of her hips drew the deputy's eye.

Jason and Uncle Harry, meanwhile, got put in charge of leading a party of searchers into territory missed during yesterday's hunt.

The scoutmaster herded his troop off in the opposite direction. Five minutes later, Hunter skidded his Fish & Game truck into the parking lot and took control of the final group of volunteers. While everyone organized, Ortiz got a communications station set up, leaving Detective Gunderson to arrive after everyone but the deputy had gone.

Truth figured it was by design. She was just glad he avoided the café.

In the first hour after the searchers departed, the little restaurant did a lot of business with her campers, all of whom seemed to believe, despite her denials, that she had the latest news. They kept her and Becca both hopping to keep up with orders.

"I can't believe you haven't heard anything," complained one, whose camper rig was parked in the spot farthest from the store. "The cops wouldn't leave you in the dark. It's your place. C'mon, Truth, spill."

Truth put on her most sincere expression. "The detective is not telling me anything, Mrs. Reardan. Really. You might try asking him yourself."

Not that the suggestion worked, and nothing Truth said dissuaded the woman.

Just in time to save her from exploding, Digbee and Sam meandered into the café and took stools at the five-person counter alongside Ken. They fielded some of the questions. Pratt, to Truth's disappointment, although why she should feel disappointment was hard to say, did not accompany his grandfather. In fact, she'd hadn't seen him around at all this morning. Strange. He'd been faithful in his lonely dock fishing since he'd showed up to stay with his grandfather.

The customers turned abruptly silent when a burly, middle-aged man wearing an expensive looking suit and carrying a briefcase pushed through the door. His glance falling on Truth's apron-wrapped form as she darted between customers, he strutted over. Standing amidst the four Formica-topped tables and seeming impervious to the eyes focused on him, he surveyed his surroundings with a lifted brow.

Is he casing the joint? Truth's first thought whipped through her mind quick as a comet. Her second was that he looked almost proprietary—or like a tax collector.

Turns out, she hit somewhere near the mark, excluding the tax collector part.

"I'm looking for the owner," the guy announced in a booming voice too loud for the space. "A Ms. Truth Diamond."

Intent until then on topping up everyone's coffee while Becca watched the timer on the next batch of scones in the kitchen, Truth almost dropped the glass carafe.

"I'm Truth Diamond," she admitted, whether she wanted to or not—and somehow, she didn't.

He charged forward with his hand extended.

She waved the pot, halting him in mid-stride. What else was she supposed to do, drop it on the floor? Her inner warning system crying out in instant distrust, she said, "May I help you?"

"I'm William Billous." He acted like she ought to recognize him. "Billous Realty."

Truth continued to look puzzled. His name rang no bells.

"My reputation for putting together property deals is second to none," he spoke louder as if sheer volume would prove his point. "You must've seen my ads on television."

She shook her head.

"Call me Bill," he went on before she could tell him she didn't watch television. His chest stuck out like the breast of a turkey. "I'm here with an offer on your property. A good one. You'll appreciate it, especially coming at a time like this."

Truth's mouth dropped open. "An offer? What are you talking about? The resort isn't for sale."

"Everything is for sale." He winked. "If the price is right." He turned to the other customers. "Am I right? Huh? Am I right?"

Like magic, a business card appeared in his fleshy hand. Twisting her neck, she managed to read the largest print on the card while he held it. Sure enough, Bill (in a puke green font) Billous. She thought the last part ought to read *Bilious.* Just like she felt, right now.

"Not right," she managed at last. "Not everything." Even to herself, Truth's protest sounded weak.

"Just listen. This is the thing. The body they found here must've been a big shock. Things like dead bodies tend to scare people off. Cause a loss of custom. Huh? Am I right?"

"Nobody has been found." Outraged, Truth eyed him as if a viper had just taken over her cafe.

He waved off her protest. "A technicality. What I'm talking about are the ladies walking around in fear of not only their lives, but their children's. Doesn't do your property value any good, I can tell you. I've got a proposal that will make you jump up and take notice. Believe me; it's plenty to free you from all this hassle—" His deep voice turned sepulchral. "—and save you from looking over your shoulder every time you go outside, wondering if you're going to be next."

"Next?" Truth repeated like ventriloquist's dummy. The coffee carafe she held suspended in mid-air shook with a steady tremor.

"The next woman found with her hand cut off." His stage whisper carried to every corner of the room. Every female—or male— in the cafe failed to suppress a shudder.

"No woman from this resort has had her hand amputated!" Truth felt her face go fiery with indignation. "That's a terrible thing to say. And untrue."

"But it's no more than everyone else is saying," Bill replied in a self-righteous voice. "I assure you, true or not, the rumor is going the rounds. You can't deny a hand was found, can you? Huh? Am I right?"

Truth gaped at him.

"Unfortunately, your property values are dropping as we speak," Billous boomed on.

Not a soul in the place had the decency to turn away from the show.

"Which is why I urge you to take advantage of the offer while it's hot." Ignoring the coffee pot dangling at half-mast, he took her arm. "Lets you and me go into your office and discuss my proposition."

"Let's not." Truth's grip on the carafe went slack. Steaming hot liquid gushed down over Bill's shiny brown wingtips like the flow of a waterfall.

"Son of . . ." Bill yelped. Face turning red with effort, he changed the course of his curse. ". . . Hercules! My shoes."

His hold on her arm tightened, became painful.

Truth failed to apologize. "Take your hand off me. I'm not

interested in your proposition. Period. Dot, dot, dot." She jerked away, rubbing the reddened mark on her skin that matched Billous's thumbprint.

Billous's bonhomie slipped. "Don't be like that, Ms. Diamond. Can't you see I've got your best interests at heart?"

She was pretty sure her spiked hair stood up like porcupine quills, not all of it due to gel and her expensive hairspray. "As a matter of fact, I can't."

"But you haven't given me a chance to present the offer," he said. "You don't even know how much my buyer is prepared to pay."

At this, Digbee Madden dismounted his stool, Sam a mere second behind him, and the two old men ambled over to flank her.

"Guess the lady has given you her answer." Sam took the lead.

Billous released Truth and allowed his gaze to sweep coolly over Sam. "Unless you're Ms. Diamond's legal representative, I suggest you sit back down, sir. This discussion doesn't include you."

"Yeah?" Digbee said. "Then you'd ought to speak a little softer—and a whole lot politer."

Truth flashed him a grateful glance and a weak smile.

"Go away, old man." Billous waved Digbee aside and grabbed at Truth again. "Come, come, Ms. Diamond. Let's talk this over. I warn you; time is of the essence. Why I can have you out of here and on your way to wherever you'd like to settle within a week."

She stiffened as she shook him off. Her eyes narrowed. "I don't want to go anywhere else. My home is here. We have nothing to talk about, Mr. Billous. This conversation is over before it begins. I'd appreciate it if you'd leave. Now."

Razz chose this moment to dash to her mistress's rescue.

Her creamy fur bristled like a Rhodesian Ridgeback's. Her snarl copied a Pitbull's. Her tiny white teeth flashed before they hooked in Bill Billous's pant leg. She shook it viciously, putting all of her four pounds into the effort.

Billous's foot swung back, Razz dangling in mid-air.

Truth's breath rushed out in a stifled screech.

Before Billous managed to complete the movement to dislodge Razz, a heavy work boot landed hard on top of the foot the realtor had planted on the floor. The same foot soaked in hot coffee.

Digbee Madden glared at Billous. "Don't even think about it." He stomped down hard.

Eyes bulging, Billous stilled as Razz continued savaging his pant leg.

Relieved, Truth glanced around. Ken, without Mandi by his side for a change, stared flatly at Billous and shook his head.

Mrs. Thompson, in for her morning pastry, glared like a white-haired gorgon. "For shame," she said.

A young man, there to rent space on the dock, muttered audibly, "What a creep. Mr. Personality in the flesh," and Dottie Amboy, of all people, rushed forward to rescue Razz before the little dog lost her grip.

Billous's face turned an alarming red, all his former heartiness dissolved. But unfortunately, he found his voice. "You're gonna be sorry you didn't listen to my proposal, little lady. I guarantee it. The offer is a lot of money for a place like this, rundown as it is." He glanced around. "Am I right? Huh? Am I right?"

It crossed Truth's mind to wonder which part he was asking about. Sorry or right or rundown? And just who was he asking, anyway?

She gritted her teeth. None of the above, by golly. The place wasn't all that rundown. It was just showing its unique claim to "oldest family run resort in all of eastern Washington." Maybe in the whole state.

"Goodbye, Mr. Bilious." She spun around and headed toward the safety of the kitchen to regroup.

Billous evidently chose to ignore her pronunciation of his name. He'd probably, she thought, heard it before.

"The offer is for two million five," he called before she managed to disappear. "Call me when you've thought it over. I'm leaving my card right here on the counter."

Truth froze. A buzz broke out behind her. She heard the slam of the screen door and Billous's heavy footsteps grinding chips in the cedar path.

"Did he say *two* million five?" someone—maybe Dottie—said in a wondering voice. "Wow. I think I'd take it. Two and a half million dollars!"

Truth was more than a little shaken herself. *Two, comma, five with five more zeros after it?* No more getting up before dawn every single day for months on end to prepare food. No more messy fish guts to clean up. No more oddball customers demanding instant attention.

A vision of Larry and Fran flashed before her eyes.

But who would make such an offer to her out of the blue? And why?

Oh, she could see why really. Any lake property went for a premium these days. But two point five? *Million?*

More importantly, why now?

She set the coffee carafe back on the burner, not noticing as it tilted and emptied the dregs all over the counter.

CHAPTER 9

AT EIGHT O'CLOCK THAT EVENING, AS THE SUN SANK BELOW THE stony bluff sheltering the bay, searchers began trailing into the resort parking lot. Disgruntlement mixed with weariness on their dust-grimed faces, making it easy to guess the results of their labor. Most, their feet dragging, made their way to the café. The Eagle Scouts, poor souls, were immediately shooed aboard the bus waiting to transport them home without so much as a bottle of cold water.

Truth commiserated with the foot-draggers. Her own hurt so badly from being on them since six a.m. she felt ready to drop. Mix that with meeting Bill Billous earlier, and her smile was not quite so sunny as normal, a fact Hunter Blaine, entering the café as most of the earliest arrivals were leaving, wasn't shy about mentioning as he straddled a stool at the counter.

Announcing he was parched, he eyed her up and down. "What's doing, Truth? You're looking a little . . . moody." He squinted at her out of bloodshot blue eyes.

"Who me?" Truth shrugged. She reached for a glass, ice, and tea, his usual, and pushed the sugar dispenser closer. "I'm just peachy, thanks. But you, from what the guys are saying, aren't so great. None of the searchers are. I'm told you had no luck finding the girl."

Judging by his wry expression, she guessed at his frustration, and was surprised when he said as if this were good news, "Tire tracks." He lifted the frosty glass she set in front of him to his mouth and chugged the liquid down. Nodding for a refill, he raised his voice to carry around the café. "Attention, folks. Any of you been driving your 4-by-4s through the draw separating Truth's buffalo pasture from the BLM grazing land within the last few days?"

Talking stilled throughout the room. Feet shuffled. A glass clicked onto the Formica counter. No one spoke. A few exchanged glances.

Hunter smiled sardonically. "Guess that's a no. About what I expected."

Truth's stomach was busy tying itself in a knot. "Nobody has any business in the buffalo pasture, on foot, on horseback, or driving. If tracks are there, it means somebody was up to no good. Is there any way to trace who it was from the tread pattern?"

Her question won a smile. "Maybe. Depends on the software the County is using. Where'd you hear about the feasibility? Some TV show?" His tongue clicked.

She didn't feel up to sparring with him. "As if I have time to watch television. In case you hadn't noticed, this is my busy season. But I read a newspaper article just a couple months ago about the city police arresting some guy because of his tires."

Hunter grunted. "You believe everything you read in the local rag?"

"I believe some of it. They can't always be wrong."

"You think?"

Becca saved Truth from starting an argument with the fish and wildlife officer by emerging from the kitchen. She homed in on Hunter as if he wore a beacon as she sauntered toward them, hips swaying.

Unlike Truth's limp spikes, every hair on Becca's head lay in tousled perfection. Her lush lips gleamed with petal pink gloss. White short shorts and a skimpy pink top fitted her form like a second skin. Gold hoops graced shell-like ears and a pretty gold bangle clanked on her arm. She was a refreshing vision at the end of a long day as she greeted Hunter, caroling, "Hi, Hunter. Have a bad day?"

Hunter's eyebrows arched. "I've had better," he admitted.

"Aww, poor baby." Becca's lashes fluttered.

"You can say that again." Hunter seemed mesmerized by Becca's lashes, especially when she obediently repeated, "Poor baby."

Inwardly, Truth gagged. Good grief, could the girl be any more blatant? Becca was too young for Hunter. Much too young. What did the girl think she was doing, flirting with him like that?

And what about Hunter, eating up the attention like a starved man? Tied with Pratt Madden for the "best looking man award" to sit at Truth's counter in a long, long time—or maybe ever—Hunter's looks obviously gave him a special edge with the girl. Anybody could see it did. Which meant he shouldn't be encouraging Becca. Leading her on. What a dolt!

"Becca," Truth's voice went sharp, "I see Jason is outside with the horses waiting for you. You rode a horse to work this morning, remember? I think he expects you to ride back."

Becca's pink lips formed a moue. "I'm not going to get on

that stinky old animal and get all dirty again. Jason can lead it home."

"Oh? You mean you'd rather walk two miles in the dark?" Truth looked down her nose at the girl.

"I won't have to walk. I can always hitch a ride with someone." Becca smiled. "Right, Hunter?"

As if guessing her annoyance, Hunter winked at Truth a second before he grinned at Becca. "You're gonna get in trouble one of these days," he said to the girl, "if you're not careful who picks you up."

"Who, me?" Becca grinned back at him. "I'm always careful."

"You better be. Especially right now." On this dark note, one Truth couldn't disagree with, Hunter disentangled himself from the stool and stretched, muscles popping. "C'mon, Becca," he said. "It'll be dark soon and I don't want you out at night by yourself. Your place is on my way. I'll drop you off." His hand on the girl's back urged her forward.

Becca turned to give Truth a little princess wave, one that said, plain as day, "Told you so."

Truth gave serious consideration to firing Becca on the spot, but doggone it, who would she get to fill the girl's job? One thing for certain, she was not about to enter into a competition for Hunter Blaine's attention.

Becca was already ascending the cedar path to the car park when Hunter came back and poked his head around the screen door. "You seen Pratt Madden anywhere today?"

Truth, wiping the counter where Hunter's glass had dripped condensation, thought the question odd. She had the sense the two men were not on the friendliest of terms.

But it was also a little odd Pratt had neither joined a search party nor been fishing at his chosen spot on the dock.

"No," she said. Then, "Why?"

A funny look crossed Hunter's face, one so fleeting she might never have seen it—except she had.

"No reason. Just—" His mouth twisted. "Never mind. Goodnight, Truth. I'll see you tomorrow."

" Night."

~

HAVING KEPT the store and cafe open hours past regular closing, Truth shooed one last customer out the door, turned the "open" sign to "closed," and flipped off the overhead lights. After setting the lock, she leaned against the door and allowed weariness to wash over her.

No baking for her tonight. Thank God the big freezer held a supply of goodies in simple need of thawing.

The click of doggie toenails on the floor warned of Razz's presence. Truth bent and picked up the dog, cuddling the blonde fur ball and receiving a nose-lick in return.

"Where have you been, little one, hiding in the stock room? Too many people around and afraid somebody might step on you? Wise girl."

Razz made a funny little sound in her throat as Truth set her on the ground.

"Yeah, it's been that kind of day, hasn't it?"

Truth removed her apron before checking the grill and stove to make sure the gas was off, the pilot lights lit, and that Becca had left the kitchen ready for the next day's breakfast rush. She was gratified to find the girl had completed her job. Consuelo Morales would be here tomorrow, and Becca often took advantage of the older woman's good nature by leaving a bit of a mess.

"C'mon, Razz, let's have a breath of air before we crash." The kitchen was stifling after the long day, even though the back door was open to the cool evening air. Truth unlocked the screen and stepped out onto the deck. Razz ran ahead into the yard and disappeared amongst some of Truth's prize dahlia plants.

Stars flickered overhead, a major perk to living at this remote lake where ambient light was almost non-existent. The campground lights didn't reach here, for which Truth was grateful. Letting her eyes become accustomed to the dark, she breathed deeply, smelling fish and water, ferns, cottonwood and pine trees. The lake lapping gently against the shore soothed her ears after the cacophony of the day.

Taking off her shoes, Truth rubbed her feet on dew-dampened grass, reveling in the pleasant chill. Beyond a fence that kept Razz corralled when necessary—as well as marked an off-limits boundary to her customers—Truth heard a soft Ker splash from the dock nearest the yard.

A fish jumping, or a night fisherman?

She took a deep breath and held it. *A night fisherman or a man who lopped off women's hands?* Mandi's words of advice came back to her and she shivered.

"Razz," she called softly, not much above a whisper. "Razz, come here."

No patter of four tiny feet; no rustle of leaves. Where had the dog gotten to so quickly?

Drawn forward despite her reluctance to leave the comparative safety of her home's beckoning door, her feet slid soundlessly through wet grass until she reached the gate leading to the farthest dock.

The gate stood wide open.

What in the world? Who has been here?

Out on the dock, a man's voice rumbled. She didn't quite pick up on his first words, except that he sounded startled.

Then he said, "What are you doing out here, little dog. Your mistress will be looking for you."

A sharp bark retorted.

What was Razz saying? That she didn't care?

Truth knew the voice and started forward. Pratt, back at last. Sounding amused, he said, "Hey you! Watch it. You're gonna fall right off the—"

CHAPTER 10

TRUTH BROKE INTO A TROT.

"Razz," she called, louder now, "Razz?" Jogging forward, she spotted them both, the man and the dog. Pratt sat on a bench at the end of the dock, his legs outstretched before him, arms linked behind his head as he stared up at the stars. Razz, in typical Pomeranian fashion, was showing off, spinning like a miniature whirling dervish. The pooch, too excited by this new audience to judge her distance, or maybe the dark played tricks on her, leapt into the air and spun herself right off the edge into the lake.

Water splashed.

"Razz!" Horrified—terrified—Truth ran, bare feet flying, the dog's name still on her lips.

Pratt got there first, a lightning-fast lunge from bench to dock edge. She thought maybe he levitated. A second later, he rose to his feet, holding a water-logged Razz by the scruff of her neck.

"She was going under like she had a concrete block tied to

her tail." Pratt's right arm was wet to the shoulder, the front of his shirt dark.

"Yes. I saw." Truth, voice shaking, reached for a dripping Razz who wriggled in Pratt's grasp as if he were to blame for her predicament. "She's not a swimmer; her hair weighs her down. Hates the water."

Amusement colored Pratt's voice. "Likes to show off though."

Truth managed a laugh. "Yes, she does. That's why I keep her corralled unless I'm on the water with her and put her in a doggie flotation vest. She usually sticks close to me." She hugged the shivering dog to her chest.

Pratt gave her a look that said, plain as day, *where were you just then?*

"My gate." Truth answered his silent question, the same one racketing around in her head. "It was open. I don't know why. The gate has a childproof—sometimes adult proof—latch, and a sign pointing outward that says No Trespassing. No one has any business trying to enter my backyard. It's off limits to the clientele."

"Off limits," he repeated as if he were agreeing with her.

"Yes."

Razz sneezed twice in succession, almost thrusting herself out of Truth's arms.

"Poor girl, you almost scared me to death," Truth crooned, settling the sopping, and rather smelly, dog under her arm. Razz sneezed again.

Truth looked up at Pratt. "Thank you for saving her. I don't know what I would've done if you hadn't been there. Dived in after her, I guess." *And maybe, in the dark and murky water, never found her.* She couldn't bear the thought. "I still don't understand about the gate."

"Accidents happen."

"Yes, but . . ." She stopped, unable to carry the thought further. There'd been something odd about the gate, hadn't there, aside from it being open? "Anyway, coffee and breakfast are on the house in the morning. I'm so grateful."

"No reward needed. I'm glad I could help." He sounded serious.

She started up the dock, a little surprised to find Pratt walking with her, guiding her and her bare feet around a splintery plank in need of replacement. Another chore to put on Eddie Morale's ever-lengthening to-do list.

"I'll take a look at your gate," he said. "If there's a malfunction, I'll fix it, either tonight or in the morning. Don't want Razz getting in the habit of falling off the dock, do you?"

"Certainly not. Not without her flotation device."

Although he didn't seem overly concerned, something about his studied quietness struck her. What? Was he thinking of the lost, no-doubt murdered girl? She was. Couldn't help it. Especially coming on the heels of Mandi's offhand warning to stay in and keep her doors locked at night.

"Then it'll be one breakfast," she said, falsely cheerful, "and a buffalo burger with all the trimmings for lunch."

"Deal."

At the gate, Truth left him to look around while she took Razz inside. She wrapped the dog in a towel and settled her in a cozy padded bed on the enclosed back porch. Grabbing a Maglite, she slipped on her flip-flops and rejoined Pratt.

Strangely, he didn't seem to have touched anything, opting instead to do his investigating visually. But when he turned the powerful flashlight onto the gate latch, it was immediately apparent to Truth that her property had been vandalized.

Something with a blade had gouged the latch receptacle until it drooped from one screw. Worse, a powerful jerk had twisted the whole gate frame on its hinges.

Truth drew in a sharp breath. "Crackerdoodles! That sucks."

"Have you made somebody mad?" Pratt took out his phone and, flash cutting into the night, took a few pictures of the damage, including a close-up of the latch.

"Not that I know of." Distractedly, she ran nervous fingers through her hair, until it stood up in a pale nimbus around her head. No. Her denial wasn't quite true. She had ticked someone off, two someone's actually, although neither was a customer. "Except . . ."

"Except?" Pratt turned the light onto the ground around the gate and took another picture. Of what, Truth had no idea. The path section under the gate was of cobblestone and appeared to her just as it always did.

"Except?" he asked again, fixing his gaze on her.

"There's detective Gunderson, of course, and have you talked to your grandfather this evening? I thought he might have mentioned the little fuss I had in the café this afternoon."

"You had a little fuss? I haven't seen my granddad since I got back from town. I think he's holed up in Sam's trailer right now, playing penny-ante poker with Sam, Dottie Amholt, and her boyfriend." Pratt stowed his phone. "So, talk to me. Who's mad at you?"

Truth didn't see any way around telling him, although she found it a bit difficult to get started. In retrospect, the whole incident struck her as ridiculous and more than a little embarrassing. But she found Pratt listened well. Or maybe it was the quiet dark and the fact he'd just saved Razz's life. Soon the whole story spilled out.

"Two and a half million dollars?" Pratt repeated.

She was getting a tad tired of people being so incredulous. Why not, after all? So, this wasn't a big Pend Oreille or Coeur d'Alene Lake resort. Or fancy and ultra-posh. The Golden

West on tiny Lost Girl Lake was still a very nice property, with the added bonus of private ownership. Some people were willing to pay good money for solitude.

Swallowing her momentary flash of aggravation, honesty formed her answer. "Yes. The dollar amount took me by surprise, too. What else strikes me as odd is Mr. Billous making the offer not only in a public place with plenty of onlookers but at this time of year."

Pratt tilted his head. "Why not at this time of year?"

"Because this is my busy season. I'm making money. Or I was, at least. I'd think his client would wait until fall or winter, maybe on a below zero day when the wind is howling, and the lake is frozen over. Or maybe even in the spring, before the season, when I have a dozen rental boats to paint or otherwise fix, docks to replace, the store to stock, the café kitchen to prepare for the health inspector. That's the time most buyers jump in, trying to get lake property cheap."

"I guess if two and a half million is on the table, the client doesn't think a few thousand is worth quibbling over."

"Several thousand, but even so." Truth looked out over the dark lake. A night bird cooed in one of the big cottonwood trees, and the scent of her luscious David Austin roses perfumed the air. "You know something else about Billous and the offer?"

"What?"

Was she mistaken, or did Pratt seem to tense up a little? She answered anyway.

"He was in such a hurry. Pressure to the max. Why the sudden rush to buy me out, Pratt? That's what I can't figure. Kind of a knock, knock, here's the cash and you're gone type of deal."

"I take it this isn't the first offer you've ever received?" Pratt grabbed hold of the gate, lifting and twisting, the hinges squealing until he forced it closed.

Truth rushed to help. "Oh, no. I get a few low-ball offers a couple times a year. Nothing worth considering. Only this kind of money has never been mentioned before, and when it comes from a . . . a . . . character like Bill Billous, well, I don't know what to think."

"You've not dealt with him before?"

"Hah! As if I'd so much as give him the time of day."

"So, the offer was completely out of the blue?"

"Yes. Strange."

"I can't wait to hear what Digbee has to say about him." He turned the flashlight onto the gate and nodded, hurrying now, as if he couldn't wait to take his leave. "Guess that'll hold for tonight. I'll be around in the morning to finish."

"Maybe Eddie or Jason—" Truth began, but Pratt shook his head.

"I expect they'll be busy tomorrow. The search goes on, you know." He grinned at her. "Don't worry. I'll get Digbee and Sam to help with the gate. Between the two of them, they've got lots of experience fixing stuff. You don't want Razz taking another flyer into the lake."

Truth nearly turned to jelly, being on the receiving end of that smile. Who would ever have thought? Sober-sides Pratt Madden had a dimple.

Flustered, she forgot to thank him as he walked off into the night. And later, it was only because she had to stay up an extra hour bathing Razz—using a sweet-smelling doggie shampoo for white coated dogs—that she caught one final glimpse of him.

He was in his pickup, headlights off, the motor a soft hum, heading up the grade from the resort to the main road. She knew it was him, all right. Revealed under the light of a million stars, there was no mistaking Pratt's rig for anyone else's. He drove an old GMC from the 60s, all cherried out fine.

Within thirty minutes he returned.

Truth's curiosity soared. So did her disquiet. Where had he gone on that quick trip? And what had he been doing?

CHAPTER 11

Groaning, Truth threw a hand over her eyes. "Up and at'em," she muttered.

She rolled out of bed, every bit as tired as when she'd lain down five hours earlier. A stiff breeze had risen during the night, keeping her awake. While it cooled her bedroom via an open window, it also caused creepy thoughts to enter her head.

Creepy, when all her life she'd felt safe here, in the old resort handed down from her great-grandparents' generation.

It had been the noise outside last night that bothered most. A dry-lightning storm brought waves beating against the shore, a loosely tied boat knocking against the dock, the wind moaning through the pine trees. Bushes had rustled, "stuff" had banged and rattled, windchimes had . . . had chimed over and over on a single note.

Truth, covers thrown back because of the heat, believed she'd heard voices underlying the clamor, and later, Pratt's jury-rigged gate refusing to hold and slamming loose. And weren't those footsteps? All of which did a great job of keeping sleep at bay. She shuddered even now, remembering.

A quick shower did little to perk her up, although an extra dab of stiff gel worked into her hair did wonders for her platinum spikes.

"Come on, Razz." Truth lifted the snoozing dog from the bed and jerked the sheets smooth. She was late already. Sunlight gleamed over the eastern cliffs and she still had to prepare for the breakfast crowd. If today was as riotous as yesterday, she'd be worn to a stub by evening.

Standing on the back stoop and keeping careful watch as Razz completed her business, Truth stared around, examining the detritus left by the storm. Pine needles and dropped cones littered the paths. One of the rental boats floated loose in the cove, riding low in the water. The gate, while not quite open, now slanted even more severely in a thirty-five-degree tilt. So not everything she heard last night had been her imagination. Truth didn't know if she should be relieved her mind wasn't playing tricks or not. Maybe this alternative was worse.

Mandi and Ken strolled along the shore, so intent on their conversation they apparently didn't see her. Going by the vigorous hand gestures, whatever they were talking about must've been serious.

Chubby Mrs. Thompson, one side of her white hair crushed flat in a case of serious bed-head, waved cheerfully as she walked out on the short dock, fishing pole in hand.

"Good morning, dear," the old lady called. "Beautiful day to catch a fish, isn't it?"

Truth, waving back, avoided calling attention to the fact fishing wouldn't be much good until the lake settled after the stormy night.

Summoning Razz with a whistle, she went inside to surround herself with a flurry of bacon and eggs, pancakes and syrup. A couple times as she set the coffee to drip into carafes, filling the café with its rich scent, she paused her work to stare out the front windows.

Deputy Joseph Ortiz, first to arrive, drove up and parked his cruiser. With Gunderson absent, the search party came under the deputy's direction. Three or four volunteers trickled into the Golden West parking lot, fewer of them than on previous days. They stood by their rigs talking, seeming to have lost their zest for the hunt. The Eagle Scouts had dropped out, as had most of the local residents. In the main, only sanctioned Sheriff's Department search-and-rescue people were on the job, and they, apparently, all needed fortification with Truth's good coffee and pecan pancakes before heading out to trudge the dusty fields.

Ortiz came in to cadge a cup of coffee, too. "Don't worry." He took a sip. "We'll find her today."

"Well, I do worry." Truth fiddled, wiping a few water spots from the counter. Should she mention her ruined gate? Nah, she decided, Ortiz looked haggard enough as it was. He must not have slept any better than she. "Even finding a body is better than this uncertainty."

Ortiz rolled his shoulders in a gesture that could've meant anything.

"Or," Truth continued, "maybe she isn't dead at all. Did anyone think of that? People survive amputations all the time, you know, even if they've had to cut off one of their own limbs. Remember that rock climber in Colorado? Or was it Yosemite? Or both?" She succeeded in confusing herself.

Joe gave her a look. "Is that what you think happened?"

Truth stared at him. "No."

"Me either, but I hope you're right. Although it's hard to figure why the hand is burned, in that case." He finished his coffee and strode out to direct his troops. Truth, watching, noticed Hunter Blaine's arrival. He was a little late, as usual, leaning against his Fish and Wildlife truck and watching the activity as he sipped from a Styrofoam cup. He had an odd expression on his face; one part bored, one-part smirk.

She had to partially agree with him. This whole thing resembled the storyline of a daytime soap opera—not that she'd ever watched one.

Consuelo and Eduardo Morales were right on time for their end of the week stint, Eduardo to fetch a rake and sweep pine needles, Connie to mind the store.

Jason, wearing his normal work clothes of t-shirt and shorts, rather than the jeans and boots required for grubbing through gullies and scabland rocks, reported for duty. With a huge sigh of relief, Truth put him to work cleaning rental boats and the dreaded gutting station.

"Oh, and bring the loose boat in, please," she added. "It looks like it's in danger of sinking."

"I'll mark it a priority on my to-do list." Jason, at least, seemed cheerful enough. "Right after I clean the gutting station. It's kind of overpowering."

Truth had no argument with that. She fancied she could smell it from here.

Busy hopping back and forth between the kitchen, the dining room, and the store, she barely had a chance to catch her breath before the first wave of soon-to-be-disappointed fisherman arrived. They'd be complaining of no fish in the lake before they left, as she knew from experience. Did they never learn a storm, especially a windstorm, turned the lake over and ruined the fishing?

The old store was beginning to heat up before she got a break.

"Take over for me please, Connie," she dabbed at a bead of sweat with her apron.

Connie looked up from stacking cans of whole kernel corn, always a big seller, in the store. "Sure."

Pouring herself a cup of fresh coffee, Truth stepped with it out into the backyard, Razz at her heels. The broken gate, completely removed now, lay on the grass. A toolbox sat beside it, a battery-driven screwdriver—sans battery—at the ready.

Truth smiled. Pratt, keeping his promise. But where was he? She strode down the path to take a closer look at his progress. She didn't see him anywhere, but out at the end of the dock from which Razz had taken her plunge, she spied Jason climbing into one of the rowboats.

Settling onto the bench seat, he hooked the oars into their locks before noticing her. "I'm going out to retrieve the loose boat," he called. "Could probably use some help if you've got a minute."

The wind had risen again, whipping white-topped waves across the bay, releasing strings of algae from the lake bottom, and making boat maneuvers difficult for a lone oarsman.

"Coming," she called back.

Stripping off her apron, she tossed it over the fence and trotted out on the dock to join him. Razz stuck to her side as if glued.

"I'm so relieved you came into work today," Truth told Jason. "Eduardo has his hands full raking pine needles and these boats are getting pretty rank."

"Tell me about it." Jason wrinkled his nose, holding the boat steady as she and Razz clambered in. "Looks like the fish have been biting the last couple days."

"Yes." Truth nodded toward Mrs. Thompson seated on the far dock, patiently casting her line into the breeze only to have it drift right back to her. "Unlike today."

With Jason pulling strongly on the oars, they bounced over

the water toward the derelict. "Look how low the boat is riding, Truth. Hope it didn't get holed."

Dollar signs ran through Truth's head. "Me too." Then, as they drew nearer, "Look, there's something in it."

Jason peered over his shoulder and snorted in disgust. "A big nasty garbage bag. I'll bet one of the campers intended to take their junk into the lake to dump it."

"The wind last night must've deterred them. Or else the boat got loose, and they were afraid to go after it in the dark. Idiots!"

They pulled up beside the other boat. Jason grasped the side to hold the two together as Truth snatched the trailing painter out of the water.

"Crackerdoodles," she said, making a face. "The boat's missing an oar. Can you tow it back if I grab the line?"

Jason grimaced. "If you can hang on."

"I'll hang on. It's only a hundred yards." She wrapped the rope around her hands and braced her feet. Helping, Razz stood on the flat seat and barked.

Jason dug in with the oars, his strong pull almost jerking Truth out of the boat as the line's slack tightened.

"Wow!" She panted with effort. Rope burns turned her palms a bright red. "This thing is heavy. What do you suppose is in the bag? Rocks?"

Sweat dampened Jason's hair. "Cannonballs."

"Whatever it is stinks."

"Maybe a dead horse, then."

Dead. *Oh, no.* Truth tried to push the errant thought away. *Please, no.* A couple minutes later, she huffed out, "Almost there."

And not before time. It felt as if her arms would detach at the shoulder socket before the boat bumped against the dock.

Jason jumped out, tying the painter to the nearest cleat while she kept the towed boat snubbed close.

The dock rocked as someone stepped onto it. Footsteps thudded on the wood planks.

"You look like you could use a hand. Let me take this." Pratt reached for the laden boat's line.

"Thanks." Brushing sweat out of her eyes, Truth tossed him the rope and got out.

From a standing position, she could see into the escaped boat. The black garbage bag, a king-size heavy ply, contained several strange appearing projections; some round, some square, some almost stick-like. And from here, it stank even worse.

Pratt's head lifted, like a dog taking scent from the wind. As did Razz's, only the dog whined.

Jason finished tying their rowboat, came and stood beside her. "What do you want me to do with the garbage?"

"Nothing." She swallowed. "Go get Ortiz. He's in the car park minding the radio."

"What? Why?"

Pratt nodded. "Do as she says," his voice was taut. "Ask him to meet us here. Quietly. We don't want a crowd following him."

The blood drained from Truth's head with an almost audible *whoosh*. So, she wasn't the only one. Pratt, too, had put two and two together. Please, please, let those numbers add up to three or to five. Anything but four.

CHAPTER 12

Pratt, reluctant to say aloud what his nose already told him was true, gave Truth high marks for hanging tough. The stench rising from the boat certainly had his stomach roiling. He glanced down at Truth's bent head where, clutching a dock support post, she leaned out over the water. Her shoulders heaved, although nothing came up. She'd gone so pale the hint of blush she'd applied to her cheekbones this morning stood out like clown makeup.

"I can't believe this is happening." Her voice came out harsh and raspy.

"You seem pretty sure the missing girl is found." He didn't mean to sound mistrustful in view of her obvious distress but knew he did.

Her shoulders straightened. "Aren't you?" She looked up at him, her pansy dark eyes meeting his gaze directly.

She might be blonde—platinum blonde, at that—but she was no airhead.

"Yes."

Gulls swept in low, their interest in the boat's contents increasing.

"Shoo," Truth yelled. "Shoo. Go away, you miserable creatures." Razz, eager to help, yapped a ferocious warning at them. Truth waved her arms and the flock fluttered upward, gliding in place on the wind and mewling. "Criminy. You'd think they were buzzards."

Pratt appreciated the bucolic atmosphere of the old resort at this moment, glad the place wasn't overrun with children and curious adults—and birdwatchers.

"Somebody had to sneak down here during the night and put the bo . . . bag in your rowboat." He watched for her reaction. "Did you see anyone after I left?"

"No. Not on the dock." Her answer came slowly, and she seemed to tense. "But I wasn't looking. I had to bathe and dry Razz after her dunking, and then I went to bed."

"Not on the dock," he repeated, picking at a certain evasiveness in her reply. "What does that mean? Somewhere else?"

He wasn't surprised when, avoiding his question, she bent down and lifted Razz, tucking the dog under her arm. Truth used the little mutt as a barrier against anyone who pushed too close. It had been his first impression of her when his grandfather introduced them and became even more apparent when she was under stress. Like now.

To his disappointment, Jason appeared just then, allowing her to ignore his last question. Ortiz followed a half-step behind.

"Finally." She hugged Razz and took a step toward them. "Here comes Deputy Ortiz."

The deputy and Jason jogged along the shoreline, jumping over rocks and the reeds that filled in the boggy low spots until they reached the dock. Sweat darkened Ortiz' uniform. All his attention centered on Pratt.

Pratt, the movement almost invisible, shook his head.

"What's up?" Ortiz, shifting his gaze to Truth, to all purposes ignored Pratt. "Jason is saying something about a boat with a garbage bag. You want to explain?" His nostrils flared, involuntary response to the odor.

Truth pointed, her forefinger shaking. "Jason and I . . . somebody set the boat adrift last night. We retrieved it a few minutes ago. That . . ." Her finger shook again. ". . . And found that."

Ortiz glanced at Jason, who nodded, then at Pratt. "What is it?" he asked Truth.

Jason stood hunched like an old man.

"We think it's . . . it's . . . " Truth stopped and tried again. "Maybe it's the missing girl."

Jaw flexing, Ortiz hunkered beside the boat and pulled it to him. "Hold the boat steady," he told Pratt.

Pratt snubbed the craft against the dock. "You're going to open the bag?"

"Think I have to. Don't want to call in the M.E. or forensic crew to deal with a dead animal." Ortiz may have been nervous, but his actions were plenty steady.

Pratt pulled out his phone. "Pictures first?"

A nod signified agreement. Jason helped Ortiz hold the boat steady while Pratt clicked away, time after time, from every conceivable angle, close-up and far away. At last, he pocketed the phone and stood aside for Ortiz to take over again. "That oughta do it."

Pulling a folding knife from his belt sheath, Ortiz flipped open the blade. Pratt, noting the deputy's careful method, said nothing as Ortiz poked the tip through the garbage bag's side, leaving the tie, complete with a knot, undisturbed around its neck.

The deputy cut a six-inch slit. "This is it. You want to do the honors?" he asked Pratt, and if Truth or Jason caught the little byplay and wondered at the deputy's deferral, it apparently went in one ear and out the other.

Pratt grunted. "Go ahead."

An overpowering stench gusted out as the deputy spread the edges of the hole with the knife blade. Flies burst through the opening, dashing against his face. He jerked and fell back, onto Pratt's toes.

"Oh, dear God." Truth turned away.

Jason gagged, leaned over the other side of the dock and vomited.

Gathering himself, Ortiz peered into the bag and gestured for Pratt to do the same.

Two seconds were enough. Both men rose to their feet.

"I'll call it in." Ortiz was already striding away down the dock, rousing a gathering flock of gulls. "Keep everyone away."

"Yeah." He had no intention of allowing either Truth or Jason a view, even if they wanted one. Which they didn't.

Truth swallowed, once and then again, her eyes big in her face. "Is it her?"

Pratt saw no point in playing it cagey. "Female, at any rate. Probably her."

"Holy . . ." Jason faltered and then fell silent.

"Ortiz won't let you leave the resort, but you can get out of the smell." Pratt took pity on the kid. "In fact, why don't we all move into Truth's yard. Nobody'll get past without one of us stopping him. Jason, you can help me finish fixing the gate while we wait."

They looked into the yard where Truth's apron, tossed over the fence, flapped in the breeze. Strange to think it looked ordinary, even cheerful.

"I saw you working there." Jason made a valiant effort to sound normal. "What happened to your gate, Truth?"

"Vandalized," she said.

"Vandalized?" Jason glanced backward at the boat. "What's going on around here, anyway? What next?" He sounded confused and angry. Scared.

Pratt had no good answer. Or any answer, come to that.

Allowing Jason to go ahead, Pratt caught Truth's arm, causing her to pause. She jerked away from his touch.

He let go, even though he'd rather have held her close and given her a shoulder to cry on. She looked like she needed one.

"You never answered me, you know," he said.

"Answered you?" The confusion she feigned wouldn't have fooled one of those little kids calling and laughing over at the swing set in the park.

"You saw something last night." He studied her, the way she avoided looking at him, the way her hands clenched into fists. "What? Or who? Who was it?"

Without speaking, she started to follow Jason, but he stepped in front of her. "Tell me."

Drawing in a deep breath, she met his eyes. He almost smiled, thinking he could see the wheels turning inside her head. "Well?"

"You," she rasped. "I saw you, driving up the hill away from the resort. And after a little while, I saw you come back."

He saw no reason to deny it. Couldn't, even though he wished she'd been tucked in bed, safe and sound. "I had to make a phone call."

The call had been to let Frank know about the untimely and fulsome offer Truth received for the resort, as well as to mention the attack on her gate. Ernhardt hadn't been impressed by either instance. Pratt had a hunch this morning's discovery would draw a more emphatic response from the senior agent in charge.

His simple explanation did nothing to wipe away Truth's expression, which leaned toward the distrustful side.

"Plenty of time to move a body, right?" He regretted the way she flinched. He knew he was scaring her. "Isn't that what you're thinking?"

"No. I . . . no." Razz leading the way, they'd reached the edge of Truth's yard, where Jason waited. "You're Digbee Madden's—"

Pratt cut in before she dug herself a deeper hole. "And right now, I'm going to take Digbee's cordless drill with its newly charged battery and attach heavier bolts to your gate. Jason—" He snapped the kid's name. "—hold this end up against the post, so I can put this screw in the right place."

Jason jumped to help. Without another word, Truth retrieved her apron and hurried away, saying she needed to give Connie a break. Pratt had no idea if he'd eased her mind or if he'd frightened her more. Better if she *was* frightened. Her gate, her boat, her resort—all compromised. Truth herself might be compromised, too.

CHAPTER 13

THE DISCOVERY OF THE BODY DREW DETECTIVE GUNDERSON back to the scene, his unmarked car stirring up a cloud of dust on the road leading into the resort. Alighting from the car, he strutted about calling orders in a loud voice, throwing his considerable weight around and generally scaring the little kids.

Truth, glaring at him from a distance, could've gone the rest of her life without ever seeing him again.

Ortiz, once more demoted to not much more than a gofer, put out a call to withdraw the searchers from the fields. Uniformed officers surrounded the resort. A van load of crime scene investigators unloaded what seemed a mountain of gear and began picking the place apart as soon as the M.E. declared the girl dead.

Truth, Jason, and Pratt, separately, of course, were the first ones subjected to Gunderson's preliminary questions. Next, he summoned the Golden West campers, one-by-one, to the café where the detective set up headquarters. Each person, excepting only the children, were put through the normal routine: "Name, address, where were you last night? Can you prove it?" And lastly, which raised the most hackles, "Don't go anywhere until I say you can."

Call them, Truth thought ruefully, the *unhappy* Golden West campers. And she didn't blame them a bit.

Speculation ran the gamut, spoken in low tones from one ear to another. Who was the woman? Where had she come from? Had anyone from the area gone missing.

Nobody wanted those answers more than Truth, but none were forthcoming. In plain language, nobody knew squat.

For now, the regulars, funneled into the café after meeting with the detective, gathered to drink iced tea or sodas or, in a few cases, beer, and dissect the unfolding tragedy. Gradually, as Gunderson released them, every table, every stool filled. The noise level became almost overpowering.

Unfortunately for Truth's pocketbook, with the road into the resort closed off at the top of the hill, rental boats remained tied to the empty docks. The only fisherman were the osprey diving from their nests atop pilings, and then swooping into the air, talons full of wriggling rainbow trout.

Gunderson, without so much as a by-your-leave, appropriated Truth's private patio in the backyard to conduct his inquiries. His action effectively trapped Razz inside the building. From time-to-time, she yapped a complaint. Truth sympathized.

Inside the café, Fran and Larry, two of the first to come under Gunderson's accusatory eye, claimed one of the four tables as soon as the detective released them. They sat talking with Dottie Amholt and her boyfriend—a strange pairing. Fran waved and gestured as she talked, her diamond rings twinkling. Dottie's head nodded agreement like a bobble-head doll.

Ken Henning stood at the counter kibitzing with Sam and Digbee. Mandi worked the room.

At least that's how it all struck Truth. What did Mandi have to say to Mrs. Thompson? Was she warning the old lady to remain holed up in her RV after dark, as she had Truth? Whatever, the old lady flinched, her wrinkled cheeks taking on a hollow look.

Maybe Mandi gave good advice, Truth reflected, hurrying a tray of soft drinks to table one. Kept on the go refilling glasses and serving the occasional sandwich, Truth finally got a chance to ask when, whirling from the kitchen where Consuelo presided over the grill, she literally bumped into Mandi.

"Oh, sorry, Truth," Mandi said, though the collision hadn't been her fault. "This place is rocking today."

But nobody was spending much money, Truth thought ruefully. "Everyone wants to hash over their interview with Detective Gunderson. Have you been to see him yet?"

Mandi made a face. "Just got back. He's on a roll, as you can imagine. But he didn't keep me long. I sleep like a baby at night and haven't seen or heard a thing out of the way since I've been here. Which is what I told him."

"Even last night with all the wind?"

"Sure. Ken says a couple gusts rocked the motorhome a little, but I never felt a thing." Her smile warmed. "That's why we enjoy vacationing at the Golden West, Truth. It's so peaceful."

"Until now." Truth heard worry creeping into her voice and sought to keep it hidden. "Did Gunderson tell you anything?"

The smile dropped from Mandi's face. "To keep my nose clean. Honestly, can you imagine? My nose clean?"

"Typical Gunderson, from what I've seen of him."

Mandi touched Truth's arm. Her voice softened. "What happened to that girl isn't your fault, Truth. Try not to fret."

Fret. A sweet, old-fashioned word for emotions she failed to hide.

Ignoring a customer calling her name, Truth hesitated. "I saw you talking to Mrs. Thompson. Is she all right? Not frightened, is she?" What would Mandi say?

"Not that I can tell. Mrs. Thompson is a brave old gal. Obviously, or she wouldn't drive that beater motorhome all over on her own. She told me to 'buck up.' She says Gunderson isn't as tough as he thinks he is." Laughing, Mandi gave a little goodbye wave and dashed over to engage one of the resort regulars, who leaned against the wall for lack of a chair, in animated conversation.

Not much comforted, Truth went to deliver a buffalo burger before it got cold.

～

THE CAFÉ HAD CLEARED OUT, except for a few stragglers, and the store completely emptied of customers before Hunter Blaine, acting now as an usher, fetched Truth into Detective Gunderson's presence. Her turn for the third-degree had arrived. For some reason, he'd left her until last.

Which suited her, actually. Razz was due for a piddle break. Truth took the Pomeranian out to the patio with her, ignoring Gunderson's frown when the little dog squatted on the lawn, a beatific look of relief on her face. The cop stationed at the detective's side smiled.

An impatient gesture indicated where Truth should sit. Pulling a lawn chair to the shady side of the table where Gunderson was conducting his interviews, she obeyed, sighing a little. It felt good to get off her feet.

"Do you know who that girl is?" Truth got her question in before the detective could speak.

Gunderson, as though he hadn't heard her, mumbled into a tiny recorder, giving the time and date and the information that their conversation was indeed being recorded.

Duh. As if she couldn't tell.

"State your name," he ordered Truth.

Scowling, Truth complied. "Is it her?" she demanded. "Is she missing a hand?"

"Tell me how you came to find the body." A rivulet of sweat trickled down his left cheek as Gunderson pushed the recorder a few inches closer to her. His shirt bore large dark circles of damp beneath his arms.

She blew out a breath.

How to begin? Where to begin? "I brought Razz"— a nod identified the dog now panting beside her chair— "outside during my morning break. Jason was down on the long dock cleaning boats. He hollered at me. Earlier, we'd found one of the boats adrift and he was going to after it. He asked if I'd come help." She shrugged. "So, I did. The boat was riding low in the water, and there was a big industrial strength garbage bag in the bow. We noticed an awful smell and . . . and . . ." She stopped. "Is it her? The girl with the amputated hand?"

"I question, you answer." Gunderson snapped his fingers. "You noticed the stink and did what?"

Truth was certain he knew. "Pratt . . . Pratt Madden saw us and came down to help with the boat and . . . and . . ." She swallowed. "He told Jason to fetch Officer Ortiz, so Jason did while Pratt and I stayed with the . . . boat." She'd almost said *body*.

"Where did Madden come from?"

Razz, ears alert, popped up from her place at Truth's side and trotted off around the corner of the Golden West building. Bored, Truth thought, and in need of exercise. Her own mind drifted for a moment.

"I asked where Madden came from." Gunderson's voice hardened.

His tone drew Truth's attention back to him. Her right eyebrow arched. "My yard. He'd been fixing my broken gate." She pointed. "There. The one with the No Trespassing sign. Someone vandalized it yesterday."

"Why?"

"Why?" Up went both brows. "How should I know? Why does anyone vandalize anything?"

Gunderson's fingers snapped. "You keep much in the way of building material on the premises, Ms. Diamond?"

"Huh?" In the act of shaking her head, Truth paused. "I don't know as you'd call it building material, exactly, but there's some stuff for fix-it projects. Bags of cedar bark, some lumber, pavers, things like that. It's kept in the garden shed with the lawn mower, rakes, shovels and what not. Why?"

"That all?"

"Yes." Restless, wondering at the direction of his questions, Truth scanned for Razz. Still out of sight. Disregarding Gunderson's sharp movement, she stood up. Then, reminded, plumped down. "No."

"No?" She swore she heard triumph in his voice.

"Maybe not. There's an old barn on the property. It hasn't been used for livestock in years, but if you go around back of the resort, you'll find a rather overgrown path. It leads to the barn. My father used it for storage. I don't think it's ever been emptied. There might be some lumber in there."

Gunderson got to his feet. "Get down there," he told the other cop. "Take Ortiz."

Truth stood up too. "It's locked. You'll need a key. Unless," she added with just a trace of sarcasm, "you intend on breaking in."

The detective glowered. "Get the key. You're coming with us."

What a treat. She got to spend more time in Gunderson's company. Truth clamped her mouth on a pithy retort.

～

THE SEARCH for the padlock key took several minutes. Unused items often have a habit of gravitating to the back and bottom of junk drawers, which is what Truth found in this case. Of course, bantering with Hunter—the Fish and Wildlife officer overseeing to ensure she didn't escape or kill anybody in the next couple minutes—delayed things as well.

"Nice place." Hunter, leaning against the door jam, unabashedly gawked around the living room in Truth's upstairs apartment.

Nice, yes, she thought, if you were a fan of Edwardian decorating and facilities. But she'd never had the heart to change the old place. Only her own room had seen a remodel and was modern as could be, the master bath a total contrast to the one off the living room that still had a claw-foot tub and a ceiling-high, wall-mounted toilet tank. A tank made of oak, no less.

"I like it," she lifted her head from pawing through a drawer in the dining room's built-in china closet. The three top drawers were full of odds and ends. Junk, for the most part. Pencil stubs, old receipts, some Christmas tree light bulbs from strings discarded years ago. Oh, yeah, and lint balls. Where on earth had those come from?

Making himself at home while she searched, Hunter took a seat in a massive Stickley chair whose brown leather seat held a few cracks. "Bet your bedroom doesn't look like this."

Funny how he'd followed her thoughts.

"What about it, Truth?" he grinned at her. "Do you have cabbage rose wallpaper and a baby angel print hanging over your bed? Inquiring minds want to know."

Dang! He was flirting with her. A little tingle fingered her spine.

She looked up and smiled. "What if I did?" It wasn't an admission.

"This I've got to see." As though with new purpose, he rose to his feet.

"Ah, ah. Not so fast. Do you have a search warrant?"

"Do I need one?"

Did he, if he wanted to push it? Truth was a little confused herself.

At last, she found the key. Maybe. She figured it must be one of the four she dug out. She held them up for him to see. "Eureka."

Hunter's grin grew wider. "In the nick of time."

Yeah. The nick of time. For her? Or for him?

"I don't know which of these might work. If any."

"Bring'em all." He stood in the doorway, business on his mind now.

He was funny that way, switching from one persona to another without effort. One moment hot, the next cool. Leading on, then drawing back. He'd been like that with Becca the other night, too. A man to have fun with, she reminded herself, but not to take seriously.

"Let's go," he said as if the previous byplay had never happened.

Razz led the way to the barn, veering from the path occasionally to forge through weeds and grass higher than her head.

Every so often she looked back, panting from effort, to make sure everyone was following her. They were, the men stumbling over ankle-breaking ruts and clinging purple vetch vines.

Gunderson, no surprise, groused loudly to Ortiz and Hunter about how they'd come to neglect searching the barn in previous days. Ortiz said he didn't even know it existed; Hunter that he'd forgotten all about it, although he vaguely remembered seeing a structure marked on an old game department map.

"I thought it was derelict, most probably fallen in by now," he said in his own defense. "The map dated from 1921."

"The barn is about a half-mile from the resort. It's located in a gully behind one of the bluffs and pretty much hidden in a grove of cottonwoods. They've grown a lot these last twenty years." By this time Truth carried Razz, who'd pooped out after a couple hundred yards, in the crook of her elbow. "It's not visible from the road or the lake. I haven't come out here to check its condition for a couple years."

But someone had been this way. Often. And recently. A hundred yards from the barn, they intersected a path ranging down from the cliffs. One too clear to be as innocent as a game trail. Trodden grass gave off a sharp, green scent from crushed stems; bits of tree and shrub branches hung broken and raw. Uneasy, she pointed this out to Gunderson.

Breathing like an out-of-shape marathoner, he glowered at the offending evidence.

A surprise awaited them when they followed the path around to the front of the weathered barn. Or a surprise for Truth, at any rate. A shiny new padlock secured the door.

"The padlock," she said, eyeing it warily. "It isn't mine."

"What are you talking about?" Gunderson gave her a hard stare.

"This isn't my padlock. Mine is old, almost as old as the

barn." She scuffed her foot through the weeds growing up by the door, scanning the ground. A rust-encrusted object bumped against the toe of her sneakers. Bending down, she withdrew a brass lock of antique status. "See. Look here. This one is mine." In proof, with a little effort, the largest of her keys fit.

Gunderson's scowl drew in his face like a wizened apple. He snapped his fingers. "Bolt cutters," he demanded as if expecting one of the cops to conjure them out of thin air.

Impossible, of course, although Hunter Blaine, acknowledging possession of said item in his truck, was ordered to the car park to fetch them.

"Take Ms. Diamond and her dog with you," Gunderson said. "She's done here."

Hunter's touch on her arm, drawing her away, intercepted Truth's fiery, and frightened, urge to ask if search warrants had become passé. The thing is, she wanted to know what that new padlock guarded as badly as anyone.

CHAPTER 14

HUNTER BLAINE RETURNED TO THE BARN WITH A SET OF BOLT cutters strong enough to slice through the cheap Chinese steel lock as if it were made of marshmallow. Ortiz flung open the doors, letting in air, if not much light.

Grunting something that might have been "Thanks," Gunderson sent Ortiz and Blaine around back to scout the area. Once they were out of sight, Pratt slipped around the corner of the barn and joined the detective inside.

His nostrils flared in reaction. The interior stank, smelling of decades-old moldy hay, ancient animal urine, mice—and more. New odors overrode old ones. Blood and human waste. That's what it was. Easily recognizable if you'd ever met it before.

He had.

Gunderson, he could tell, also knew the scent.

They had the barn to themselves for the moment, not that Pratt believed any of the campers from the resort were likely to find their way here. None had so far. Or not that he knew of.

And the lock. Was it meant to keep people out? Or in?

Gunderson cursed loudly as he stumbled over an object that rattled and clanked. A chain.

"You all right?" Ortiz called from outside.

"Fine," Gunderson yelled back, his displeasure clear. "You and Blaine, start cordoning off the area with crime scene tape. I'll let you know if I need you."

"You got a flashlight?" he asked Pratt. His tone was noticeably quieter, less aggressive since being apprised of Pratt's undercover status with the FBI. Thoroughly verified, of course, him not being a man to take anyone's word for anything. Pratt didn't blame him. Much.

And give the man some credit for a modicum of sensitivity, the atmosphere worked to keep his temper under control.

"Ortiz probably has one." Pratt stood still in the quiet—quiet except for Gunderson's heavy breathing—absorbing the feel of the place. The hair on the back of his neck prickled. The barn felt like death. He'd had the same feeling in the ruined villages of Afghanistan, only this place was dank and old instead of crackling dry.

The only light came from through the open door, sunlight creating a path down a center aisle in which dust motes rose in an agitated flurry. The window beside the door had been boarded over from the inside. Gradually, as his eyes became accustomed to the dimness, he made out more details. A pile of old fence posts occupied the middle of the barn which still contained a few blackened bales of crumbling hay. There was also a roll of rusty barbed wire and some lumber. Concrete blocks were stacked in a corner, although from the lack of symmetry, it looked as though a few might be missing.

Pratt knew where to find them. In the bag where they'd found the girl. Weights meant to take her to the bottom of the lake and keep her there. He wondered why the sinking hadn't happened. The storm?

Off the center room, slightly darker rectangles indicated openings into the portions of the barn where the livestock had been kept. One to the right; one to the left.

He nudged Gunderson, pointing out the doorways.

Gunderson nodded.

Using his cell phone to throw a glimmer of light at his feet, Pratt headed left. A hunch. Without speaking, the detective went right, his own phone glowing.

As soon as Pratt entered the enclosed lean-to—meant for cows if the stanchions were anything to go by—he knew he'd chosen the correct area. The odor of death was strong here. Blood, feces, fear.

He pressed the button on his phone again. Yes. The dark smear spread over a two-foot area was blood. A lot of it. Enough to soften the earthen floor as it had seeped in. He stared around, absorbing details and aimed his phone at a bloodied chopping block where he suspected the murderer had cut off the girl's hand. He took pictures, hoping the light was enough to show detail, without being seen by the men outside. Only Ortiz and Gunderson knew he was FBI. He wanted it to remain that way for now.

"Other side is empty," Gunderson said, rejoining him and watching as Pratt finished photographing the area. "At least these phones are good for something, even if there isn't any cell service." He stared down at the tell-tale stains. "You think this is it? The crime scene?"

"Looks like."

"Unless they been butchering cows in here." The detective hesitated. "I'll get my officers on it." He waited a tic as Pratt shot another photo. "Or are you taking over?"

"Not at the moment," Pratt said. "If this is a local girl, it's your murder and I'm out of it. If it turns out she's not local, the case is ours and I'll take the lead. Let's wait and see."

"Yeah, yeah. Same old, same old. I do the grunt work; the feds take the credit."

Pratt, as though cheerful, nodded. "Always better when you don't need federal resources, isn't it?"

"So, you done here?" The detective rubbed his fingers together, just short of a snap.

Keeping his tone even, Pratt said, "Until we find out more."

Gunderson nodded. "Fine. Then clear out. I'd like to get to work sometime today. Rodriguez will keep you posted."

"Ortiz."

"Huh?"

"The deputy's name is Ortiz."

"Yeah, whatever. Same, same."

Shaking his head, Pratt left the barn as stealthily as he'd entered. He hated leaving the investigation in Gunderson's hands. The detective took his arrogance to extremes, using a bullying attitude to get results when a simple approach would do better. Pratt didn't trust him. The man seemed careless to him, too impatient, and always in a hurry. How much experience did Gunderson have? Enough to cover all the bases without mucking up the evidence? Pratt hoped so.

At least until they knew if this murder was connected to Pratt's human trafficking investigation.

Those snapping fingers, for instance. Pratt, hiking swiftly along the trail to the resort, smirked. How would Gunderson cope if, say, one of them accidentally got broken?

He'd rather have his FBI team processing the evidence, but for now, the Feds were keeping a low profile. Cooperation between them and the locals depended on honesty and openness. On how much information the two were willing to share.

Pratt could be tough when necessary. He admitted his own

tactics lacked finesse upon occasion. But what was the point of intimidating an old lady like Mrs. Thompson? Or a former hooker like Dottie Amholt, trying to clean up her life. Or even, he paused in thought, a hard-working resort owner like Truth Diamond?

Cutting off the path in time to avoid an influx of deputies carrying armloads of equipment toward the barn, Pratt approached the resort from the far side of the car park. He was surprised to find Hunter Blaine had beaten him back. Evidently, Gunderson had sent the fish and wildlife officer after more gear.

Even more surprising, Blaine sat half in, half out of his truck, butt on the seat, feet on the ground. Almost as if he were trapped by the woman standing in front of him shaking her finger in his face.

Who the— Pratt stopped short, just out of their sight. His curiosity flared. What had Mandi Hennings so het up? Soundlessly, he inched forward.

All he could hear of their conversation was small snippets of sentences. The woman's voice carried better than the man's, good since she was doing most of the talking. But too bad, too. From the way Blaine flushed, both sides might be illuminating.

"You promised . . ." Mandi was saying. "No . . . more. You . . . all done. Well, guess . . . lied. Now . . . customers . . . leave it to Ken?"

"Hold on!" Blaine's protest came through loud and clear. ". . . can't help . . . night . . . walking . . ."

A big skip where Pratt couldn't make out any words, then Blaine said, "I'll . . . bargain. Give . . ."

And Mandi said, "You'd better. . . . . stake. Don't . . . they'll wonder!"

With that, she stalked off, and for some reason, even her walk struck Pratt as much more aggressive and confident than he'd ever seen her. Completely different than when she was rounding up little kids to keep them out of harm's way.

Passing Blaine on the way to the Golden West café, he gave the fish and wildlife officer a friendly salute—and received a cold, distant stare in return.

～

PRATT FOUND his grandfather and Sam perched on stools in the café, engaged in earnest conversation with Truth. She stood behind the counter wielding a white cloth, wiping an already spotless area in a dispirited kind of way.

The café was nearly empty. A lone couple sipped from tall, ice-filled glasses containing a fizzy drink of some sort. The three little kids from the playground huddled around the candy display in the store.

Business, he observed, was *not* booming. He took the stool on the other side of his grandfather.

Truth's smile seemed forced as she greeted him. "I wondered where you'd gotten to. I was beginning to think Gunderson arrested you and took you off to jail." She stopped, apparently a little embarrassed. "On general principles, I mean. He doesn't seem to like you much."

"Oh, you noticed?"

One of her eyebrows arched upward. "I'd say he's made that pretty clear."

"Guess that's the breaks." Pratt shrugged.

Digbee nudged him. "Everything all right, son?"

"Sure. No problems."

Sam leaned across Digbee, the corner of his mouth quirked. "You should've been here when Gunderson was questioning Mrs. Thompson, Pratt. I think you'd've got a kick out of it."

"What happened?" Pratt wasn't so sure he'd get a kick out of anything right now, unless it was catching the murderer.

Sam outright laughed. "For one thing, she told him he was a blundering ass if he thought Truth had anything to do with that poor girl." His voice rose to a shaky falsetto. "If it hadn't been for Truth and her little dog, you wouldn't even know anything about this. What if she'd just swept up that hand without noticing and put it in the trash? Nobody would've been the wiser."

"Bless her heart," Truth said, her polishing cloth finally stopping its sweep of the counter. "I'll have to thank her next time she comes in. A dozen cookies oughta do the trick."

Digbee nodded, eyes snapping. "She didn't stop there. She told him there might be some questionable characters here. Asked him why didn't he think logically and pick on them?"

"Make that two dozen cookies," Truth said. "Maybe some nice soft chocolate ones with macadamia nuts."

"Did Mrs. Thompson mention anyone specific?" Pratt didn't discount the old lady's instincts.

"Oh, she pointed a finger here and there. Nothing too explicit."

"But Gunderson said that's profiling," Sam said darkly. "He can't do it. It ain't politically correct."

"I can't imagine so minor a point as politically correct stopping him," Truth threw in.

From what he'd observed of the detective, Pratt had to agree.

Truth squirted soap into the little stainless-steel sink under the counter and ran water over a scant collection of used glassware—hardly worth her while. "Has anyone heard anything about the girl? Who she is, or where she's from?"

"Not that the cops are telling," Digbee took upon himself to answer. His glance slid to Pratt. "Probably too soon for them to identify her."

The glasses rattled as Truth plunged her hands into water hot enough steam rose above the counter. "I wish I knew what the police found in my barn—if anything." She looked up. "I know there must be something. Probably awful. Otherwise—"

Short-circuiting the direction of their conversation, the children came over to the cash register to pay for their collection of candy bars and chips. Good healthy fare, Pratt thought, smiling inwardly, remembering when he'd done the same. He was aware of Truth trying to pull herself together, chatting with the kids as she took their money and made careful change.

"Where's Razz," one little girl asked. "Can she come out and play?"

At the sound of her name, Razz, tongue curling in joy, came bounding out from behind the counter where Truth kept a cushy doggie bed.

The exchange brought forth one of Truth's flashing smiles. "You kids can use the side yard here. There's so much traffic right now I don't want you or Razz too close to the parking lot."

Agreeing, the kids ran out, Razz yapping gleefully at their heels.

She glanced at him. "Which reminds me, Pratt. I put your tools on the back porch before they walked off with someone. Thanks' so much for fixing the gate. Anytime you're ready for your reward, just say the word."

A reward other than the offered meal flashed through Pratt's mind. One that included kisses and maybe more.

Fool!

"No reward necessary," a slow smile curled his lips. "I was glad to help." Too bad he couldn't have electrified the whole fence, done something to provide a real deterrent to anybody sneaking into her yard. The hand, the body, the barn. They all indicated she had become a target. Maybe not even an intended one, but a target all the same. And where did an out-of-the-blue offer for the resort fit?

To his relief, the atmosphere relaxed. Some of the tension went from Truth's face—until Jason pulled into the car park, dust swirling around his Samurai.

The screen door slammed as he strode into the café and glanced around. "Where's Becca?" he demanded. "I need to talk to her."

CHAPTER 15

"Becca?" Truth wiped her hands on her apron and stared at Jason in bewilderment. "She's not here today. It's Thursday, remember? Connie's day." A cold frisson of apprehension traveled up her spine. Or was it annoyance? What was the girl up to now? Considering his and Becca's constant sibling squabbles, Jason acted a lot more concerned than one might expect.

"I worked today," he pointed out as if she didn't know.

Truth had sent him home only an hour ago, early, because he'd been sick as a roadkill eating dog after they found the dead girl. A lengthy grilling by the police, followed by Gunderson flat out accusing him of murder, had done him in.

Of course, the detective had gone around accusing every man in sight of murder, so Jason wasn't unique. And, as far as she knew, Gunderson hadn't gotten very far with this tactic.

Anyway, Jason only came in today because he'd missed a couple days work while helping search for the girl with the amputated hand. He and Becca nearly always worked the same shift, so his question caught Truth off guard.

But they hadn't, she remembered, been together the previous evening, either.

"Are you sure Becca didn't go shopping with a friend?" she asked. "Yesterday was payday, so she had money to spend."

Shopping, as Becca herself was fond of saying, was her second favorite thing in the world to do, right after flirting with guys. Well, sometimes maybe even before. Depended on who was around to flirt with—like Hunter Blaine. Truth had a hunch Becca wasn't quite the innocent her mother might hope.

"Mom says no." Jason truly seemed alarmed now. "She says Becca's purse is still in her room. She never goes anywhere without that big ole suitcase of hers, you know. Gotta have something to haul around the stuff she sprays on her hair every five minutes."

The two old men, Digbee and Sam, hung on Jason's every word, but it was Pratt, eyes alert, who had the questions. He sat poised on the counter stool facing Jason, one foot on the floor as if to spring into action. "When did you last see Becca? When did your mom?"

Jason turned to him. "I haven't seen her since yesterday evening, right here, when she told me she'd find her own way home. Remember, Truth? Anyway, I got there before she did and went to bed. Mom says she saw her come in last night, though."

"She tell your mom why she was late?" Pratt asked.

"Don't know."

Pratt glanced at Truth. "When did she leave here?"

"Soon after Jason. She caught a ride with Hunter Blaine—at least I think she did. I didn't actually see her get in his rig. He told her she shouldn't be out walking by herself, especially after dark."

"Can't argue with him there," Digbee said. Sam nodded.

"They went out together, although Hunter came back in for

a second." Truth frowned. "I'm surprised they didn't pass you on the way, Jason." Or maybe not all that surprised considering the banter between the two of them.

A contemplative expression on his face, Pratt grabbed up a waitress's order pad and a ballpoint left lying on the counter and wrote something down.

Not the best handwriting, Truth observed, attempting to read his scrawl wrong side up.

With a heavy stroke, he traced a question mark at the end of a line, left a space, and wrote down another question.

Truth craned her neck to read. The first sentence asked, *Did mom physically check Becca's room, or did she just give a holler this morning?* The second, *Was her bed slept in?*

"What're you writing?" Jason stood on his toes, trying to see over Pratt's shoulder.

"Just a couple questions you should ask your mother," Pratt said easily, without any great emphasis.

"Me?" Jason's mouth opened in protest. "Not me! Why do you think I'm here now? Mom started bawling, so I said I'd come over to the resort and ask around. I don't want to get her going again."

Digbee took the notepad from Pratt and read it too, as Sam —who wasn't known as Silent Sam for nothing—watched. Taking the pad and pen, Digbee ripped off the page with Pratt's questions and wrote down one of his own on a fresh sheet. *She got any transportation?*

"Sorry, Jason." Digbee tore off the note and held both pages out to the kid. "Looks like you're elected to do the talking."

Jason pushed the notes away. "You do it."

"Can't. If your mom gets a call from a strange man, it'll scare her to death. Especially with this girl being found here today." Digbee extended the pages again and gave them an emphatic flip.

Everyone but Jason murmured agreement. "Maybe Pratt—" he said.

Pratt shook his head. "Same reasoning. Less alarming if it comes from you."

So, it hadn't been Truth's imagination, the concern she felt, the same as she sensed from the three men.

Steeling herself, she snatched the notes from Digbee. "I'll do it. Jason, you're too upset. You'd probably forget the answers." She was pretty upset herself, when you came right down to it, but figured she was actress enough to pull off asking a few questions. A better actress than her young employee was an actor, for sure.

The men following like puppy dogs, she stepped into the kitchen, to the phone. From a list of frequently dialed numbers taped to the wall, she selected the Keene kids' home. Punched in the digits.

"Hello? Becca?" Sandra Keene answered on the first ring. Her voice sounded thick; evidence of her tears.

Truth turned on the speakerphone feature so everyone could hear. "No, Sandy. It's Truth Diamond. Jason is here. He says Becca seems to have . . . um . . . he says you can't find Becca." *As if they'd lost or misplaced the phone or a TV remote. How clumsy can you get?* For a moment she blanked.

"Have you seen her?" Sandra quavered.

"Not since last night. But a couple of us were wondering, did you actually look in on her this morning, or did you just call her name? Are you sure she's not just sleeping late?" Truth couldn't imagine sleeping until the afternoon, but she knew some people who did. And teenagers were notorious. Her pencil hovered above the order pad, ready to write down anything Sandra Keene had to say.

"I looked in her room," Sandra said. "Of course, I looked. I wouldn't get all stirred up for nothing. Becca is . . . well, Becca is—" She couldn't go on.

Truth swallowed. Wrote down 'yes' in answer to Pratt's questions. "I see. Has her bed been slept in?"

"I don't know. She's not good about making her bed. It could've been a day or two, maybe even a week, so—"

"Uh huh." *Undetermined*, Truth wrote, *too messy*.

Pratt scrawled another question, ripped off the page and passed it to Truth. "Can you tell if her room was disturbed in any way? Or if anything is missing?"

Sandra's voice grew louder, more strident. "Her room is always a mess, Truth. And my Becca is missing. That's all I know, and I don't care about anything else."

Pratt wrote. *Favorite hangouts?*

Patiently, Truth repeated the question.

"I don't know," Sandra wailed despairingly. "She doesn't talk to me anymore. She says she's a grown up now. My baby is all grown up."

Finally, Truth came to Digbee's question, the last on her list. "Does Becca have any transportation? You know, someone to pick her up and take her somewhere?"

Sandra paused. "Maybe."

Ah ha. Encouragement. "Who?"

"She's got lots of friends. They're always in and out around here. I . . . I'll have to think of which ones have cars."

She'd not gotten very far, but Truth had a few ideas on that score, herself. Her hand tightened on the phone.

"Did any of her friends come around yesterday evening after she got home?"

"Maybe," Sandra said again. "I went to bed. But I've already called her friends, Truth. Everyone I can remember." She hiccupped on a sob. "They all say they haven't seen her."

Pratt scribbled another note and thrust it toward her, Digbee nodding a kind of agreement.

"Do you think any of them could be lying?" Truth parroted.

"I don't think so. I can't imagine why they would. I'm sure they're not." But Sandra *didn't* sound entirely sure. Actually, she sounded like maybe a little lie or two would be a good thing.

Truth kept going. "What time did Becca get home last night, Sandra?" She caught Pratt's thumbs up out of the corner of her eye.

"Around ten or so." Sandra seemed on surer ground with this. "I asked why she was so late and she told me she'd been with a friend." Her voice faded again. "Hooking up with a friend, she said. Was she saying what I think she was saying, Truth?"

Hooking up? Becca and Hunter? Truth scowled, realizing it only when she intercepted Pratt's inquiring stare. And because her forehead hurt.

"Could mean a lot; could mean nothing. It seems pretty certain she was with a guy," she explained.

"Not unusual," Sandra said. "She dates a lot, but hooking up? I just don't know. Becca always has lots of boyfriends."

Boyfriends! Truth inhaled. "Did she happen to mention who brought her home?"

"No."

"So, how did she seem? Happy? Maybe a little broken up? Disappointed?" *Disappointed because Hunter is a tease and he couldn't possibly be serious about a sixteen-year-old girl?*

"Not broken up at all. More, oh, euphoric may be the proper word, like a kitten at the cream. I kind of thought . . ." Sandra faltered.

"You thought what?"

The men encircled Truth like chicks around a hen, openly hanging on both sides of the conversation.

Sandra breathed in and out before saying, as if the words were dragged out of her, "It struck me that she might've been . . . you know . . . making out with someone."

So what else did she think "hooking up" meant? Truth, visualizing Hunter and Becca together, wasn't sure whether those were her teeth grinding together, or Sandra's. Certainly, she heard Jason snort. "What makes you think so?"

"Oh, like I told you, the kitten-at-the-cream thing. I've been around the block a time or two myself, you see. Often enough to recognize the look when I see it."

"Oh." Truth avoided looking at Jason. She was thinking that Becca and her mom most certainly did resemble each other, in more ways than one.

"What should I do, Truth? Do you think I should wait until Becca comes home, or should I talk to the police? She's never done anything like this before. You know, gone somewhere and not told me." The quiver was back in Sandra's voice. "And there's that girl, the dead girl—"

Truth opened her eyes wide at Pratt. He'd know. Sure enough, he mouthed the word, Police.

"I think you should call the sheriff's office, Sandra. Right away. In view of—" Oh, mercy! She really did not want to harken back to the girl they'd found, not when Sandra already had. Better to downplay that aspect.

"Can you?" Sandra whined. "I mean, the police are still there, aren't they? Jason told me about finding her, the girl. If you could just mention—"

But on this point, Truth was firm. "I can't, I'm sorry. I'm pretty sure a missing person has to be reported by a family member."

Actually, she wasn't sure at all, but no way was she going to be drawn into the Keene family's dysfunction.

Jason muttered, "Oh, man. This isn't going to go over well."

Sure enough, Sandra started crying again. In consequence, several minutes passed before Truth got off the line, and when she did, her hands were shaking.

"You'd better go home," she told Jason. "Your mother needs you."

"I'll have to make sure she actually calls the cops." He sighed. "Sometimes Mom isn't real reliable. If she starts— Yeah." Without another word, he walked out, shoulders drooping. A few moments later his Samurai roared to life.

"If she starts what?" Pratt gazed after him.

This time it was Truth who heaved the sigh. "Sandra has been known to take a drink or three. And when she does, well, Jason will probably be on his own."

"Well, now," said Sam, master of the understatement, "this kinda sucks, don't it?"

CHAPTER 16

SAM HAD IT RIGHT, PRATT THOUGHT, DRUMMING HIS FINGERS ON the counter. The Becca Keene situation did suck. The whole thing. He hated that his hunch meter had clanged into operation, insisting Becca was in trouble and not simply hanging out or overnighting with some guy.

They were back at their places in the café, he, his grandfather, Sam, and of course, Truth, who stood behind the counter, elbows propped, with her chin cupped in her hands. From a strange little swelling of her eyelids, he judged tears were waiting to fall.

Beyond them, in the kitchen, Consuelo had returned from her smoke break and begun forming patties of ground meat. Beef or buffalo, he made no guess. She, uninformed of this newest wrinkle, sang the chorus of some repetitious song in Spanish.

Silent, each of them seemed lost in his own thoughts. Pratt figured they were mulling over this new development, same as him. Finally, Truth's head came up. She laid her fingers over his, stilling their restless motion, her touch cool—almost icy—

even as the ancient air conditioner fought a noisy, though ever-losing battle against the summer heat.

She blew out a breath. "What do you think? What should we be doing? We should be doing something, right?"

Digbee took over as she hesitated. "Is there a specific time frame for reporting this kind of thing, Pratt? Twenty-four hours, maybe?"

Pratt shrugged. "Depends. Amber alerts go out right away."

"I wonder if Becca qualifies for an Amber." Sam nodded wisely. "Whether or not, these here are special circumstances. If she . . ." He didn't finish. Didn't have to.

Turning his hand, Pratt squeezed Truth's fingers, then let go. He got up. "Guess I'll have a little talk with Blaine. Becca may have told him her plans for today. He might have an idea where she is."

Relieved expressions, almost identical, crossed the faces of the two old men. Only Truth's remained every bit as concerned.

"I suppose Sandra and Jason may be making waves where there's no water," she said. An apparent agreement, only she didn't sound like she believed it. Not to him. Well, he didn't either.

Escaping from the oppressive atmosphere in the café, he strode down the now well-worn path to the barn. Gulls wheeled through the sky, mewling as though starved. Sunlight sparkled on the waters of the bay, visible through breaks in the trees. Once he saw a fish jump. Nature showing off its serene beauty.

But the children had been chased indoors, kept close under their parents' supervision instead of running wild. He missed the cheerful, homey noise of their laughter. Campers sat in groups around tables set outside their own RVs instead of gathering in the resort café, fishing from the docks, or taking boats for a spin. From the path, it appeared every single one of the rental boats was snugged to a cleat. No wonder Truth worried about her bottom line.

And now Becca.

Was this, by chance, a conspiracy by Bill Billous's client to force Truth to sell the resort? Would Becca be willing to play along with the man in an underhanded ploy like that? Maybe, if enough money were involved. He'd heard Becca talk about buying a car for her senior year in high school, and Truth had been a little rough on her lately. Payback.

A possibility, a concept with merit—except he just didn't buy it. As soon as they had an identity on the dead girl, he'd have a better idea.

"Hola," he called out as he neared the barn. He ducked under the yellow crime scene tape encircling the building and found Ortiz working under the boarded-up window. The deputy was poking through weeds grown tall enough to hide the sill. He carried a canister of plaster foam, so he may have found a viable footprint.

Ortiz waved him over. "Anything happening at the resort?"

"Could be."

Ortiz's face screwed into a frown as Pratt explained about Becca. Then he heaved a long-suffering sigh. "This means Gunderson will be off on another rant the second he hears." The deputy snorted. "And I suppose I'm the one elected to report and get him started."

"I'll tell him, not that I'm overjoyed about it." Pratt looked around. "First, I want to talk to Hunter Blaine. Where is he?"

"In the barn." Ortiz resumed his search through the weeds, a variety with yellow flowers with an acrid, pungent smell and stems that exuded a sticky white latex. A butterfly hovered nearby. "I think he's holding Gunderson's flashlight."

Pratt smothered a laugh. "Helpful."

Hunter Blaine wasn't literally holding a flashlight for Gunderson, although his show of readjusting some spotlights hooked up to a small portable generator seemed remarkably like busy work. The lights were pointed at the bloodstained chopping block where a tech with a better camera than the one in Pratt's phone snapped picture after picture, sometimes with the lens only inches away.

"Blaine," Pratt called from the entry into the lean-to, "You got a minute? I need to ask you something."

In reply to the photographer's incremental move to the side, Hunter tweaked the light. "What is it, Madden? I'm kind of busy. Can't it wait?"

"No."

Gunderson hunkered by a pile of what looked like rags in a dark corner of the shed, lifting each object and putting it in a bag. Pratt, aware of the chains anchored in one of the posts holding up the roof, gave him kudos for not delegating this part to Ortiz or one of the techs.

"Detective Gunderson," he said, "this is something you need to hear too."

Gunderson's knees popped as he arose. "Found another body?" He didn't sound pleased.

"Not yet," Pratt said with a certain grim emphasis.

"What's that mean?" Scowling, Gunderson came to meet him.

Blaine was slower to respond, leaving the lights with notable reluctance.

"Let's go outside," Gunderson said. "Into the sunshine where it's warm."

The barn was stifling. Gunderson apparently owned more sensitivity than Pratt had given him credit for.

Once outdoors, Gunderson turned his face to the sky and took a deep breath. "What is it?"

"Maybe nothing, maybe a lot. Jason Keene—" With Gunderson's furrowed brow indicating he had no memory of who Jason Keene might be, Pratt stopped to explain. "The kid returned to the resort a few minutes ago, asking if his sister came to work today. Ms. Diamond said no, it's the girl's day off. Trouble is, Mrs. Keene hasn't seen her daughter since last night. Apparently, no one else has either. To all appearances, she's disappeared."

Gunderson let loose with a fiery obscenity. His fingers snapped twice in quick succession. "A runaway? How old is she?"

Pratt looked questioningly at Hunter Blaine, who shrugged. "Don't look at me," the wildlife officer said. "How should I know? Sixteen, seventeen, maybe?"

"Underage." Gunderson was disgusted.

Pratt nodded, and Hunter said, "Yes."

Gunderson nodded wisely. "Runaway for sure. And we don't have time to deal with some spoiled kid running off, worrying her folks just to get attention. Statistics—"

Pratt's gaze hardened. "Considering the age and circumstances regarding the girl we just found cut up in a garbage bag, I don't believe your normal statistics can be applied in this case. Especially since Becca's mother says her daughter's handbag is still in her room with everything intact and, as far as she can tell, none of the girl's clothing is missing. A runaway would certainly take a change of clothes and her money. And her phone."

Hunter studied Pratt as if wondering how he fit into this equation. "Maybe she has a rich boyfriend," he suggested after a pause.

"Maybe you can tell us that. Ms. Diamond says you took the girl home last night."

Hunter stiffened. His voice rose, matching Pratt's in hard

intensity. "Just you hold it right there, buster. I don't answer to you. I don't know what makes you think you can butt in. And I don't like your insinuations."

Is this the time to reveal my FBI credentials? Pratt, though loathe to reveal his undercover status just yet, thought he might have taken stealth as far as practical. What's more, he had a hunch Gunderson was thinking the same thing.

The detective surprised him by stepping forward. "Madden may not have any jurisdiction here, but I do, and I'd like to hear the answer to that, too. What did you and this girl have going on between you?"

Hunter's face changed from belligerent to calm and collected in the blink of an eye. "Nothing went on between us. I didn't do anything. We didn't even talk. As it happens, I didn't take her home. I was going to, even told her to get in my truck, but at the last minute I went back in the café to ask Truth a question, and when I came out she was gone. I saw some lights topping the hill above the bay. I just figured a friend had come by and picked her up." His gaze shifted from the detective to Pratt and back again. "Ask Truth, if you don't believe me."

"Oh, I will." Gunderson nodded even as Pratt, having already heard Truth's version, made a mental note to ask about another vehicle.

"You see what kind of a rig?" Gunderson asked.

"No. Just ordinary taillights."

Pratt spoke without thinking. "Truck taillights? Car? Motorcycle? Take a guess."

Hunter glared. "I don't know. Didn't think I'd need to write a report on it." He paused. "Not a motorcycle."

"Good choice. Someone might have noticed a bike."

A short, tense silence fell over the group, one that Hunter broke, his voice a bit overloud. "Maybe somebody oughta question Dottie Amholt's boyfriend. He looks an unsavory character if I've ever seen one. Tattoos, baggy jeans and that chain."

"Profiling," Pratt said, "and not real helpful."

But Gunderson nodded. "Yeah. No smoke without a fire. I'll be talking to him. If this goes any farther. Which I doubt." His face lifted skyward again, although Pratt didn't think he was watching clouds. Proving his hunch right, the detective's voice bellowed out, making both Pratt and Hunter jump. "Sanchez!"

Pratt noticed Ortiz, still making a slow and careful search of the terrain, jump too, although he put on an act as though he hadn't heard.

"His na . . . " Pratt began.

"Rodriquez!" Gunderson roared, putting his substantial gut behind it. "Get your rear-end over here. I got another job for you."

"Might help if you asked for Deputy Ortiz," Pratt finally got in, earning himself the honor of becoming the next man on the receiving end of Gunderson's glare.

The detective settled for crooking a finger when Ortiz's glance shifted his way. Pratt nearly, but not quite, laughed.

Ortiz, tarrying to pick up his equipment, made the detective wait. But not too long. "Sir?"

"Got a situation," Gunderson exhaled a gust through his nose, making his displeasure known. "A new situation. You're elected." Rapid fire, he set out Ortiz's orders. "Talk to Mrs. Keene. See if this Becca girl has come home. I figure her for a runaway but tell her to call tomorrow if she isn't back yet."

A sick look on his face, Ortiz nodded. Like every other man who came into the Golden West, he knew Becca and enjoyed bantering with her. Pratt felt sorry for him.

"I'm on it." The deputy headed back toward the resort, his footsteps hurried.

Gunderson turned his glare on Hunter. "All right. We're done here for now. Get back to work."

As soon as the wildlife officer disappeared inside, presumably back to the job of focusing the tech's lights, Gunderson said to Pratt, "What do you think? We got another victim here?"

"I'm afraid of it." Pratt hated making the admission—absolutely hated it. And Gunderson. What was the matter with him, delaying a search. What an ass. "And the quicker we move, the better chance we have of finding Becca Keene alive."

"You think these cases are related?"

"Don't you? It's a major coincidence if they aren't. Young pretty girls, this resort."

Gunderson breathed out heavily through his large and slightly sunburned nose. "Nah. I figure her for a runaway. You'll see."

"I think you're wrong." Pratt's voice turned arctic. "Dangerously wrong."

"You don't like it?" Jaw jutting, Gunderson challenged him. "Think you can do better? Maybe you want to take over, huh?"

Oh, yes, he did. Pratt seethed, staring through the doorway into the barn until he gained control of his temper. "Not just yet. Not until the report is back on the dead girl. If she's one of yours, I'm out of this, except I'm going to help find Becca Keene."

Mention of her name diverted Gunderson. "Blaine is wondering about your role here already. You could see the wheels turning in his head."

Pratt didn't care much about Hunter Blaine and his wheels, turning or not. "Let him wonder a while longer."

~

AT EIGHT O'CLOCK THAT EVENING, as an unnatural silence settled over the resort and a quiet so profound, waves lapping the shore were discernable as far as the car park, word came through on the girl. Forensics, to Pratt's satisfaction, had been working in quick time.

Gunderson, summoned from the barn by the deputy manning the communications center, took the report. His fingers snapped, once, twice, slipped on a third. Before long the results spread to even the least of the police on site. Pratt was first in line.

She'd been a small, blue-eyed blonde. Definitely pretty, once upon a time. She'd been between sixteen and twenty years of age, pregnant, and a bit malnourished. She'd been beaten and brutalized before she died.

Her ethnicity was apparently eastern European. Ukrainian, for a guess. No records, so far, had been found to help in identifying her, although the bits of clothing she wore was of foreign manufacture and of poor quality. No matching missing person report had been filed on her—in this country, anyway. They'd have to wait on Interpol. It seemed likely she was an illegal alien.

She'd been dismembered before being stuffed in the garbage bag, and the original hand belonged to her. The mystery of how her body and her hand had gotten separated remained. They were stilling working on the implement used to dismember her.

Pratt passed only part of the information on to Truth and Digbee.

Truth got sick. Digbee got mad.

But not as mad as Pratt.

CHAPTER 17

Truth, too weary for words, sent Consuelo and Eddie home a couple hours early and not only closed the store and café but locked the doors tight. Not that it made much difference that she could see. Customers were on the sparse side anyway.

In fact, she reflected as she stared up at the half-moon shining down on her private patio two hours later, the day had been a total disaster.

Leaning into the slightly damp chaise lounge cushions, she breathed deeply of the pine-scented air and attempted to relax. As soon as the Morales couple had left, she'd forced down a BLT on a homemade Kaiser roll, showered, and donned sleep-shorts and shirt before coming outside. A little light remained in the darkening sky. The quiet gave her an illusion of peace.

Illusion? If only it were real. If only Becca were to waltz into her home as if nothing had happened.

Not going to happen. She knew it.

Put together, the discovery of the missing girl's body, Becca's disappearance, and the news that her . . . *her* . . . own barn had been used as a stopping off point for a murderer, made her stomach, let alone her mind, churn in protest. Had her asking, what next?

Oh, please, don't let there be a next.

Razz, curled in a tight little ball at Truth's side, licked her hand in a comforting sort of way. Suddenly, the Pom sat up and let out a sharp, imperative bark.

Truth, holding the dog, leapt to her feet. "Who's there?" Peace broken, a chill ran up her spine. What was she doing out here, sitting all by herself?

Razz struggled in her arms until, perforce, Truth let her down. The dog ran off across the yard, yapping her duck-like quack.

"Razz!" she yelled, like she was mad.

"Truth," a man's voice carried to her, so softly it was almost inaudible, "it's Pratt. I need to talk to you. May I come in?"

He was at the gate at the bottom of her yard. A rush of relief swept over her. Thank Mandi for making her so paranoid about—well, about *everything*, really, and most especially voices in the night. But Pratt? He was safe.

Wasn't he?

Yes. Of course.

"Yes. Come on in," she called before remembering her attire. Oh, well, her garb was modest enough. He wasn't likely to see anything that filled him with raging desire. Anyway, while it wasn't totally dark, there were no artificial lights, either.

The gate latch clanked. A blur in the dusk, Razz's light-colored fur shone as she pranced around Pratt's feet. He bent and swooped her up. They met Truth a few steps from the patio.

Pratt nodded toward the chairs grouped around the white

resin table Gunderson had appropriated earlier while doing interviews. The overhead umbrella had been closed and tied.

"Shall we sit?" Pratt handed her the little dog.

"Sure." Pulling out a chair, Truth sank down, the resin cold against the backs of her bare thighs. She shivered. "What's up? Is it Becca? Have you heard anything about her? Has she come home?"

"No word, I'm afraid. Not yet, anyway."

She patted Razz, little hollow sounding thumps on the dog's back. "That's bad, isn't it? It means she's not with friends. And I know Becca. She wouldn't leave without telling someone. Jason, most likely. For all their arguing, they stick together. Because of their mom being sort of..."

Finishing the thought, Pratt said, "Unreliable. Yeah, so I hear. Jason tells us his mom hits the bottle pretty hard at times."

Truth, about to agree, frowned. "Tells *us*? Who's '*us*'?" The word had invisible quotes around it.

Pratt shifted in his chair, its legs scraping on the concrete. "I'd prefer you didn't spread this around, but I think you deserve to know."

"Know what?"

"I'm with the FBI, Truth."

Her mouth dropped open. "The FBI?"

"Yes. I'm afraid my visit here has been under somewhat false pretenses."

"What false pretenses?" She went cold, a condition reflected in her voice. "Why? Aren't you Digbee's grandson? Or has he been lying to me, too?"

Pratt smiled his crooked little smile. "Digbee's my grand-dad, all right. But I'm not on vacation, or resting up after serving in Afghanistan, like you were told. It's true I was in Afghanistan, but not in the last year. I'm working a case of human trafficking and staying out of the public eye. You didn't need to know. Moreover, you weren't to know."

The news struck her dumb—but only momentarily. Her voice rose. "Human trafficking? Here? At the Golden West? But why? What makes you think . . . Do you suspect . . . me? Ohmygosh, you don't suspect me!" She felt as if a fire had lit in her core. *How dare he?*

"Not now. Not ever, really. Digbee said you couldn't be involved, and after the first couple days here, I agreed with him. But there were—are—other considerations, reasons to bring me to Lost Girl Lake and the Golden West."

"For instance?" Razz squeaked as her grip tightened.

Pratt didn't hesitate. "Convenient crossing from the Canadian border, for one thing. For another, this place is remote, while still being convenient to a large city and an international airport. It's also a family-friendly area known for having almost zero crime. No crime, no cops to nose around and stir the pot. But in the FBI's eyes, when you add a transient clientele to the area, there's room for suspicion. And," he hesitated, "there were one or two other, er, items of interest."

"Don't you mean one or two other *people* of interest?" Truth bristled. "Who, besides me?" Her customers, people she trusted, whom she thought of as friends? Well, maybe not all of them. Fran and Larry might be exceptions.

Pratt folded his arms over his chest. "I suspected everyone but Digbee, to begin with, and then Sam. I crossed you off by my second night here."

"Yeah? Why?"

Good grief! She sounded belligerent even to herself. Did she want him to suspect her?

No. Just not to treat her like the breakfast toast.

Thankfully ignoring her silly outburst, he said haltingly, as if trying to placate her, "You work too hard at running the resort to head-up a trafficking ring. You get up at 5 a.m. and are in bed by 10 - 10:30 at night. And you never prowl outside at night."

"Yeah? How do you know?" More belligerence, justified this time.

He shifted in his chair as though the seat had suddenly grown super hard.

Oh. He'd spied on her sleeping habits and watched when her bedroom light went out, that's how. When else had he watched her?

She leaned forward, challenging. "So, you're saying you've been sneaking around, keeping an eye on me."

"I don't care for the word 'sneaking,' but yes. Early on, and now for these past few days. Long enough to exclude you from my list. You should be relieved. I mean to cut off the head of this ring, you see, and serve it up to the justice department on a silver platter."

He sounded fierce, so much so that Truth shuddered under the force of his conviction. She forced her anger down. "So, who *didn't* you cross off? And why are you telling me now?"

"This is where we get into the need to know category."

"*I* need to know."

"I agree. Although my boss doesn't." He watched her. His dark eyes narrowed as though wary of her reaction.

She'd show him a reaction, all right. If necessary. But for now, she wanted to hear what he had to say.

"As far as who hasn't been eliminated," he said slowly, "let me put it this way. Trust Digbee and Sam. Dottie Amholt is all right. So are the couples with kids. Jason checks out, although I wouldn't tell him anything I didn't want the whole world to hear. I'm still working on the others."

Her mouth dropped open. "Really? All the others? Are you kidding me?"

"Nope. This isn't a kidding situation. I'm not saying any of your guests are guilty. They may be pure as arctic ice. Most of them probably are. For your sake, I hope all of them. On the other hand, they may not be. I'm just recommending you be wary and careful what you say to people. And stick with your routine. Up early and to bed at ten. Don't wander around at night."

Truth's stomach churned as if she were going to barf. "And tell you if I see anything odd."

Pratt nodded. "Goes without saying."

"Of course, without saying, you being FBI and all. Funny though, you're not the first to warn me about that."

Aha. That got his attention. "About what?"

"Going out at night. Oh, it was nothing really. Mandi and I were talking, and she said—"

"Said what?" Pratt asked after an uncomfortable little pause. "Don't stop mid-sentence, Truth."

"Just that after I found the hand she became nervous enough to be glad she has a husband to protect her. She felt bad because I only have Razz." She glanced down at the little dog sleeping in her arms. "And Razz is so tiny. Not much protection. But she is," Truth added loyally. "She's got a fierce bark."

"Willing, but not necessarily able." The corner of Pratt's mouth quirked up briefly. "I agree with Mandi. Better to stay inside. The foreign girl is one thing. Becca Keene going missing strikes too close to home. These human traffickers—" He shook his head. "I don't want you becoming a target."

"Me?" Her voice cracked. "Why would anyone target me?"

"In their business, they like girls with pretty faces. Put that with your hair and, well, depending on the customer, you'd be a prize, Truth. A certain class of men is apt to find that white blonde hair of yours irresistible."

"Gah," she choked.

"Yeah." Pratt got up. Evidently, he'd said all he meant to say.

She got up, too, shaking all over, so that Razz awakened with a whimper. "Are you deliberately trying to scare me? Because if you are, it's working."

"Is it? Good," he said and strode off.

Too soon, the night hid him from view.

TRUTH, even though she knew Pratt was still within hailing distance and that a single cry would bring him on the run, stared around the familiar perimeter of her yard. Her eyes stretched wide, trying to see everything at once. Danger, new to her, lurked in shadows cast by overgrown lilac bushes. The fluttering wings of a night bird hinted at sleep disturbed. A big pot of wildly flowering clove-scented petunias seemed muted. Was it possible someone, a murderous pervert of the worst sort, had his eye on her?

She clutched Razz against her chest, thankful for the dog's warmth.

"No," she whispered. "We're not afraid, are we, Razz?"

But then, who'd ever think of the Golden West as a hub for a human trafficking scheme? Cops had been running in and out of here for days, from the moment she'd raked up that hand. No one would dare—

Taking long steps just short of running, Truth reached the door into the building, scooted inside and with shaking fingers, set the latch on the screen door. Slammed closed the thick, old-fashioned wooden door. Snapped on the locks, checked and double-checked for security.

No one would dare?

Then where was Becca?

For the first time in years, Truth barred the door between her private section of the old building and the public portions. Even then, every creak as the place settled and cooled stretched her nerves.

Jump in bed and cover up your head. The line from a childhood poem echoed. She stopped short of taking so drastic an action as that; it was far too hot for one thing. But she lay in bed with her arms behind her head, listening . . . listening.

Concentrate then on Pratt.

"He's FBI, Razz. Imagine that."

Razz didn't say anything, though her tiny body tensed as if she were paying strict attention.

"He didn't even tell Gunderson. No wonder he wasn't worried about the detective on that first day." She sighed. "I wish I'd known."

She closed her eyes, which shot open again as something down at the dock thudded. Another loose boat? Another body? She resisted the urge to look out the window. Think of something else.

Think of Pratt, who'd said, "Pretty face."

Think of his dark eyes, sometimes hard and unreadable. Sometimes not.

Think of . . . No. Don't think. Sleep.

Hard to do when you're angry. And scared.

CHAPTER 18

DIGBEE STIRRED NOISILY ABOUT IN THE TINY KITCHEN SECTION of his fifth-wheel, awakening Pratt much too early. The old man ran water and banged a grease-splattered enamel coffeepot under the water faucet, the clamor magnified by the small space. A burner on the gas stove started with a pop.

Muttering under his breath, Pratt cast aside the light blanket and sat up, his feet thumping to the floor. He stretched his arms over his head until his back gave an audible crunch. He couldn't wait until this business finished and he could blow this place. Sleeping on a sofa tucked into the RV's slide-out made his bones hurt. And that was on a good day when he actually got more than four hours in the sack.

He yawned. "Anything happen on your watch, Granddad?"

Digbee hooked down a couple mugs from the overhead cupboard. "Nope. The light in Truth's bedroom went on at five a.m. as usual. She let the dog out and stood at the door watching Razz do her stuff. Didn't go into the yard. But Pratt —" The old man's bushy eyebrows drew together.

"What?" Alarm touched him. He didn't care for the way his

147

grandfather's wrinkled lips twisted. "Did you notice anything that looked wrong?"

"Yeah. I did. Pretty sure I saw a pistol in her hand. Don't look like our girl is taking any chances. You must've been kind of rough on her."

"Spooked her, huh?" Pratt grabbed his jeans from a chair and stuck his legs into them, got to his feet and drew them over his hips. He avoided meeting Digbee's accusing eyes. "I meant to. Can't say as I like her carrying a gun, though. Do you suppose she even knows how to use it?"

Digbee, shrugging, looked like he didn't know whether to be sad or mad. "And I don't like her so scared she thinks she needs one. Hope she doesn't shoot one of her own customers. You should talk to her. Let her know she's got people looking out for her."

"Better if she doesn't know. Better if *no* one else knows." *Dammit, it!* He should've been prepared for her to take matters into her own hands. The business she was in didn't propagate shrinking violets. She might well have run up against a variety of rough customers before now and, since she was still in business, managed to hold her own. Still, a gun?

He should've been prepared for Digbee's protest of his methods, too. "I'll have Ernhardt get someone here today to keep an eye on her," he assured his grandfather. "On the whole resort. But until then—"

Digbee turned down the flame under the coffee pot from which a rich aroma spread through the trailer. "Good. Sam's sticking to her tighter than duct tape at the moment." He poured a few drops of cold water down the spout to settle the grounds. "You've got me a little puzzled, son."

"I do? About what?"

"About Truth. Why her? What makes you think she's in any more danger than any of the other women at the Golden West?

Why not Dottie Amholt? Or Mandi Hennings, even if she is a married lady?"

Pratt pulled a clean gray T-shirt over his head and reached for the mug Digbee held out to him. "Call it a gut feeling. There's also the matter of Truth's gate being vandalized for no apparent reason. Put together with using her barn as a kill site, and her boat as a disposal unit, that makes her too closely involved for comfort. Hers or mine. The kicker is the unexpected cash offer she's gotten from Bill Billous. It's got me wondering if this is a sign Truth is number one on a hit list."

"You think whoever is doing this is stupid enough to stick around since the girl's body has been found?"

"I think it's obvious, now Becca's gone missing." Pratt viewed Digbee with some surprise. "Don't you?"

Digbee grimaced. "I suppose. So, are you afraid Truth will go missing like Becca, or that somebody might try to kill her, like the other girl?"

"Both." Putting a voice to the possibility made Pratt nervous. He took a big swallow of scalding coffee.

"Ortiz and Blaine, you can count on them. They're her friends. They'll see nothing happens to her."

It sounded to Pratt like his granddad was grasping at straws. "Well, yeah. About them—"

Digbee slammed his cup onto the counter. Coffee sloshed as far as the window over the sink, a few drops running down the glass. "Don't tell me they're under suspicion, too."

"Right now, I consider everyone at the Golden West a suspect except you and Sam and Jason Keene." Pratt's answer came out sour.

The old man's shoulders bowed, but only for a moment. "Well, then, it looks to me like you'd better get your butt in gear and figure this out."

"I plan on it." Pratt checked his pockets for phone and keys.

His Glock 26 went into an ankle holster. "First I'm going to take Truth up on her offer of a free breakfast. I used your tools. Maybe if we're real nice, she'll feed you, too."

Digbee cocked his head.

"Payment for fixing her gate," Pratt explained and smiled wryly.

Although it was early, 6:30, as Pratt found upon consulting his watch, a few fishermen were trickling into the resort. Three or four boats were backed up at the boat launch, waiting for their turns. A trio of boatless anglers went inside the store, either to buy time on the dock or rent one of the Golden West's flat-bottoms. He figured Truth was probably feeling a little relief as a few dollars dropped into the till.

Gulls, already in action, swooped and screeched overhead. Somewhere, a dog barked, and another answered. The lawn, damp with morning dew, released a new-mown scent. Tracks through the grass showed Pratt that he and his grandfather weren't the first campers to be out and about.

The parking lot was empty of law enforcement vehicles. Apparently, Gunderson had finished at the barn and moved his operation back to town to help law enforcement personnel put a joint task force together. As for Becca, the twenty-four-hour waiting period was nearly up. Pratt figured the detective would make it official and get his deputies out talking to friends and neighbors soon.

Unless the girl had returned home during the night. A possibility, although not one he believed had a chance of working out. Another gut feeling, this one as uncomfortable as the first.

At least Truth was safe for the moment. As Pratt and Digbee started down the cedar chip path to the store, she came around the side of the building lugging a green hose, spraying water over the plantings and washing down the porch. Razz frisked around her feet as Truth stretched to tidy up big pots of brilliant red geraniums hanging from the eaves on each side of the door. The warm scent of apples, cloves and cinnamon escaped from the building.

She wore denim capris and a yellow tank top, with another of her ubiquitous white baker's aprons wrapped around her slender middle. A bulge in the shape of a small pistol showed under the apron, although Pratt figured nobody else would notice. He only did because he was looking for it.

Spying the two men, Razz ran to meet them. Digbee laughed as the tiny dog's plumey tail waved a greeting. She jumped up on Pratt's knee, halting him midstride.

"You've got a friend," Digbee said.

Pratt's lips twitched. "Yeah. I had to fish her out of the lake the other night. Don't tell anybody. I'll get laughed out of the agency if the men think I'm partial to four-pound dogs. No, I'll take a big guy, maybe a malamute. That's the breed for me. Make a statement."

"*Are* you partial to four-pounds dogs?"

"Just this one. I'm a sucker for cute." He reached down to ruffle Razz's ears. "Yeah, and you know it, don't you?"

Razz barked. Digbee laughed.

"Morning, Truth," Digbee said as they mounted the two steps to the resort porch. He stuck his nose into the air and made a production of sniffing. "Do I smell apple pie?"

"You do, but I'm not cutting into it until lunchtime. If you want a piece, you'd better tell Connie and she'll set some aside for you." She sprinkled water over her geraniums as if it were the most important task in the world.

The short rejoinder was unlike her. Pratt suffered an inner twitch. "Sleep well last night?"

Raising brown eyes made larger by the raccoon-like dark

circles beneath them, Truth glared. "What do you think? After . . ."

Pratt lifted a forefinger, the small gesture stopping whatever she'd been about to say. Just as well, too, because Mandi Henning, carrying a clear plastic bag with three bananas and a few containers of yogurt inside, exited the store just then and stopped beside them.

"Good morning, Digbee, Pratt." She seemed disconcertingly cheerful, especially when compared to Truth. "You guys coming to breakfast? Truth has homemade beef hash and it looks and smells divine." She held up her grocery bag. "Makes me wish Ken and I weren't on this health kick. We're trying to cut down on fried food." She took on a woebegone expression. "All the good stuff."

Digbee patted his stomach, only recently grown a bit paunchy. "I'm too old to worry about my health."

His own stomach growling, Pratt agreed. Not about the too old part, but the worrying about his health. He kept looking at Truth, willing her to meet his eyes. "That offer of breakfast still hold good?" he asked, his voice soft.

The reminder worked as an attitude changer. She took a deep breath. Her smile seemed natural. "Of course. You and Digbee both. I'm so grateful to have my gate fixed; your labor and Digbee's tools. I'm sure all potential bogeymen will be kept away."

Something still a little facetious there, Pratt thought.

Overhearing, Mandi broke in, "What did happen to your gate, Truth? I noticed Pratt working on it yesterday, but when Ken and I walked past the night before, it was perfectly all right. Did the storm damage it?"

Truth glanced at Mandi and shrugged. "Maybe the storm. Or maybe vandals."

"Vandals?" Mandi's mouth rounded. "Here?" Then, hair

flying, she shook her head. "Well, of course, in view of . . ." She paused and took a deep breath. "I'm so sorry, Truth. Is there any news about that poor girl?"

There wasn't. Or at least, none anyone was willing to discuss. Pratt said nothing, his shrug an eloquent enough denial.

When Mandi finally moved on and the men went past Truth into the café, Digbee nudged Pratt none too gently in the ribs. "She mad at you?"

No question which *she* he meant.

"A classic case of killing the messenger," Pratt growled.

AFTER A HEARTY BREAKFAST of the beef hash special that included a side order of buttermilk pancakes, Pratt left Digbee, who said he wasn't sleepy yet, on watch. He got in his pickup, drove out of the canyon to the top of the hill, and stopped. His cell, upon receipt of a requisite number of bars, chirped to life. Pratt tapped in numbers.

Earnhardt answered a nano-second before his voice mail kicked in. "What?"

Pratt's report was almost as short as the boss's greeting. His requests made up a longer list: IDs to be checked, credit reports and bank statements verified, his request for back-up cleared.

"One more thing," Earnhardt said. "I've got a name for you on our victim."

A surprise. Pratt had worried the girl's body would remain unnamed and unclaimed for months. "Which is?"

"Yudif Maruseva. She turned up on a state department report. She's from Ukraine. No question it's the same girl." He stumbled a little over the girl's name, but Pratt got the gist.

And once identified, finding the girl's killer became a more personal quest.

"Think we might be dealing with the Russian mob?" he asked.

"All things are possible," Ernhardt replied.

Yeah, it had always been a possibility, given the large Russian and former USSR population base in the area. The information ticked over in Pratt's mind. A real lead, at last. And among his wide circle of—call them acquaintances—he knew just the woman he needed to talk to. Excitement tweaked his hunter's blood.

Ernhardt was still speaking, although Pratt missed part of what he said.

"Madden?" Ernhardt sounded impatient. "You still there?"

"Yeah. I'm here."

"That name mean anything to you?"

"The name, no. The country, maybe."

"I hope so. We've been on this job for two months. It's time we wrap it up."

We? Two months? Ernhardt was a short-timer. Pratt had been on his own and tracking this ring much longer than Ernhardt's measly two months. "You get a man out here to the resort today. I want a visible FBI presence here at all times. Give the folks someone to point at while I go in a different direction."

"Consider it done. I'll have the information you want by tonight. And Madden—"

"Yeah?"

"Stay in touch."

"Wouldn't dream of anything else."

Ernhardt hung up, chuckling.

CHAPTER 19

Truth cleared dirty dishes from a table into a plastic tub for transportation into the kitchen. Crockery clattered, silverware banged, water glasses pinged. She paid no attention. Her mind whirled; angry, confused, miffed—mostly miffed. How could Pratt make a dramatic announcement that he was FBI last night, then waltz into the café this morning as if he were just anybody? Shouldn't he be out detecting and making arrests? Preferably before anyone else got hurt. Which reminded her—

As though her unfinished thought conjured him, Jason arrived in his Samurai, only driving at half his usual rate of speed. He stopped and simply sat there, staring off into space. Finally, instead of leaping over the side of the topless rock crawler, he opened the door and got out. Feet dragging, he headed into the store.

The screen door slammed behind him as he entered, not even flinching as the door caught him on the heel.

Truth drew in a deep, apprehensive breath. *Uh oh. This is bad.*

He spied her watching him and gestured, indicating he wanted her to join him in the kitchen. She cleared one last place setting before following him, pausing to deposit her load by the sink.

"Becca hasn't come home, has she?" she asked, trying to mask her anxiety. "Is there any news?"

Jason looked as if he'd aged ten years from the time he left the resort yesterday. "Nope. Mom is still in denial, but I'm asking the sheriff's department to start looking for her. The twenty-four hours is up. More than up."

Tears welled in his eyes, matching the ones in Truth's. She put her arms around him and gave him a hug. "I'm so sorry, Jason. Try not to worry. Maybe—"

"Yeah. Maybe."

He obviously wasn't in the mood to listen to platitudes and she didn't blame him. She wouldn't be either if their positions were reversed. "Have you spoken to Detective Gunderson?"

"Not yet." He pulled away and straightened. "I didn't want Mom listening in when he gets going. You know how he is." He peeked around the corner and surveyed the tiny dining room. "I hoped he'd be here by now. I wanted to talk to him in person."

Truth wrinkled her nose. "He hasn't shown up this morning. Your best bet is to call Deputy Ortiz and report to him. He's probably the one who'll do most of the work anyway." Truth had no illusions about the ill-tempered detective and his methods of delegating.

Jason nodded. "Okay if I use your phone?"

"Sure."

Setting his lips in a firm line, Jason crossed the room to the kitchen phone, turning his back on her.

Consuelo stood at a cutting board chopping onion and celery for yet another batch of potato salad. She widened her eyes and raised her shoulders in mute question. Truth, beyond trying to explain the dynamics of the Keene family, shook her head.

At the phone, Jason talked, listened, talked again, listened. His shoulders slumped, then jerked as if hit with a taser. "No," he shouted into the receiver. "No, no, and no. How many times do I have to tell you?"

Connie looked at Truth; Truth looked at Connie. Both women stood still as museum pieces, trying to understand the gist of the conversation. Things obviously were not going well and from Connie's round-eyed wonder, she was even a little alarmed by Jason's outburst.

Jason got quiet and tense again, then said in a taut-sounding voice, "Fine. I'll wait for you at the resort." He slammed the receiver onto the hook, nearly pulling the phone from the wall. "Stupid cop," he muttered, swiping at his eyes with the back of his hand. He rubbed any residue off on his pant leg. "If he had a brain he'd be dangerous."

Truth shared another look with Consuelo.

"Is Deputy Ortiz giving you a bad time?" Truth dared to ask, surprised at the deputy rousing so much ire. He'd always seemed to get along well with Jason. Actually, with everyone here at the resort.

"Not Ortiz. I talked to Gunderson, after all." Jason's face glowed an angry red. He took a couple deep breaths as though he'd been running a race.

Connie murmured something in Spanish, something that started with, "*pobre chico.*"

"Oh." Truth could guess where *that* was going. She waited a tick, and when Jason forbear to say anything further, went ahead and asked, "The sheriff's department is going to instigate a search for Becca, isn't it?"

Sarcasm colored Jason's voice. "Yeah. Sorta. He finally said he'd put out a BOLO, whatever *that* is, and send Deputy Ortiz out to ask the neighbors and Becca's friends if they've seen her." His lip curled. "Dude must think we're stupid as a box of rocks. As if Mom and I haven't already talked to everyone we know. Twice. I tried to tell him."

Truth nodded as if agreeing with him, but she guessed the police had a protocol for dealing with cases like this. And experience. Too much experience, probably. They had to ask the same questions again and again and maybe compare notes. All old buildings—just like her barn—must be searched. Any lead, no matter how small, followed to the end. At least, she trusted the latter was the case, and done quickly.

A sense of foreboding shivered through her. Time must be important. Gunderson and Ortiz and, yes, Pratt Madden, even if this wasn't exactly his jurisdiction, must see that what had happened to the dead girl might also become Becca's fate. They had to find her. Soon.

"Try not to fret," she told Jason, even as Consuelo returned her attention to the chopping block and started whacking through a big Walla Walla sweet onion. The pounding seemed more vigorous than usual. "Becca's a smart girl. Too smart to . . ." She broke off, mentally snorting at the thought. Actually, she'd never been overwhelmed by Becca's intelligence.

"They'll find her," she went on. "Wait and see. Becca will be fine." Only somehow Truth found her own words less than convincing.

THE DAILY LUNCH rush was in full swing before Deputy Ortiz finally arrived, looking hot, tired, and hungry. Unhappy, too.

Jason, who'd been on the look-out for him, fidgeted on the counter stool where he'd been waiting the last two hours. He scowled as Ortiz, claiming the empty stool next to him, beckoned Truth over.

With a wary side glance at Jason, she approached. Why didn't Ortiz just get to it? Couldn't he see the boy was on the verge of a breakdown?

Apparently not.

"Cheeseburger, spud salad and iced tea," the deputy ordered. "I'm starving. Been a busy morning."

"You're going to eat? *Now*?" Jason's starkly pale face reddened. "We don't have time for you to screw around feeding your face. You've gotta get out there and find my sister." His voice rose and broke. The conversation between a couple women seated at the nearest table stilled.

"I can eat and listen to what you tell me at the same time. Like who she's dating, her friends . . . her enemies." A shake of Ortiz's head sent Truth into the kitchen.

Behind her, she heard Jason say, "Enemies? Becca doesn't have any enemies. All she's got are friends. Tons of them."

She kept an eye on them through the open doorway. While the burger cooked, she brought Ortiz his tea, a slice of lemon on the rim and condensation running down the side of the glass. She was hoping to overhear their conversation. And she did, a little, although as far as she could tell Ortiz was just discussing the steps Jason had already completed, that of talking to everyone Becca knew. The deputy pulled a ballpoint from his shirt pocket and wrote down something—several somethings—in a small spiral-bound tablet.

A newly arrived customer called her away, and in the flurry of taking an order for a club sandwich and fries, she lost track. She was hurrying from the kitchen to serve the sandwich when Pratt strode in.

He stopped, scanning the room before going over to where

Ortiz and Jason sat. He lay a hand on Jason's shoulder and gave it a squeeze.

"You been briefed?" she heard him say to Ortiz as she rounded the counter.

"Yes."

"Been briefed about what?" Jason's angry question followed her.

Cat's out of the bag, she thought as she served her customer, pausing a moment to chat and answer his question about the best fishing spot on the lake. She made sure to warn him about rocks in the shallow water at the other end of Lost Girl. Too shallow for his 25-foot Seaswirl. When she turned around, the three had retreated to her private patio without so much as a by-your-leave, Ortiz carrying his lunch out with him.

Through the side window, she watched them take chairs at the table. Pratt tilted the umbrella to shade them from the sun, also hiding their faces from view. A short while later, Ortiz threw down his napkin. He and Jason jumped up and left, the deputy getting in his patrol car and following in the Samurai's dust toward the Keene place. Jason drove a whole lot faster than when he'd arrived.

Pratt stood outside and watched them out of sight, before coming back in. He appropriated Jason's place on the end counter stool and, although she hadn't meant him to, caught her looking at him. The corner of his mouth twitched up.

"I'd like to place an order," he said.

Reaching for her order pad, a farce since her memory functioned quite well, thank you very much, she moved to stand in front of him. "What'll you have?"

"A piece of that apple pie you promised, and a couple minutes of your time." His expression turned serious. He wasn't smiling now. Not even close.

"Digbee asked for the pie, not you," she reminded him, trying for light and coming across surly.

Pratt studied her, his eyes narrowed. "Still mad at me, Truth? Why? I'm just doing my job. Nothing personal."

Why? He asked why? Nothing personal? Really? She felt ready to explode. All this going on in the background of her resort and she not informed? Yes. She took all of it personally.

She spoke through gritted teeth. "You should have warned me there was . . . is . . . a problem. That you suspected someone of using *my* resort as a criminal way station."

"Warned you? Listen, honey, when an agent is on undercover assignment, it means the operation is a secret. Means *nobody* is told, who doesn't have to know. You didn't." He toyed with the salt shaker on the counter in front of him, spinning it around and around. "What if you'd been one of the . . . schemers?"

"Me? A schemer?"

His pause meant something. What?

"That's ridiculous." Her retort sounded a tad squeaky.

"Is it? Remember that farmer and his wife down around Odessa? A couple well-respected in the community, farm been in the family for more than a century. Then it turns out their biggest cash crop is marijuana sold on the black market. The case belonged to the DEA, but everyone in law enforcement heard the details."

"No comparison," she countered. "I've not murdered anyone, and what's more, neither did they." She reached out, took the salt shaker from him, and sat it down with a snap. "And I'm not growing marijuana, either."

Pratt sighed. "I know you're not. Why can't you accept that I'm trying to look out for you? Stay innocent, Truth. Better yet, stay ignorant. You'll be safer."

As if she were able to unknow what she knew, little as it

was. She took a deep breath, her glance going around the café, emptied now of customers, and on into the store where she heard the bait refrigerator door close. "Ignorant. Oh, that helps. And safe from what? Anyway, why aren't you out chasing bad guys? Or looking for Becca?"

"Ortiz can handle the preliminaries of finding Becca without my help. That's his job, not mine. And I am chasing bad guys, right here, right now."

Was he talking about her? Truth narrowed her eyes. "What do you mean?"

"Don't look so guilty, sweetheart." Pratt reached for the pepper shaker and started it spinning. "I mean I'm still keeping my presence here quiet. You know I'm FBI. You, Digbee, Gunderson, Ortiz and now Jason. That's all. And Truth, pay attention to this. No one else is to know. No one. Got that?"

He'd called her sweetheart. Mockery? "No one else? Not Sam? Not even Hunter or the other cops?"

Pratt shook his head.

Truth took refuge in cynicism. "Aren't I the privileged one? And why all the secrecy now the girl with the amputated hand has been found? Do you—the FBI—even know who she is? Who she was?" She watched the shaker, ready to make a flying catch.

"No other information is being released to the public," he intoned, like someone making a press release on the evening news. Then less formally, "We found a body. We still don't have the people who killed her."

That was true. Nor had they, from what she could tell, even a hint as to who the killer might be. She nodded.

Pratt pressed home the point. "It wouldn't take much for word to get around. A slip of the tongue. Talking too loud. Any little misstep. Any of which could put Becca in danger."

If she isn't dead already. "And you think the killer-slash-kidnapper is one of my campers." She felt sick saying it out loud.

Pratt shifted on the stool. "Possible. Not written in stone."

"I hope you're wrong."

"So do I," Pratt said. "Now, do you think I could get my pie?"

"Of course," Truth said through clenched teeth. She took the pepper shaker from him ever so gently and put it beside the salt and the sugar jar. Even so, she made a point of going over to the store side of the building first, to take money from a fellow who bought a couple dozen worms. She wanted to show him . . . what?

CHAPTER 20

PRATT FOUND HIS GRANDDAD HAD GONE OFF SOMEWHERE—MOST probably hobnobbing with his pal Sam—when he stopped by the fifth-wheel to collect his fishing gear. Following his afternoon routine of previous days, he ambled down to the dock. He needed an hour or two away from the case. Something to rest and refresh his mind.

He found Dottie Amholt already there, dangling a line in the water. Old Mrs. Thompson sat next to her, her wild white hair protected from the beating sun by a ragged straw hat.

Pratt took a seat on the backless bench on Dottie's other side and unscrewed the top of his jar of salmon eggs.

She looked over at him. "Everything all right? You've been spending a lot of time with those cops."

"Everything's hunky dory." He forced a smile. Except it wasn't so hunky dory. Wouldn't be, not until whoever kidnapped, mutilated and killed Yudif Maruseva was found. And Becca. What about her? Where was she, and why did he have such an awful premonition Truth also might suddenly disappear?

Pratt fit a couple fuchsia-colored salmon eggs onto his barbless hook and tightened his line. Rearing back with his arm, he cast the line out over the lake, nearly reaching the rocky shore on the opposite side of the bay.

"Beautiful cast." Mrs. Thompson nodded admiringly. The line from her pole drooped into the water a mere three feet in front of the dock. A bright red and white bobber moved with the gentle lapping of the waves.

Leaning back, Pratt let his bait sink slowly to the bottom of the lake. He lifted his face. Sunshine beat down on his head, dark glasses sheltered his eyes. It should've been peaceful. He found no respite, though. His mind kept going over the scant facts of the case.

Mrs. Thompson, a great chatterer, leaned around Dottie to speak to him. "I've been worried that detective is going to arrest you, Pratt. We all are. He isn't, is he?"

Pratt barely withheld his chuckle. "Arrest me? Not that I know of, Mrs. Thompson."

She blew out a breath. "Whew, that's good. Something like that would break your grandfather's heart. He dotes on you, you know."

Dotes? Digbee? "I hadn't noticed," he said.

Beside him, Dottie smothered a giggle.

Pratt turned serious. "I'm afraid Detective Gunderson may have a difficult time pinning anyone down."

Dottie sobered. "Really? Why? I mean, I've wondered if he's very, you know, sharp, but who am I to judge?"

Time to speak out? Pratt wondered. Reveal a little bit here, a little bit there. Wouldn't hurt to stir the pot. Let a few facts go the rounds. You never know what might rise to the surface.

"Not because of Gunderson's failings. Because of the time of the girl's death. Yu . . ." He broke off. Almost a beginner's slip of the tongue. No way he should know the girl's name, even though most everyone knew he'd been in on the discovery of her body. The rest of it was too graphic to relate. The decomposition, the presence of insect larva, the fact Yudif had been stowed in a black garbage bag with the sun glaring down on her. No need to present them with this vision. He didn't care for it himself.

He was getting sloppy, working in this laid-back place. "From what I understand . . ." He hesitated again.

"When did that poor girl actually die?" Mrs. Thompson picked up on the hint, seeming not to notice as her fishing line, its bobber bouncing up and down, plunged beneath the surface of the lake. "Has Officer Ortiz mentioned anything? I've seen the two of you talking."

Pratt shook his head no.

"Think about it." Dottie wasn't giving much heed to her fishing, either. "If they don't know when the girl died, they can't establish a reliable timeline."

"True." Pratt agreed, and at Mrs. Thompson's still-puzzled expression, he elaborated. "No reliable timeline, like Dottie says, and the detectives can't prove anyone's whereabouts or alibi, good or bad. Timewise, it'd just be a guess."

Mrs. Thompson's mouth rounded into an O. "My goodness. So you mean *any one of us* could have killed her? No one is cleared? Even me?"

"Exactly." Pratt and Dottie responded in unison.

"Oh, my goodness." The old lady gulped. "Well, I wish I'd noticed something that points to the murderer. I mean, holding the girl right under our noses? Someone should've noticed."

And wasn't she right about that? Guilt drew a black cloud over Pratt. He'd been on the scene here at the Golden West. Yudif Maruseva had been killed on his watch.

"You couldn't know," Dottie said, and although she spoke to

Mrs. Thompson, the words were apt for him as well. He hoped.

"But I should have," Mrs. Thompson insisted. "I don't sleep well, you know. Not even here where it's always so quiet. Sometimes I get up in the night and walk around until I can drop off again."

Pratt came to attention. "Do you ever see anyone else out?"

"Once or twice, but never any strangers. Old Mr. Pearson walking his dog. A woman, coming out of the public restroom."

"A woman? Who?" His voice sharpened.

"I'm sorry, Pratt. She went around the corner before I got a good look. I don't see all that well at night, you know. Cataracts."

They all fell silent as Mrs. Thompson absently dealt with a tiny sunfish that had stolen her bait.

"Pratt?" Dottie, who'd been replacing a chewed worm on her hook, looked up at him, squinting into the sun.

"Huh?" Thinking he felt a tug on his line, he gave his pole a little jerk. Nothing jerked back. He reeled in the slack.

"On my way down here, someone told me Becca Keene has gone missing." Dottie ignored Mrs. Thompson's gasp and said, "Do you think it's for real?"

News got around fast in a closed environment like the Golden West Resort. "Afraid so," he said. "I was in the café when Jason reported to Deputy Ortiz this morning."

Dottie tossed her baited hook into the water. "Becca is a bit of a show-off, in case you haven't noticed. Well, being a guy, maybe you haven't, but she is."

"Are you saying she might have staged a disappearance?" Pratt picked up on Dottie's barely veiled hint.

"Oh, she wouldn't do a thing like that," Mrs. Thompson cut

in before Dottie could say yes or no. Then, more doubtfully, "Would she?"

"I hope not," Pratt said. "Her brother or her mother certainly don't think so."

Dottie bit her lip. "I hope not, too, but she does like being the center of attention. Besides, what do brothers know?"

A man without brother or sister, Pratt gave a helpless shrug.

"She's a pretty girl," Mrs. Thompson said as if that explained anything.

"So?" Dottie gave her pole a little yank. "Doesn't give her the right to eyeball every other girl's guy."

Had Becca done that to Dottie's boyfriend? Maybe. Pratt remembered an incident last week where Dottie had been spitting fire but refused to speak about it except for one disgusted, "Becca!" He decided to stay out of the women's way and listen to their gossip.

"Oh, but—" Mrs. Thompson floundered.

"You can't deny she does." Dottie's voice sharpened, carrying over the water and causing a low flying gull to bypass the group of humans. The other end of the dock dipped a little as someone stepped out onto it. A man, silhouetted by the sun at his rear.

"Maybe Becca is a bit of a flirt," Mrs. Thompson said, "but I'm sure she doesn't mean anything by it."

"Hah!"

"No, really, Dottie. She's naturally friendly, is all."

"Too friendly."

"But charming, too. Don't you think so, Pratt?" Mrs. Thompson drew him into the discussion again whether he liked it or not.

He shrugged, and the old lady said, "Come now, Pratt.

Admit it. I've seen you smile at her, and you don't smile at many people. Not even Truth, who is a lovely person."

The mention of Truth set his mind off on a different tangent.

"Truth *is* nice," Dottie agreed. "If she weren't, she wouldn't put up with Becca always being late to work and then sluffing off her job when she gets here. And I know Becca can actually do her work—when she feels like it."

Apparently, Mrs. Thompson couldn't deny this part of the argument. She leaned in closer to Dottie, saying, "Well, there is something to that, I must admit. And she does manage to finagle special treatment for herself. For instance, the night before last, just about dark, I saw Becca get in Hunter Blaine's SUV and ride off with him. And we all know Truth has been sweet on Hunter for a couple years."

Truth was sweet on Hunter? Pratt felt a twinge of disappointment at Mrs. Thompson's comment. *Not* the kind of stuff he wanted to hear. But what had she said before that distraction? About Becca? About Becca and Hunter Blaine?

He sat up straight, nerves blaring.

"We all thought something was going on between them, but it seems to have petered out," the old lady went on. "Becca's fault, do you think?" Her wrinkles folded one into another like an accordion as she frowned. "Although if you ask me, Becca is much too young for Officer Blaine. Don't you agree?"

Although the two women didn't seem to notice they were about to have company, Pratt was hyper-aware of the man who clumped to a stop beside them. He had a good look at the hiking boots on the man's feet. His stomach muscles tightened.

"You ladies having any luck? It's a fine day for fishing." Fish and Wildlife Officer Hunter Blaine's words were pleasant, although Pratt understood he'd been included in the "ladies" sobriquet.

Languidly, Pratt adjusted his sunglasses and peered up into Blaine's face. Although a smile curved the man's mouth, his blazing eyes reflected something different. As if realizing this might be so, he took mirrored sunglasses from his shirt pocket and slid them on.

Pratt didn't laugh, even though the guilty exchange of grimaces Dottie and Mrs. Thompson shared struck him as amusing. As funny as he and Blaine, each concealing whatever tale their eyes might tell behind darkened lenses.

Mrs. Thompson found her voice first. "It is a fine day, Officer Blaine, even though the fish aren't biting worth a hoot."

"No?"

"No." But she sounded uncertain.

"Mind if I poke around a little?" Blaine asked. "Just to make sure."

"Make sure of what?" The old lady blinked.

Blaine's toe touched the equipment scattered around her feet: the Styrofoam cup of worms, a Plano tackle box, a red Coleman cooler. "You know I can't take anyone's word when they tell me they're not catching anything. You'd be surprised how often folks are mistaken." His tongue clicked. "A shame when I have to levy a penalty over such a simple error in judgment."

"I'm not mistaken, but you do what you must." Her voice quavered.

"No?" Blaine's tone went soft, yet Pratt fancied he heard something menacing in it. "But you're mistaken about seeing Becca in my truck."

Mrs. Thompson set her mouth in a firm line. "I know what I saw."

"Evidently not." The menace sounded stronger as Blaine added, "You should be careful what you say, Mrs. Thompson. People can find themselves in big trouble, spreading rumors."

"But—" she faltered. Stopped as his message sank in. Her chin trembled. "Well, maybe I'm wrong. My eyes. They aren't so good anymore."

As Dottie took a breath as though to speak, Pratt squeezed her arm in warning. He shook his head.

The wildlife officer made a production of "poking around," emitting short grunts ever so often. Mrs. Thompson's face flamed, although she refrained from challenging him.

Pratt didn't much care for the man's method of retaliation. Harassment as payback, if that's all it was, seemed petty to him, and yet, put himself in Blaine's place and he might do the same.

He huffed through his nose. Or not. He knew bullying when he heard it. He fought down the urge to take the wildlife officer on, head to head. Not now, he told himself, even as he made a mental note. A further check into Hunter Blaine's history struck him as an excellent idea.

Blaine didn't seem all that surprised when his search came up empty.

"I'm next, I suppose." Dottie sounded hard, not at all like herself.

"You over the limit?"

"No."

Blaine waved a hand. "Then not today." He looked at Pratt.

"Sorry, all I brought to the dock was my pole and this jar of salmon eggs." Pratt smiled easily. "Catch and release—if I ever get a bite."

"I'll take a look at your license," Blaine said.

"Oh—" Dottie began, but Pratt cut her off.

"Sure. No problem." He reached into his hip pocket and found his wallet. The slip of paper showed he was legal.

"Fine, that's fine." Blaine gave the license a cursory glance. His mouth turned up in that cool smile again. "Just doing my job." He gave a little finger wave as he retreated down the dock.

"Well! I certainly don't understand what Becca sees in him. How rude!" Mrs. Thompson failed to lower her voice.

Blaine kept walking, his chuckle carrying back to them over the water.

"Nevertheless," Mrs. Thompson said in a whisper, "I know what I saw, and I saw Becca get in his SUV."

Pratt believed her. "I wonder why he denies it?" he breathed without realizing he spoke out loud.

Dottie answered anyway. "Bet we find out." She didn't sound happy.

CHAPTER 21

"Alone at last, Razz." Truth set her cold drink and a book she'd been trying to read on the patio table. Sinking onto a lawn chair, she kicked off her shoes and gave her toes a vigorous wiggle. Immediately, she felt ten degrees cooler. "Ah. Just you and me, kid."

Razz, ever curious, came over and gave her feet a sniff and a lick.

Truth laughed. "Cut that out. It tickles." Bending over, she gave the Pomeranian a scratch on the head.

The mid-afternoon doldrums had settled over the resort. Dogs lay in the shade and panted. Too hot to swim or fish, too hot to play ball or even swing, kids napped while adults sat at picnic tables sipping iced drinks. And talking. Oh lordy, how they talked!

Heaven knows they had plenty of grist for the rumor mill. Becca's disappearance, the dead girl, even so minor a thing as the vandalism to her own gate, all of interest to gossipers.

And the barn, of course. "How delightfully creepy," she'd

overheard a woman say. *Delightfully*. Was the woman out of her ever-loving mind?

Pratt's warning nagged at her. Adding Mandi's frightening hints to the ones he'd mentioned made Truth's headache with worry and stress. So much that a few minutes ago she'd knocked back three ibuprofen, locked the door to the resort and put out a closed sign. If anyone had a real emergency, they could give the night bell a yank. What she really wanted—no, needed—was an hour to herself.

Sitting back, she raised the iced tea glass to her forehead and rubbed it over her temples. The glass contained an herbal concoction with a slice of lemon, even though what she really craved was a strong margarita. Or two. Or maybe even three. By that time she'd be passed out and wouldn't have to think about what was happening around her resort.

She sighed. Trouble is, it'd all still be there when she woke up.

Razz had the right idea. The little dog stretched out with her tummy pressed to the cool grass. Her eyes drifted closed.

Leaning back in her chair, Truth propped her weary legs on a footstool and opened her book. A bumblebee rumbled as it flitted from lavender to delphinium to veronica in the blue garden. A hummingbird's wings thrummed at the feeder. Far off, maybe mid-lake, a boat motor's sudden full-throated roar told her some hardy souls were cooling off via water skis. Her eyes, like Razz's, drifted shut.

The night bell jangled its alarm.

Truth's feet, heels first, fell from the stool and hit the pavers. "Ouch."

Razz, also startled, jumped up. Her sharp yelps shattered the calm. The raucous noise of the night bell almost put Truth's heart into a spasm, worse even than when she was awakened at two a.m.

Imperiously, the bell pealed again.

Wincing, Truth ran. *Save me, please Lord. What now?*

She wrenched open the door and flung it wide. Bill Billous, broad grin intact, stood there, his meaty hand still on the bell rope. "Good day, Ms. Diamond. A fine day for selling real estate, isn't it? And an even better day for buying it." His laughter boomed out, breaking the afternoon stillness.

Heart still pounding, Truth stared at him. "What are you doing here?" It came out a snarl worthy of Razz. The dog sat at her feet, head cocked as if trying to decide whether a nip at the real estate agent's heels might be a good idea.

Billous feigned not to notice the dog, truly an impossibility the way she was growling. Truth knew by the way his eyes shifted to the dog, then back to her.

"Oh, now," he said, grinning like a jack'o lantern on Halloween night, "you can't be surprised to see me. The dollar number I mentioned the other day must have told you my buyer is serious. His offer is for a lot of money. A lot."

Truth, shaking her head, drew in a breath.

He held up a hand as if the slight movement had been as loud as a shout. "I understand a body has been found on the property. An awful thing. Awful. Certain to scare most people away. Think about it. Am I right?"

"But not *your* buyer. He's not scared." An imp took possession of her tongue. "Am I right?"

"You are. Absolutely right. See, the buyer has developed a yen for this old place. He's fallen in love with it and all its history, and he has the means to bring the Golden West up to date. Did I say to date? I mean into this century." His laughter thundered, his eyes swiveled in their sockets, gaze fixed on a corner of the porch that had developed a slight sag this past spring when the snow went off.

She'd meant to have Eddie and Jason—

Truth cleared her throat, a rasp that returned his focus to her. "Still not interested," she said. "Not now, not ever."

"Madam," he knocked away a tiny black insect hovering around his head, "I understand. I do. This old . . . er . . . lovely resort has been in your family since the early 1900s. But you're young. Don't you want something more than this? I know how hard you work, keeping up appearances."

Madam? Condescending ass. She hoped the bug was a black fly hungry for blood. His blood.

"You do, huh?" she said.

"Why, yes." He seemed to think he was making progress. "People tell me—"

"What people?" she cut in.

Porch creaking, he shifted his considerable weight. "What people?" He spurned her interruption with a flap of his hand. "Take my word for it. I've been in this business a long time, Ms. Diamond. You know, you should get some financial advice." He seemed much struck with this portion of his argument, but had an even better one. "I know the very person."

She just bet he did.

"Look around you," he went on before she could get a word in. "The Golden West has fallen into a state of disrepair, and you haven't had the wherewithal to address its needs. I know what your property taxes are. I looked them up. They must be tough to meet, a real burden. Huh? Am I right? So why don't you save yourself the worry? Sell out now. Opportunity is knocking."

Gads, was there a cliché he hadn't used?

Beyond him, Pratt Madden was hiking down the cedar chip path toward them. Tongue curling, Razz raced to meet him. Truth had to admit she wasn't exactly disappointed, even if she was still a little irritated about the secrets he'd been keeping from her.

Either Billous didn't see Pratt or didn't care. He was too busy trying to urge her inside the building, his sweaty hand on her arm.

Truth didn't budge. She closed the door, trapping both of them outside.

"Is the price going up?" she demanded, brushing off his offending appendage.

"Huh?"

"I asked if the price is going up. It looks to me that you, or your buyer, is getting desperate. Here you are again after I distinctly told you my property isn't for sale. I wondered if there'd been an increase in the offer."

Billous chortled as if she'd said something funny. "Oh, you're a tough young lady, aren't you? What'll it take? What do you want? Give me a number."

Pratt halted within easy earshot, unabashedly listening. Oh, yes. Truth was definitely glad he was there.

"Three million? Four? I wonder what your client would pay?" She put a forefinger to her lips as if she were thinking hard.

"Whoa. Let's not get carried away." Billous went still.

"How's this sound? You tell me your client's name and what he plans on doing with the Golden West, and if I approve, I'll . . . um . . . *entertain* the offer."

Billous's already squinty eyes narrowed even further. "Oh, no. I can't do that. I told you before my buyer prefers anonymity. That's why the big bucks in the first place. No messing around. Privacy is a valuable commodity in this business."

Truth shrugged. "That's it, then. Any deal is off. I must say this whole song and dance seems shifty to me, anyway."

"Shifty? I'll have you know I'm an honest man. Ask

anybody." Apparently, he thought he could convince her if only he yelled loudly enough.

"Forget it. We're done here." She turned to go inside but, hand on the screen door latch, she paused and swung back toward him. "Don't come ringing my bell again, Mr. Billous. You won't be welcome."

His fist clenched. Red crept from beneath his shirt collar into his fleshy cheeks. Truth stepped back, wondering if her dismissal of him had gone too far.

Maybe the same thought occurred to Pratt because suddenly he was beside her, with Razz acting as though she were once more ready to go for Billous's pant leg.

And Pratt, Truth admitted to herself as she plucked Razz up and tucked the dog under her arm, looked tough enough just then to scare anybody, including Bill Billous.

"So that's the famous real estate entrepreneur Bill Billous. Granddad told me about him." Pratt stared thoughtfully at the man beating a retreat to the car park. Billous drove a fairly new Cadillac Escalade. Evidently, the shocks were already worn because the car dipped as the realtor got in.

Pratt made a note of the license plate.

"Famous! I'd say notorious," Truth muttered. She set Razz down, only to snatch her up again when the Pom made a move to charge after Billous.

Wise of her, Pratt thought. He wouldn't put it past the man to run over the little dog if he got the chance.

"A real charmer," he said.

"You noticed."

"I did. I see Granddad was spot on with his description. I wonder—"

He lost what he was going to say, although Truth picked up where he left off, almost as though she channeled his thought.

"I wonder why he's so persistent," she said. "After Digbee and Sam ran him off the other day, it's odd he's back again this soon. Who wants my property so badly they'd resort to hiring him? And *why* do they want it?"

Pratt shrugged. He wondered too, maybe even more than she did.

"Well," she released Razz as Billous's Caddy disappeared over the hill, "I doubt he'll return any time soon. He refuses to give his client's name, and I refuse to sell. Not," she added, "that he gave away any privileged information. I didn't expect him to, although I'd sure like to know what's behind the offer."

"Yeah. So would I." Although he had an idea and planned on finding out more. Get the name of Billous' client and he'd soon know where to look for the girl's killer. "Leave it to me. Shouldn't be much of a problem."

Truth's smile flashed. "Well, well. The FBI at work. I hope you'll let me know what you find out."

He guessed he was on his way to being forgiven. "I'll do that. Maybe not right away, but at some point."

"I guess I'll have to be satisfied with that." She eyed a plain, dark blue sedan chugging down the hill into the resort. "Actually, I was hoping you'd heard something about Becca by now."

"Me too," he answered grimly. "Soon I hope."

The sedan drew to a halt and a guy wearing slacks and an aqua-hued polo shirt got out. He stood by the open car door as if fixing the terrain in his mind. He didn't look especially happy. Maybe the sun on his buzz-cut head was too hot or the squalling gulls too loud.

Pratt grinned. The newest FBI recruit in the Spokane office had arrived to provide on-site back-up. Pratt had seen him, Roy Something or another, in the office working at a computer the last time he met with Ernhardt. He'd been wearing a suit and tie, then. His present attire must be what he considered fishing camp casual.

Truth's lips quirked as if she found the way Roy shuffled down the path funny.

Like he expected to find dog poop beneath his feet with every step, Pratt thought, in tune with her humor.

She looked up at him. "Now here's one who doesn't even pretend to be a fisherman, unlike some I could name. In fact, he's not any kind of outdoorsman at all. Can you guys be any more obvious?"

Arms folded across his chest, Pratt winked at her. "You aren't supposed to notice things like that."

"Pu-leez." She shook her head as the man stepped onto the porch.

Turned out Roy—actually Rory, so Pratt wasn't far off—must have formed some conclusions of his own. The new agent's gaze settled on Pratt.

"You're Madden," he said, dead on in his reckoning. He didn't offer to shake hands. "And this must be Ms. Diamond, owner of this fine establishment, whom I see has put a period to any attempt to keep my affiliation with the FBI secret. You tell her?" It was like he wanted to blame Pratt.

Truth snorted, and not in the most ladylike manner. "As if I need anyone to tell me," she said. "You might as well be wearing a sign."

Razz lifted her upper lip in a soundless snarl.

"Really?" Rory brushed at a bug and stared from the woman to her dog. "A matched set of blondes. This should be interesting."

"Oh, my. Don't tell me!" Truth's dark eyes narrowed to slits. "He's been taking personality lessons from Detective Gunderson."

Choking on a laugh, Pratt jerked his head at Rory, indicating they should get out of sight and talk. His assistant needed to be filled in before he got himself into serious trouble.

On the other hand, the new man did distract Truth's ire away from him.

Not a bad thing, all considered.

CHAPTER 22

PRATT LEANED AGAINST THE FENDER OF HIS PICKUP, HANDS IN HIS pockets, listening more than talking. His '64 GMC, plus two sheriff's department vehicles, Ernhardt's dark sedan, and a rig from the medical examiner's office were all parked in a rest area off the Interstate. Four men and one woman stood clumped together for the impromptu task force meeting, a rare cooperation between local and federal law enforcement.

Evening shadows gathered under the tall pine trees shading the rest area picnic tables. In the pet area, a small woman walked two Bernese Mountain dogs on leashes. Pratt wondered if she'd be torn in two if the giant dogs decided to go in opposite directions.

Ernhardt and Gunderson were arguing over calling out the volunteer search and rescue people again. Gunderson for, Ernardt against.

Gunderson, true to form, had plenty to say. "The county can always use the free labor."

"No overt search parties," Pratt roused himself to insist.

"Whadya mean, no *overt* search parties?" Gunderson acted as he'd never heard the word before.

"Pratt means no *full-out* searches at this point," Ernhardt, who'd called the meeting, amended in a soothing-ruffled-feathers tone of voice. "For now, it seems wise to keep a low profile. We don't want to spook whoever has Becca Keene into either killing her or spiriting her out of the country."

"If they haven't already. How are we supposed to find her, by using our *intuition?*" He might have been questioning Ernhardt, but Gunderson's gaze was on Pratt.

Pratt shrugged. "Tell him, Frank."

"I think I'll let Dr. Holt say her piece first. She's got information that's been withheld, per my request. Just the people here right now are being informed." Ernhardt deferred to the M.E. "Doctor?"

Dr. Holt, a thin, middle-aged woman with chin-length dark hair and a pleasant smile, drank from her designer water bottle before speaking. "As I've informed the sheriff and Mr. Ernhardt, our murder victim, Yudif Maruseva, didn't die because her hand was amputated. She died at least a week later. It's hard to pinpoint when, exactly, give the condition of the body. Certainly, a week, although we're still working to be more precise."

Pratt straightened.

Ortiz looked puzzled. "But the blood— So what did she die from? Infection?"

"Oh, no," Dr. Holt said. "Exsanguination. Massive blood loss. Her throat was cut and then her body dismembered. A bit of a mess, unfortunately. But before then, the stump of her arm had begun to heal."

Ortiz's dark face faded to a sickly pale amber color.

"So, there's more to her death than the simple cover-up of a possible accident," Ernhardt explained further for the benefit of anyone who might not have grasped the fact. "That might explain how her hand came to be separated from her body."

"Yes," the M.E. agreed. "You'll also be interested in learning that at some time the hand had been holed and a string passed through the holes, as if intended for display."

"Why would anyone do that?" Ortiz asked.

Dr. Holt shrugged. "I really couldn't say. That's for you to discover. The why of it, I mean. I've done my part."

"So you have," Ernhardt said, reaching forward to shake her hand. "I know you're on your way to a conference in Seattle, Dr. Holt, so I won't keep you longer. Thank you for stopping. I wanted these officers to hear your report directly."

Dr. Holt drank another swallow of water before climbing into her car. Checking her rearview mirror, she waved and drove off, foot heavy on the gas feed.

Even Gunderson was silent, watching her go.

Ortiz cleared his throat and spat into the dust at his feet. "You think this girl, this Yudif Maruseva, was killed because we were looking for her?"

Ernhardt glanced at Pratt, who answered. "Seems a possibility, Joe, when the search called too much attention to her. It's hard to fathom what goes on in the criminal mind, but they may have figured it was easier to get rid of a body than move a girl with that kind of wound out of the area."

"So that's why you don't want an overt search for Becca." Ortiz nodded his understanding.

"Yes."

"This girl, Yudith, she probably lost her value in the sex trade, anyway," Gunderson said.

"You'd be surprised," Ernhardt said darkly. "There's a certain kind of man who gets off on mutilations and scars."

"You mean they'd do that to a girl, deliberately cut off her hand, because some pervert takes pleasure from it?" Ortiz's expression showed shock. A little naive, in Pratt's opinion, though justifiable.

"My guess is the mutilation originally served as an object lesson to keep the other girls under control," Pratt said, staring off into the trees.

"Other girls?" Ortiz asked.

"Human trafficking on a large scale," Pratt murmured.

"These girls they bring in, they're considered expendable." Ernhardt's explanation covered the situation well.

"Do we know other girls are at risk?" Ortiz fidgeted uncomfortably.

"Pretty certain," Pratt said. "They're usually moved in groups rather than individually. More cost-effective."

Except for Gunderson, whose spate of cursing faded into background noise as an eighteen-wheeler rumbled past them into the rest area, they remained silent.

Absently, Pratt eyed the semi. *Washington Fresh Produce*, it said on the trailer, which had a garish picture of a watermelon painted on the side. Melons being trucked out of the rich Tri-City area to Canada and markets farther east.

"So, the girl was in the old barn the whole time we were looking for her." Ortiz's sneer seemed aimed at himself, but Pratt could relate. He'd been at the resort for three weeks and hadn't known an empty barn stood on the property. No excuse that he'd done most of his scouting of the area at night. He had maps, although in his own defense, only new ones. He should have expanded the area, been aware of what lay outside the resort itself.

How had the perps found the old building, a perfect way station from which to carry out their crimes, when no one else seemed to know it existed? But they had, which indicated someone with close ties to the area. Someone with a handle on the terrain.

But not Truth, he was sure, although Gunderson was quick to point a metaphoric finger at her.

"If we don't find this latest missing girl, this Becca Keene, real soon we're apt to have another murder on our hands," Gunderson said. "If we don't already. I figure Ms. Diamond knows more than she's letting on and we oughta pressure her until she talks. Forget all this pussyfooting around." He aimed the comment at Pratt.

"It's not Truth," Pratt stated, certain.

"It's not." Ortiz backed him up, even against the detective's sneer.

Although a semi-logical conclusion, Gunderson rubbed Pratt the wrong way. Probably because when the man said pussyfooting, it sounded like he meant something else.

"You're right about one thing," he said through gritted teeth. "We have to find Becca before they have a chance to move her out of the area."

"If they haven't already," Ortiz muttered.

Pratt nodded. "There is that."

A loud snort reflected Gunderson's opinion.

"You spent the morning talking to Becca's friends and neighbors, Deputy Ortiz. What have you learned so far?" Ernhardt asked.

"Nothing new." Ortiz kicked at a rock. "Her mother's story of when Becca came home night before last is identical to what she told us yesterday. Jason, the girl's brother, talked to the same people I did, and that all matches up, too. It like she got taken up by a UFO."

Gunderson made an indecipherable sound in his throat.

"You checked the house inside and out?" Pratt asked.

"You bet." Ortiz sounded defensive. "A thorough once-over. I had Ms. Keene and Jason go through the house with me. I checked the screens on the windows. I checked beneath the windows, even though the girl's room is on the second floor of an old farmhouse. I saw nothing to show a girl was dragged out of there kicking and screaming. Becca is not a tidy sort of girl. Clothes are scattered all around the room. Makeup spilled in the bathroom, bed unmade. The mother says this is how her daughter's room always looks, and the brother agrees. Neither noticed anything unusual, except that Becca is gone."

Pratt took a deep breath. "You figure she might've walked out on her own?"

Ortiz's lips tightened. "Possible. More than possible."

"So, no leads." Ernhardt, his face nearly hidden as evening settled in around them, sounded disgusted.

"No leads," Ortiz agreed.

"A runaway," Gunderson said. "Just like I figured."

The others joined Pratt in acting as if they hadn't heard him.

"Nothing to specifically connect Becca Keene with Yudif Maruseva," Ernhardt persisted.

"Oh, I wouldn't say that." Alarmed, Pratt wondered if his boss was about to pull them out of the hunt.

"No? What would you say?" Ernhardt peered at him through the dusk.

"Becca's disappearance is too pat to be a coincidence."

Ortiz nodded. "Exactly."

"We'll play this close to our chests," Ernhardt said after a pause. "Follow procedure on getting her name and description out on the news, but any local searching will be done solely by law enforcement. We don't want to scare these people so badly they take off and we never find the girl."

Gunderson rolled his eyes but nodded. "Ortiz, get that Fish guy back on the job, and I'll call a deputy or two in on overtime." He sighed as if he'd personally been the one traipsing all over Truth's buffalo pasture and the rocky bluffs.

Pratt stood erect. "Sorry to disagree, Detective, but I'd prefer just myself for the FBI, and Ortiz for the sheriff's department assigned to this at present. No one else. We'll keep a low profile."

"Blaine knows the area," Gunderson protested.

Deliberately, Pratt shrugged. "So, does Ortiz and he's already working the case. This has been his territory for a couple years. Isn't that right, Joe?"

"Yes."

"And I'm familiar with it, too," Pratt went on. He noticed the look Ernhardt shot him, the unspoken question of why he'd turn down help. "Joe and I, we'll concentrate on finding Becca. The rest of you can work on tracing the dead girl."

"Should be the other way around," Gunderson grumbled, and as a general rule, Pratt agreed. But not this time.

Their meeting broke up on uneasy terms.

"Madden, call me in the morning," Ernhardt ordered before he drove away.

Pratt headed back to the resort alone.

TRUTH'S BEDROOM was only a little less dark than full night when she awakened. Four-fifteen a.m. Too early by far, her tired body announced, even as she opened her eyes. Razz's fault as the dog tromped back and forth across her chest, ears pricked toward the open window.

The little dog turned her head to look briefly at her mistress before tiptoeing stiff-legged to the foot of the bed. A low growl indicated full alert.

"Don't tell me," Truth begged in a whisper, "I don't want to know." Why was she whispering when alone in her own house? *If she was alone.*

Goosebumps dotted her bare arms.

Common sense reasserted itself when Razz's attention stayed directed to the outside. Of course, she was alone.

As soundless as a specter, Truth got up and went to the window, standing at the side to make it harder for anyone outside to see her. Not that anyone could see in anyway unless he free-floated twenty feet off the ground.

The previous night's moon had faded against the coming daylight, a bare lightening of the eastern sky. Sleepy birds murmured in the trees. Water lapped against the dock with a steady *shlip-shlop*. The fragrance of night blooming stocks rose all the way to the second story, the scent a comfort to her senses. All normal. With a soft sigh of relief, she turned away.

Until a noise, like someone crying out, broke in the distance.

Razz, still on the bed, growled again, louder than before.

"Hush, girl."

Truth hunkered down, crossed to the other side of the window and looked out again. There. Who was that? Someone —two someones—mere blobs, really, moving down by the far docks. They were too far away for her to identify given the murky light.

Then, frightening her even more, she saw they were dragging something heavy along the beach.

Her beach. Rage zinged along her veins.

Call 911.

But even as she grasped the beside phone, her hand stilled. What if it was nothing? What if Razz—and she—were tilting at nightmares? The FBI agent Pratt had introduced to her yesterday, Rory, he was supposed to be keeping watch over the resort. It must be him out there. Him and someone else, maybe Pratt.

Still, it was odd, how furtive they seemed. And what could they possibly be dragging?

Her resort. Her business.

Pausing only to pull a sweater over her PJ top and to stick her feet into sneakers, she grabbed up the little Ruger LCR from the nightstand where she kept it in case of emergency.

"Stay," she told Razz, lifting a warning finger to show she meant business.

Truth ran down the stairs, oblivious to Razz's bark of indignation at being left behind. Without stopping to think twice, she let herself out the resort's back door, the sturdy lock snicking back.

A chill sensation, kind of damp, kind of cold, raised the hair on the back of her neck as she stepped out onto the patio. A preternatural stillness encased her. She felt as though she were walking in a bubble as she took the path through a stand of trees, striding quickly toward where she'd seen the activity. She held the Ruger out in front, ready, she told herself, for anything.

Off to her right, a camper loomed. No lights showed. She heard someone snoring inside as she passed almost directly under the window. A few steps farther on was Mrs. Thompson's old motorhome. No lights were on here, either, although the old lady had mentioned to Truth several times that she always rose before dawn. A rickety lawn chair was turned on its side under the open awning.

Truth glanced around. Still pretty dark. It probably didn't count as dawn just yet.

She picked up her pace. Almost there. The path would bring her out of the trees only a few yards from where she'd seen those people with their burden.

In fact, she expected to hear the low murmur of voices, but she didn't. Only silence. An uncomfortable, foggy silence.

At first, she didn't realize what the object abandoned on the sandy beach was—not until she stood right beside it. Then she did.

"God Almighty! Who—"

The two people she'd seen had dumped someone, someone's body, that is, in such a way the torso folded over the legs, bent in the middle, so the blob was as tall as it was wide. In addition, a covering of some kind had been flung over the top, so that the whole looked like a heap of garbage.

Garbage. Oh, no. Not again.

But then Truth saw the foot. A broad, chubby foot, encased in an easily recognizable rundown slipper and she knew.

Mrs. Thompson.

A soft cry chuffed out of her.

Out on the lake, a loon woke up and laughed.

And the bubble around her disappeared, leaving her as exposed as the corpse.

CHAPTER 23

ALTHOUGH IT WAS TOUCH-AND-GO, TRUTH MANAGED TO swallow the scream rising in her throat.

Best not scream, she told herself. Screaming made too much noise.

A noise certain to attract anyone within hearing distance to her—which meant both the good *and* the bad. Only a few minutes had passed since she'd seen two people dragging Mrs. Thompson's body. They couldn't be far away.

Her flesh quivered. Perhaps they were watching her now.

The Ruger hung slack in her hand. She flexed stiffened muscles, snugging the grip into her palm, keeping her finger off the trigger with an effort.

As the light grew, she could see the body was humped in an odd position. Both the old lady's head and her knees rested on the sand. Her killers had flipped her robe carelessly over the top. Even as Truth watched, gravity took over. The body flattened by slow degrees as it slid forward in the slippery sand. White hair became visible, one side of it stained red.

The old lady's feet, both of them now, showed beneath the

hem of her ratty robe. Only one foot bore a slipper—the tell-tale bunny slipper—the other was bare.

Truth clapped her hands over her mouth, muffling a moan, and almost knocking a tooth out with the gun she'd forgotten she held. The pain in her lip brought focus.

"Mrs. Thompson." Her whisper echoed like a shout in her ears. "Mrs. Thompson?" She bent until she could see into the woman's face, needing to make sure.

Eyes open. Utterly blank. Nobody home.

She placed a gentle finger over the carotid. No discernable pulse.

Mrs. Thompson's right temple bore a large dent. A gush of blood had covered the side of her face and painted wrinkled skin with red.

Dead.

Pratt. She had to find Pratt.

Ninety seconds later, Truth dashed up to Digbee Madden's fifth-wheel, barking her shin as she stumbled on the steps. Barely registering the small hurt, she pounded on the door with her fist.

"Pratt," she cried, not too loud. "Pratt, open up."

It was far too exposed here. Looking over her shoulder, she kept knocking. After what seemed like hours, she heard someone inside stir. A light came on above the door, spot-lighting her. A lock turned.

"Pratt," she said before the door fully opened. "Hurry up. Mrs. Thompson has been murdered."

Pratt, bare-chested and clad in red plaid sleep shorts stood there. "What's wrong?" He scrubbed a hand across his stubbly chin. "What did you say?"

Half falling, she pushed her way past him. No way she was going to stand exposed on his doorstep a single second longer. No blinking way.

"I said Mrs. Thompson has been murdered. She's down on the beach with her head bashed in." Truth knew no other way to say it. "And your FBI lookout is nowhere around. C'mon. You've got to do something."

Digbee's head poked around the door separating the tiny bedroom from the rest of the RV. "Did you say Mrs. Thompson has been murdered?" he repeated.

"Yes!"

Pratt reached for his jeans and stepped into them. "Are you sure she's dead?"

"I'm sure." The horror of it was beginning to catch up to her. Tremors started in her belly and moved upward through her limbs.

"How do you know?" Pratt's question was muffled as he drew a t-shirt over his head.

"I felt for a pulse. I saw her eyes." Truth shuddered. "I saw the hole in her head. Will you hurry up?"

A false accusation, as if Pratt were delaying, even though it had taken him less than half a minute to dress, settle his Glock 23 at his hip and activate a walkie-talkie device. He pressed in a code. "F1 to F2," he said into the radio. "F2, you there."

A blare of static answered. Pratt gave radio a shake.

"Where is she?" he asked Truth.

She lunged for the door. "I'll show you. She's on the beach near the long dock."

Digbee intervened. "Shouldn't Truth stay here with me?" he asked his grandson.

"I'm going with Pratt," she said.

Pratt's dark eyes surveyed her, seeming to judge her determination. He tried the radio again. Again, no answer. Worry manifested itself in the grim set of his jaw.

"You'd better get Sam," he told Digbee. "Meet us there. If Truth is right, we'll need somcone to help cordon off the area."

"I'm right," she said, although she'd give anything if when they got to the beach, she was proved wrong. If they found Mrs. Thompson sitting up and saying she wanted one of Truth's excellent sticky buns.

Pratt held Truth back when she tried to plunge through the door ahead of him. "Wait." He took a few seconds, scanning this way and that, another extra second to peer into the bushes halfway obscuring the camper in the next space. Apparently satisfied, he said, "Put that pistol away; I don't want to be shot in the back. And stay behind me." He skimmed down the steps that only a few minutes earlier had proved a barricade to Truth.

She was right on his heels, the pistol she'd forgotten still in her hand. He hadn't really noticed her, she thought, more than a bit disgruntled, otherwise he'd know she had no place to put it. Last time she heard, PJs weren't endowed with pockets, let alone holsters.

Twice, on their way to the beach, Pratt stopped, keyed the button on his walkie-talkie, and tried to raise Rory Whatshis-name, aka F2, the FBI agent having been tasked as an overnight lookout.

The last time, Truth let out a soft moan. "Do you think something has happened to him, too?" She didn't actually say so, but substituting the word "killed" for "happened" made more sense.

"I hope not," Pratt said, his voice rough.

So did she.

They broke away from the path through the campground and headed down to the beach. It was almost daylight. Ahead of them, Truth could see Mrs. Thompson's body all too clearly, rising from the sand like a low, flat rock. She pointed.

"I see."

When they were several feet away, he stopped her. "Those

your footprints?" He indicated the size seven tracks beside the body.

"Yes. But see, there are others, going toward the car park." One set large, one set small, they'd passed right by her side yard. She must've missed meeting the killers face-to-face by no more than a minute. If they'd seen her, would she, too, be an indiscriminate lump lying on the sand?

Probably.

Pratt grunted. "Smart. As soon as they hit the car park, there's no way to track them."

"Get the dog handler back," Truth said. "His hounds can take scent not only from the ground but from the air. I'll even pay for his time."

She felt, more than saw, his sharp stare.

She avoided looking at Mrs. Thompson, or at Pratt as he went through the same process she had, feeling for a pulse, checking those dead eyes.

Surreal. The beach, the lake, the sky, the birds. All familiar and loved.

Except for the body of one of her best customers.

Pratt stood up and tried the radio again.

And was rewarded with first a burst of static, then a moment of clarity. And was that a soft groan?

"Hamaker? That you?" Pratt stiffened.

A mumble seemed to mean something to him.

"Where are you?"

Another mumble.

"I'll be right there. Hang tough."

Truth, not understanding a word from Hamaker's side of the conversation, put two and two together. "He's been ambushed, hasn't he? Is he badly hurt?"

"Doesn't sound good."

It struck her that Pratt was at something of a loss. Grim. If ever a man needed to be in two—or three—places at once, he did.

She swallowed hard. "You'd better go help him. I'll stay here with Mrs. Thompson." Dear Lord, she'd rather sit down beside a rattlesnake. Poor Mrs. Thompson. She didn't mean to imply—

Pratt wasn't blind to her reluctance. "Don't be afraid, Truth. Be cautious but warn anyone who comes along to keep away from the crime scene. I'm pretty sure you're in no danger, now, but if anything happens, fire a shot. That ought to scare anyone off. Stay until Granddad and Sam get here. Then go back to the resort and call the sheriff's office. Ask for an ambulance."

Not waiting for agreement, he turned away, muttering something about backwater joints where you couldn't even get cell service or back-up when you needed it. Oh, and he was cursing as he jogged off toward car park.

She couldn't have agreed more.

CHAPTER 24

DIGBEE AND SAM RELEASED TRUTH FROM HER LONELY, FEAR-filled vigil moments later. Pressed, she had to tell her story of discovery again. She didn't mind. It helped keep her eyes off Mrs. Thompson.

Sam insisted on walking her back to the resort and checking the building from top to bottom before he'd leave her alone. And, although she wasn't exactly confident of his ability to protect himself, let alone her, from a determined killer, she thanked him wholeheartedly.

After making the call to the sheriff's department, she hurried to pull on jeans and a shirt. Nothing would keep her from discovering what else went on outside this room. Her resort, her business, and if Pratt or Gunderson or anyone else didn't like it they could just—

Truth slammed down a bowl of kibble for Razz and dashed out again, locking the door behind her and stowing the key in her pocket. She wore a jacket, this time, no matter how hot the day promised. A jacket with pockets. The Ruger, and a place to put it, went everywhere she did from now on. If anyone asked, she would tell them she was suffering from shock.

Not a lie.

After a short search, she found Pratt up at the car park. He was kneeling beside Rory's supine body, pressing a suspiciously red cloth to the other FBI agent's head.

Another head wound. A pattern.

"Deputies are on their way," she said, a little breathless.

"The ambulance?"

"That, too." It felt like she'd been holding her breath for an hour when she finally let it out. "Is Agent Hamaker badly hurt?"

"I'd guess a concussion. He keeps going in and out of consciousness. He's lucky he has a hard head. Somebody slammed him good, just not quite good enough to kill him."

Truth felt ill. *Good enough?* "Like they got Mrs. Thompson, only her head wasn't as hard."

"Sounds about right." Pratt rose to his feet. "I want you to do me a favor, Truth."

"What?" She'd rather climb in bed and cover up her head, but a girl couldn't turn down the FBI when they asked a favor.

His smile crooked as if guessing her thoughts.

He wanted her to go door-to-door, or, more precisely, campsite-to-campsite, around the carpark. She should ask people to stay inside, and for anyone with children to keep them away from the beach for a while. "It's gonna get ugly this morning when everyone wakes up and the news gets around. For now, just tell them there's been an accident."

She approved. It sounded better than the truth.

"Okay," she said.

"Say nothing about Mrs. Thompson's death. They'll find out soon enough." He crooked a finger, stopping her when she would've turned away. "Stay within sight of other campsites.

Don't go off alone. Leave those farthest from the resort for the police. They should be here soon."

Not soon enough to suit me, she thought.

"Okay." It was beginning to seem like the only word she knew.

She stopped first at Larry and Fran's trailer, situated on the site nearest the car park. They were not exactly happy to see her. Fran, quick to tell her so, considered her repeated knocks on their door a rude awakening.

"I'm sorry," Truth said. "But I wanted to warn you that there's been an accident." *Liar, liar, pants on fire.*

"What now?" Fran grumbled, her face so haggard Truth figured she was one of those people who required a gallon or so of coffee each morning and the application of a pound of makeup before she became human. The woman growled over her shoulder to her husband, "Larry, I thought it was supposed to be quiet here. You lied. I'd get more peace out at the airport."

Truth's ears perked. "What do you mean, Mrs. Er..." She'd forgotten the woman's last name.

Fran, who looked like she'd been attacked by the Wrath of God, squinted at her through a cloud of cigarette smoke as she lit the first of the day. "I mean on account of people running up and down the road most of the night. Trying to be sneaky, and all the more obvious because of it. Taking shortcuts through the brush and panting like dogs. Grunting and groaning. I guess you know what that means. Teenagers carrying on like rabbits, that's what."

She spoke in a severe tone of voice, as though she couldn't quite settle on which animal she meant, dog or rabbit.

"It's not the first time I've heard them, either," Fran's rant continued. "You oughta put a stop to it if you want a respectable class of people here."

"Really? You heard all that?"

"I just said so, didn't I?" Behind her, Larry protested with a weak, "Fran."

"Why didn't you report the disturbance?" Truth demanded. Fran just sneered.

Glad it wasn't her job to actually interrogate the woman, Truth delivered the assigned message and left the pair grumping at each other instead of at her.

Mandi and Ken's motorhome occupied the next campsite and with dragging footsteps, she made her way there.

A light went on inside before she quit knocking. Ken opened the door, rubbing sleepy seeds out of his eyes. He wore jeans and judging by the way they hung from his hips, nothing else.

"Hey, Truth. What's up?" Since she stood on the bottom step leading into the RV and he was several inches taller than she anyway, he squinted over the top of her head. "Is that Pratt over there? What's he doing?"

She hadn't realized he was short-sighted. "Yes, it's Pratt. I just wanted to warn you. There's been an acci—" She just didn't feel right, giving the accident spiel to her friends this way. "Mrs. Thompson has been killed and a . . .a . . . law enforcement agent hurt," she amended her statement. "The police will be here soon. I wanted to let you know so you won't be so spooked when they show up."

Behind them, she heard Mandi gasp. "Did you say Mrs. Thompson is dead? Are you kidding?"

"Wish I was, but I'm not." As if she'd kid about yet another death at her resort.

Wearing a light robe gripped around her, Mandi peered over her husband's shoulder. From the expanse of bare breast peeping around the robe's edge, it seemed obvious she, like her husband, wore nothing beneath the flimsy garment. Her hair was tousled, a lock hanging close to her ear with something that looked like a clot of strawberry jam stuck to it.

Apparently, Truth had interrupted the pair at an inopportune time.

Mandi, regardless of her attire, started forward. "Is that her, with Pratt? What on earth was Mrs. Thompson doing up here in the car park?"

"Pratt's with the other person. Mrs. Thompson is on the beach."

"Ohmygosh." Mandi put her hand over her mouth. "Who found her?"

"I did."

Mandi reached out, clutched her gaping robe closed and stopped. "You poor thing. Come in, Truth. I'll start some coffee. You look like you could use a cup."

"Preferably with a shot of Johnnie Walker in it," Ken added, hitching his pants a bare inch.

Truth smiled weakly. "Thanks, guys. You're good friends. But I've got a couple more people to awaken. Pratt thinks everyone around the car park should be alerted before the police get here."

"Good thinking," Ken said. "Probably scare the pants off them otherwise. Want some help?"

Pretty sure Pratt would have a fit if anyone—meaning anyone else not in law enforcement—were roped into this, she shook her head. "I'm good, thanks anyway. I only have those two young guys, the people with twins, and Dottie and her friend. The coffee sounds good, though."

With a wan smile, Truth backed down the steps and headed over to the next campsite with its tiny teardrop trailer.

Funny, or more precisely, odd, she thought, frowning a little, but she wouldn't have guessed Ken or Mandi people who'd come to the door in that blatant state of dress. Or undress. It embarrassed her. Was she a prude or what?

One of the boys opened a tiny window in the teardrop and spoke to her through that. The people with children merely nodded and went back to bed.

Dottie opened her door before Truth could raise her fist to knock on the battered screen. She was clad in a modest t-shirt and shorts much like the ones Truth wore to bed, no bare boobs here. And evidently, her boyfriend had gone back to town, since Truth didn't see him anywhere.

"Come on in." Dottie ushered Truth into the meticulously neat little trailer. Her eyes were wide with apprehension. "What's going on? I heard you talking to the boys, but it's worse than what you said, isn't it? Is . . . is someone else dead?"

She couldn't lie to Dottie any more than she'd been able to lie to Mandi. The difference was, Dottie cried and admitted she was scared.

That made two of them.

Although it felt to Truth like hours, no more than twenty minutes after making her 911 call, flashing blue lights showed at the top of the hill heading into the Golden West.

An ambulance followed right after. Medics scooped Rory onto a stretcher and carried him away, although she heard him complaining about leaving. To her immense relief, he sounded lucid now, and in no immediate danger.

Gunderson, driving like a fat Michael Andretti, raced into the parking area in a dark Ford sedan, glowering and snapping his fingers as he got out. Ortiz wasn't far behind him, and then Ernhardt, looking barely awake. There must've been a dozen uniformed people on scene. Following Pratt, they all trooped down to the beach.

The assistant medical examiner, when he arrived, looked unhappy at being called out at this time of the morning. Even more so when he left ten minutes later. Truth, glancing at her watch, noted the time. Barely 6 a.m. A lifetime.

She felt helpless with nothing else to do. Drained of energy. Except she needed to talk to Pratt if she could ever catch him alone for a moment. He seemed to be everywhere, talking to everyone. She figured his cover to be well and truly blown by now. The way the others deferred to him made his position rather obvious.

Feeling like a lost soul, she went to open the resort, certain her only customers would be police, her business ruined for the season, if not forever. She should've taken Bill Billous up on his offer, she told herself. Made beaucoup bucks. Gone to the Virgin Islands to live. Or even better, Bora Bora.

And yet, it wasn't long before the rich aroma of her brewing coffee brought campers into the store, where the cash register soon pinged with reassuring regularity as she rang up bread and milk and popsicles for the kids.

In the café, she brought extra chairs out of storage, which people drew up elbow-to-elbow around the four small tables. A few people took their coffee and sour cream apple scones, all she could find in her freezer at a moment's notice, out onto the patio. A panicked call to Consuelo brought her helper in an hour early to wield a spatula at the stove. Soon the scent of frying bacon and eggs filled the air.

The police toiled on. Gunderson, too late to claim the patio, set up shop under a hastily erected canvas canopy in the parking lot. The line of campers filed up to him, answered his questions, and strolled back down to the resort for yet another cup of coffee, changing to ice cold pop as the morning wore on and the temperature soared. His questions were all about Mrs. Thompson, they reported, each shocked to learn their elderly neighbor had been murdered.

Truth raced to and fro, waiting tables, minding the store,

even cooking when Connie needed a break. She missed Becca, who was a good little waitress when she was in the mood.

Has everyone but me forgotten about her? Truth wondered, wiping her hands on her apron before picking up a heavy tray and toting it outside.

~

PRATT FELT his precarious hold on the situation at the Golden West slipping away. Two murders and a kidnapping, all perpetrated on his watch. Now people with whom he'd previously enjoyed good rapport knew he was FBI, they were less willing to talk with him. Gunderson's abrasiveness as he ran roughshod over those least likely to be suspects didn't make anything any easier. The investigation dragged along.

Joe Ortiz had the best luck with the campers. Calm, reassuring, a man of the people with whom they could relate. Plus, the locals all knew him and didn't give him any static. Strangers took their cue from them. Too bad Gunderson refused to let the deputy take charge.

Stomach burning, head aching, Pratt stopped to regroup. He claimed an empty stool in the café a nano-second ahead of a man he knew only as Fred, who'd once sat next to him on the dock as they fished.

This time, Fred didn't speak, even avoided looking at him. But maybe Gunderson was to blame. Taking the only empty spot in the room, Pratt sat down next to the detective. Gunderson, jaws working like pistons, chomped steadily through a buffalo burger. A dab of ketchup spotted his shirt. Pickle juice ran over his hand.

"Good food," he grunted as Pratt sat down.

"Never had a bad burger here yet." He looked around.

Truth, her short spiky hair appearing more frazzled than stylish, had what he suspected were stress-induced red streaks
glowing on her cheekbones. She halted at the counter in front
of him. His heart lurched. She looked beat.

She looked scared.

"Is anyone trying to find Becca amidst all this hoorah?" she
demanded.

Nope. Unbeaten and unbowed. Pratt's mouth twitched.

"Got a BOLO out," he told her. "As soon as Gunderson has
the preliminaries done here, they'll transfer men to start a
ground search for Becca. Same process as before."

Truth frowned. "BOLO?"

"Be on the lookout. We'll get her picture on TV and in the
newspapers. Somebody will have seen her." He sounded more
confident that he felt.

"I hope so." She didn't sound especially optimistic.

Her shoulders straightened. "Have you had anything to eat
today? I doubt you've had a break since I woke you up this
morning."

"I haven't, have you?" He'd bet good money she hadn't,
either.

She shrugged. "What can I get you?"

Pratt nodded toward Gunderson's empty plate. "Whatever
he had, please."

Nodding, she called the order into the kitchen for
Consuelo, but returned almost immediately, ignoring a couple
hands waving for her attention.

"This morning, when I notified the campers around the car
park—" She frowned, brow crinkling into lines so tight he
figured they hurt.

He took a sip of ice water from the glass in front of
him. "Yes?"

She rubbed her forehead. "Fran, well, you probably heard her."

His nod encouraged her. Yeah, he'd heard the irate sounding rasp of her cigarette thickened voice. Hadn't made out what she said and didn't want to.

Truth acknowledged a demanding customer with an uplifted forefinger indicating he hold his horses and went on talking. "Fran told me she heard people running up and down the road during the night. They were grunting and groaning, carrying on, according to her description, like rabbits. 'Or teenagers,' she said, but I'll bet what she heard was the attack on Rory. Was he able to tell you anything? Did he see who hit him?"

"Says he didn't see or hear a thing. Seems unlikely, doesn't it, in view of Fran's rant."

"Probably asleep." Gunderson broke into the conversation.

Internally, Pratt agreed. He believed the agent had taken his watch over a bunch of quote, unquote "hayseeds" too lightly. He glanced across at Gunderson. "You talked to Fran, didn't you? Did she tell you what she heard?"

Gunderson made a production of wiping his chin with a napkin. "She may have. The woman is a bi...witch. Sounds to me like she made up a story to make herself important."

Pratt sighed. "I'll talk to her again." He grimaced. "Oughta make her day."

Truth emitted an unladylike snort.

"What about the others?" he asked. "Did anyone else mention hearing a disturbance?"

"No." She cocked her head. "But Fran and Larry's trailer is closest to the road. They'd be the ones most likely to hear or see anyone stirring around there. Traffic is probably why the coyote dropped the hand along that section. I still wonder how it got hold of it." She faltered to a stop.

"Don't we all." Pratt thought a moment. "I'll have a conversation with those others just in case any of them noticed anything. Thanks, Truth."

They were interrupted by a deputy who came in, hovered at Gunderson's elbow, and murmured in his ear. Whatever he said caused Gunderson to burp and rise from his stool, making a production of dropping a ten-dollar bill on the counter.

"Investigators are done on the beach, Ms. Diamond," he announced. "You're free to take down the tape and let people back on."

"Did you find anything?" she asked. "You know, to show who—"

Gunderson being Gunderson, he refused to give a straight answer, or any answer, for that matter. He snapped his fingers at the deputy and started off, then turned back. "A word of warning. It's a mess down there. You might want to throw a little clean sand over the blood."

A deep silence fell over the room at his all too audible announcement.

He and the deputy strode out together, the deputy throwing wistful glances at Pratt's plate as Connie brought out his burger.

Truth glared after Gunderson. "What an ass!" Propping her chin on her hands, she watched Pratt attack the potato salad. "There's something else. I didn't want to mention it to Gunderson. He's so heavy-handed—" Again she failed to complete the thought.

Pratt chomped off a portion of burger, chewed, and swallowed. "What else?"

"At one of the other RVs, I saw something odd, but I don't know if it means anything."

Setting down his burger, Pratt reached out and tilted her chin toward him with a forefinger. She has the prettiest dark eyes, he thought, reining himself in with an effort. "Just spit it out, Truth. Let me be the judge of what it means."

She winced. "I feel like such a traitor."

But she told him nonetheless.

CHAPTER 25

LIVING UP, OR MORE ACCURATELY, DOWN, TO TRUTH'S WORST expectations, as soon as Gunderson finished questioning the campers, they began a slow exodus out of the resort. By three o'clock, the Golden West had become a wasteland of empty RV spaces featuring crushed grass and trash left in firepits. Abandoned toys, soggy towels, and even barbeques were left behind. She could see three multi-colored beach balls rolling across the playground from where she stood on the store's porch. A pickup pulling a 25-foot trailer churned up the hill to the main road, a cloud of dust rising in its wake.

Extra chairs now took up floor space in the café. Only a few Golden West diehards still sat at the counter stools talking in muted voices, their heads close together. She wondered if any of them would still be around when night fell.

On the other hand, why would they want to be? If she had any place to go, she'd leave too. Even for just one night, she and Razz, to some trouble-free zone where she wouldn't hear about awful things, like a woman being killed. Where she wouldn't have to be afraid. If any such place existed.

As the dust kicked up by the pickup finally settled, she sighed sadly and went inside. "Connie," she called into the kitchen, "I have outdoor chores to do. Can you handle the café and the store for a while?"

Consuelo's dark head appeared around the corner. "Sure. It's not like we're being overrun by customers."

Truth would've been happier if she'd kept her opinion to herself.

Wincing, Consuelo studied Truth's wan face. "Sorry. I should keep my big mouth shut. You want some help? I can call Eddie, have him come over."

Truth shook her head. "I won't put anyone else through this. I'll clean the beach myself."

"Eddie isn't all that squeamish. He was in the service, you know."

"I do know." She sighed. "But it's my job. Thanks, though. Keep Razz with you, please. I don't want her down there." The thought of her little companion sniffing blood and brain matter turned her stomach.

Although Razz vocally protested being left behind, Truth went off to find gloves, garbage bags, a rake and a shovel. She paused in front of the storage shed where she kept the tools, hesitant to open the door. Heaven only knew what she'd find inside. More bodies? Pieces of bodies?

Becca's body?

Idiot. The cops have already searched the shed.

Logic didn't keep her from holding her breath as she unlocked the door, or from huffing out air when the familiar, normal stuffiness greeted her. The shed contained only what it ought, including the odor of gasoline-powered tools.

Even so, tension crackled through her veins without let up.

To her disgust, the path down to the beach had lost its usual freshness; the cedar chips, their scent drastically diminished, were crushed and scattered, the lawn beside the path scuffed down to the roots in places, a planting of sweet-smelling shrubbery and a grouping of white Shasta daisies almost torn out. To all appearances, the cops had gone out of their way to destroy her property. Gunderson's fault?

Making a mental note to replenish the chips and trim the shrubs and daisies, trundling the wheelbarrow carefully so the rake and shovel didn't spill, she broke out onto the beach.

"Oh, my gosh!"

Looking over the scene, it appeared that when the investigators finished working the scene, they'd simply walked off and left the site. Crime scene tape fluttered brokenly from anchor points, which consisted of wobbly stakes poked in the sand. Seaweed had been hauled up onto the beach and dumped there. Only a psychic could guess why. Rocks, pieces of driftwood, Styrofoam coffee cups, waxed paper and sandwich bags, candy wrappers, broken glass—the list went on and on. Her normally pristine beach had been turned into a disaster area.

Far out on the lake, the hum of a boat motor grew louder as it entered the Golden West's bay, then cut off. A fisherman, Truth figured, spreading the mouth of the garbage bag wide and adjusting her gloves. But not one who'd launched from here. Not today. Frowning, wondering, she slapped at a huge fly buzzing around her head, one as noisy as a small plane.

She forgot the boat as she bent to retrieve the lid from a Starbucks cup, a written complaint to the sheriff's office forming in her head. There was no excuse for this.

Even so, she could've handled the garbage without balking too much. It was the all too obvious signs left from Mrs. Thompson's death that made her stomach lurch. The blood-stained sand and gory bits she feared to categorize. The indentations gouged by the old lady's knees still showed clearly in the sand.

One strong swoosh with her rake obliterated that portion of the evidence. Truth dug out deep shovelfuls of darkened sand and flung it as far into the lake as she could. Let the moving waters wash it clean.

But she would put up markers and keep them up for at least a couple days, saying this part of the beach was off limits. Not, she remembered bitterly, that there'd be anyone left at the resort who wanted to swim.

Forty minutes later, with the beach so well raked even she, looking behind her, couldn't tell precisely where Mrs. Thompson's body had lain, Truth finished the job and started up the path again. She had a full garbage bag of debris piled in her wheelbarrow, but there was room on top for a bit more, so she tidied as she went. The mangled daisy plant called for attention.

Reaching down to snip away a broken portion of the tall plant, the gleam of gold caught her eye.

"Hello, what's this?" she breathed, not quite out loud. Silly question, even to herself. She knew very well what she was seeing; a bangle bracelet.

Her heart thudded. What's more, she recognized the bracelet. A pattern of flowers was incised in the metal, the details enameled with white and green. Expensive looking. Distinctive.

Even before she plucked the bracelet out from under the daisy's trampled leaves, a memory kicked in. She knew just where she'd last seen it. And when. On Becca's arm as she flirted with Hunter Blaine, on the night she disappeared.

"What have you got there? Find something interesting?"

Truth jumped, heartbeat accelerating.

As though her thoughts had conjured him, Hunter Blaine's voice came from behind her. Her gloved hand closed over the bracelet. Without thinking twice, she thrust the bangle inside her other glove and made a show of breaking off a stem of the daisy.

She turned to face him, forcing a smile. "Oh, hi, Hunter. You startled me. I didn't know anyone was around."

He didn't apologize. "But here I am."

"Yep, here you are." *Sneaking up on me* remained unsaid. "I wondered what happened to you. Haven't seen you today."

"I was on the lake checking for boating infractions and fishing limit violators." His voice turned caustic. "My job. The great Pratt Madden has the FBI involved now. They don't need a lowly Fish and Wildlife officer's help anymore."

Internally, Truth squirmed. "Oh, so that was your boat I heard coming in a while ago." She wiggled her fingers inside the glove, adjusting the bracelet to fit in her palm.

"Probably."

"I didn't see you go out this morning," she said, making uneasy conversation.

"You don't have the only boat launch on Lost Girl Lake, you know." He craned his neck, trying to see around her.

She frowned. "Not quite, but I have the best and only commercial one able to take any boat larger than a canoe." And the one he always used.

"What have you found?" Hunter asked again, patently ignoring what had actually been her question.

"Junk. You can't believe how much trash the cops left on the beach. And just look what they've done to my plantings. This daisy will never be the same." She held out the stem to show him. "I might as well grub the whole thing out by the roots."

Hunter's gaze darted from her face to the flower. "Oh, I don't think the daisy is irreparably damaged. Did I see you pick up something else?"

She wadded the flower and stuffed it in the open garbage bag. "You mean aside from a candy bar wrapper and a filter tip cigarette butt? No." She paused, unable to let the question rest. "Why?"

"If you've found anything that might be evidence, you need to turn it over to the police, Truth. Or to me and I'll make a report."

"Evidence? Me?" She stared at him, puzzled by his attitude. And her own attitude, too. Maybe she was hyper-sensitive today, but he seemed determined to ruffle her fur. "The police have been digging around here since early this morning," she went on. "I'm sure they were very thorough. What could possibly be left to find? Except for their trash."

Had he seen her palm the bracelet? She didn't think so. Her back had shielded his view as she reached into the plant to pick off the broken piece.

Her itch to get away from the beach, and from him, grew. She wanted a shower, her dog, and a nap. And most of all to see Pratt and show him what she'd found.

Making a production of the movement, she arched her spine as if it were aching—no lie—and stowed the rake and shovel over the top of the garbage bag. "I'm done here." She looked behind him at the beach, now clean and tidy. No possible trace of blood remained to be seen.

She reached for the wheelbarrow handles, but somehow, he got in front of her. "The path is kind of steep and it looks like you have a load," he said. "Let me help."

"Okay. Thanks." The load wasn't really heavy, just a little bulky, but why, she figured, should she complain?

He took off in a rush, Truth jogging after him. "Hey, what's your hurry?" she asked.

Her question was answered a few seconds later as Hunter came to a turn in the trail. He'd been going too fast, as she'd tried to tell him, and as he gave the wheelbarrow a mighty shove, it tipped.

The contents spilled. Shovel and rake flew forward, the garbage bag doing a slow slide onto the path. The top of the bag, not yet secured, gaped open. Out came the coffee cups, the plant remnants, the aforementioned cigarette butts and candy wrappers. All the stuff she'd so painstakingly gathered

Hunter stood there eyeing the mess with a comical, if rueful, look on his face. "Well, dang, Truth. Sorry about that. The tire hit a tree root or something."

It had been deliberate. She'd seen him twist the wheelbarrow handles.

She managed a smile and said, as if it didn't matter, "I hope you're going to help clean this stuff up."

"Sure. I'm on it." He knelt, blocking her line of sight, and started throwing the least repulsive items back in the bag. After a few moments of selective retrieval, he made a production of looking at his watch, and jumped to his feet. "Is it that time already? I'm due to meet a guy over at Sprague Lake in an hour. Sorry, I can't finish here, Truth. I'm sure you understand."

"Yes." She stood rigid, heart beating fast. "I understand." She did, too, since he'd used almost the same ploy to hide his actions as she when she'd hidden the bracelet from his view. Only he'd done it to obscure his search of the garbage. Why? What was he looking for?

She was afraid she knew.

Wishing him gone, the sooner the better, she said, "It's all right. I'll finish here."

"You sure?"

Best not to be too conciliatory. "I don't appreciate having to do the same work twice, but I expect if you've got somewhere else you have to be—" She let the rest of the sentence hang.

"Yeah. Yeah, I do. I owe you one, Truth." With a cocky kind

of quasi-military salute, he strode up the path without another word.

Truth let out a breath. "Yes, you do," she whispered. And, "Wow."

There she went, talking to herself again.

In a matter of minutes, she'd collected, or recollected, the trash, tossed the bag into one of the barrels she kept at strategic points around the camp and locked away her tools in the shed at the edge of the woods. As she started across the children's park on her way to the resort, a furtive kind of noise coming from the trees stopped her. Bushes rattled, insects went silent. Then the flash of a brightly colored T-shirt at the rear of the shed drew her eye. To her surprise, Mandi strolled from the woods. She was alone.

Truth took a breath, then called, "Hi," and waved.

Mandi hesitated before coming to meet her. "Hi, yourself," she said. "What's up, Truth? You look positively frazzled."

"Yes. I've been cleaning up after the cops. They left garbage all over the beach."

"Ick." Mandi wrinkled her nose. "That must've been fun."

"Oh, yeah. Lots." Flapping her dusty gloves, one of which still contained the bracelet, Truth cocked her head. Mandi's hair was shining clean, the sunlight glinting on blonde high-lights. "Where's your hubby? I'm surprised to see you out walking alone. Not," she added hastily, "that I think there's any danger, but—"

What the heck was she doing? *Trying* to frighten her few remaining customers away? Anyway, hadn't it been Mandi who first suggested to Truth that she should not go out alone? Of course, she'd been talking about at night, not during broad daylight, but still, the warning had been graphic.

"—but this has been a crazy, scary day," she finished.

"I know." Mandi's voice thickened, rich with a kind of

warmth. "You poor thing. This is so traumatizing for you. How're you holding up, Truth? Maybe you should actually consider that awful realtor's offer to buy you out."

It was eerie, the way Mandi echoed Truth's earlier thought.

Truth shuddered. "Please, don't even joke about such a thing."

Mandi laughed. "One of those 'I'd rather die' situations, huh?"

"You said it!"

"I'm with you, girl." Mandi turned her wrist to glance at her watch. "Gosh, is that the time? I promised Ken a pasta salad for dinner, and it needs time to chill. See you later."

She took a step past Truth.

"Oh, wait," Truth said, wondering at the other woman's rush. "I wanted to ask, have you seen Pratt. Maybe at the old barn."

Mandi arched an eyebrow. "Old barn?"

"Yes. You were there, weren't you? The path you came out on . . . well, hardly a path, as overgrown as it is, but—"

"That was a path?" Mandi laughed. "Could've fooled me. I didn't go near the barn, Truth, and believe me, I'm glad. No, I was wandering around and fought my way through some bushes until I popped out here. And now I'm late. Anyway, sorry. I haven't seen Pratt all afternoon. Tell you what, if I do, I'll let him know you're looking for him, okay?"

With that, fingers wiggling a cheery ta-ta, she strode quickly away.

Truth, standing still as a pillar of salt, watched her go, tidy, cool, and not a hair out of place. Not at all as if she'd been fighting her way through bushes. She had to have been on the path.

Why had Mandi just lied?

CHAPTER 26

PRATT PULLED OFF THE FREEWAY INTO THE REST AREA. Ernhardt hadn't yet arrived for their meeting, so he parked his pickup in the shade of a huge fir, close to where travelers with pets walked their dogs. The rest stop, he reflected, was beginning to feel like his own open-air office.

Ernhardt was late, no big surprise.

Pratt didn't mind. He shoved back his pickup seat, toggled the recline feature, and stretched out for a nap, sleep having been a commodity in short supply lately.

Twenty minutes later, metal pinged as Ernhardt tapped on the pickup door, startling him awake. The vehicle's interior was sweltering, even with the windows rolled down and a slight breeze stirring the air.

"This all you got to do? Sit around and sleep?" Ernhardt grinned, flapping a sheaf of papers at him.

"No. All I've got to do is sit around and wait on you." Feeling worse than when he'd drifted off, Pratt made a grab for the documents.

Ernhardt held them just out of reach.

The senior agent blinked at Pratt's tone. "Yeah, well, wake up and look at what I have for you. Some people have been working their collective behinds off."

"Who? Your secretary?"

"My, my, you are in a mood. Maybe a cup of coffee will improve your outlook." Ernhardt smirked and released his hold on the papers. "A quick read through these might not hurt, either."

The name on the top sheet caught Pratt's eye first thing. A flare of excitement stifled a building yawn. He stepped from the pickup—pushing Ernhardt aside with the door—and led the way to a redwood picnic table with plenty of room to spread out the papers.

"I'll get the coffee while you read. Do you suppose the kiosk has any that's drinkable?"

"As long as it has caffeine," Pratt answered absently.

Ernhardt headed over to the rest stop refreshment stand where the aroma of a freshly brewed pot had enticed a couple of long-haul truck drivers and a rumpled woman driving an old Taurus with North Carolina plates.

Pratt, speedreading, was already halfway through the first report he'd requested the Spokane office research for him. He looked up, assimilating the information.

Ernhardt, he saw, stood at the kiosk, and was amid a four-way chat with the coffee server, the woman from North Carolina, and one of the truck drivers. The senior agent wore a smile when, returning, he placed Pratt's coffee in front of him. "Find anything that whets your hunter's instincts?"

Pratt twisted his head and stared at his boss. "Well, well, well. Marko Kravtzov? Manya Kravtzova?"

"I thought you'd like that."

"Like it?" Pratt thumped the table. "Why didn't I have this information going in?"

Ernhardt sat, legs sprawled outward from the table. "My fault. I'll admit we didn't dig deeply enough, took their application information for granted." He shrugged. "As you see, the name changes were legal."

"This one, we missed this one, too." Pratt pulled one of the sheets from the stack and waved it in front of Ernhardt's nose.

"He's been clean a long time. We just didn't go back far enough."

Pratt stopped reading and took a long gulp of his coffee, sputtering a little as it burned his mouth. "Did you notice his employment record?"

"You bet. The family connections are well established. Should be fairly easy to shut them down now we know who we're looking for." Ernhardt glanced around, smiling as though enjoying a view almost obscured by the trailing exhaust of a big diesel as it headed out of the rest area onto the highway. "And where they do business."

Pratt eyed the departing truck also. "Not a big rig, Frank. Forget that. They're not using semis for this operation. Look for something local, a delivery van, most likely."

"Local? That doesn't give them much space."

"Yeah, but how much do they need? Moving three or four girls at a time. Don't forget their pick-up point. I guarantee you no eighteen-wheeler has tracked down the road into the Golden West resort. Not as long as I've been there."

Knees stiff, Ernhardt got to his feet. "Next thing is, I suppose you want me to run a check on every outfit that delivers supplies to the resort. Got a list made up?"

Pratt took a page from his notebook and scribbled down some names, handing the list to Ernhardt when he finished. "I'll have any I missed for you later tonight. I'll talk to Truth. She can help."

"Good enough." Always impatient, Ernhardt fumbled car

keys from his pocket, anxious now to be on his way. "Are we done here?"

Pratt stopped him with a gesture. "Almost. Just a couple things more. First, I have a little something more for you, too. You can thank Truth Diamond for this. After I found Rory this morning, I had her go around the car park notifying campers to stay inside. She noticed something odd."

Ernhardt gave him a hard stare. "Are you involving civilians, Madden? Is that wise?"

"It's her resort." No, it wasn't wise. Pratt knew that as well as the boss did, but he'd take any help he could get.

"So, what did Ms. Diamond notice?" Ernhardt asked.

"What she's afraid could be blood, in a place she never expected to see it." Pratt remembered how reluctant she'd been to impart this observation. Her faith in her fellow man had suffered a blow and Pratt had an idea the situation was only going to get worse. "She found some of her guests already up when they're normally late sleepers," he went on, flipping through the papers his boss had brought and stopping again on the Manya Kravtzova document. "Definite out-of-character behavior." He met Ernhardt's eyes. "And guess who she was talking to?" He flashed the page.

"No." Ernhardt's face lit up. "Put that together with the one thing Rory remembers and we've got the case nailed."

Pratt nodded, not quite so elated as his boss. "So, what does he remember?"

"Perfume. A distinctive perfume, one he recognized because his wife wears it. Guess what it's named."

A shake of Pratt's head answered.

Ernhardt laughed. "*Tatiana*. How's that for funny?"

"Or ironic."

"True." Sobering, Ernhardt had a final question. "So, this other missing girl. What's her name again?"

"Becca—Rebecca Keene."

"Yeah, her. You sure they've got her?"

Pratt's lips tightened, his fist slammed the picnic table. "Too big of a coincidence otherwise. But I think she has a chance. I don't think they've moved her out of the area yet."

"You think. Be better if you were sure."

"Got that right." Pratt swallowed the last of his coffee and stacked the papers, ready to head back to the resort. The meeting was about over. "One thing more. How is Rory? He gonna be okay?"

"You oughta know the Bureau doesn't hire anyone with a soft head," Ernhardt said. "Look at you. He'll be fine."

SHAKEN NOT ONLY by her odd encounter with Hunter, followed almost immediately by the one with Mandi, Truth speed-walked toward the old resort building as fast as her feet would carry her. A glance at her watch indicated Consuelo's shift had ended a few minutes ago. There'd probably be a few customers at the store yet, coming in for milk or bread or eggs before closing time. She couldn't wait to lock the doors, front and back, and go upstairs and sit in her living room with Razz curled on her lap. Try to read or watch a rerun on television. And keep her pistol handy.

Except she still had to find Pratt and talk to him.

Inwardly, she seethed. Why in the world didn't they have cell phone service here? Lost Girl Lake wasn't *quite* at the end of the universe, after all. Pratt had darn well better show up before dark. She really, *really*, did not want to go looking for him after sunset.

The screen door slammed behind her as she hurried into the resort.

Consuelo peeked around the corner from the kitchen, an alarmed look taking the place of her normally placid expression.

So, Truth thought, Connie is not immune to atmosphere, either. In a funny sort of way, she felt better knowing.

"Oh," Consuelo said, "it's you. I thought for a minute that real estate guy was back. Mandi told me how rude he was, talking loud and bulling around like he owned the place."

Mandi had? "When did you talk to her?" She couldn't even think about Bill Billous.

"Not long after you took off for the beach. She said she was going to give you a hand." Connie brought in a stack of clean dish towels from the kitchen and placed them under the counter, ready for the morning.

"She did?" Truth's forehead puckered into a frown. "She never showed up."

"Didn't she? Funny. I saw her going that way."

Why hadn't she? Because Hunter was already there? Or because once she knew Truth was occupied, she went off walking in the woods near the old barn? And why would Mandi do that—and then deny it?

Truth's tummy lurched as she poured herself a glass of sweet iced tea and swallowed more than half in three fast gulps.

"No reason why she should, I guess. It couldn't be a very pleasant job, and she *is* a guest." Connie shrugged and got her purse from an under-the-counter shelf, sifting through a side pocket and coming up with car keys on a chain bearing a yellow smiley face. "So, will you need me tomorrow?"

Unable to stand the thought of being here on her own, Truth nodded. "If you don't mind."

"I can use the hours." Smiling, Consuelo left, allowing two

kids to enter before, early or not, Truth had a chance to lock the door behind her.

Some brave parent—or maybe just a stupid, unaware one— apparently didn't feel the same unease, same fear she did, letting the young ones out alone.

The kids headed straight for the chest-style ice-cream freezer, taking their time selecting and giggling periodically. Upstairs, Razz gave a couple sharp barks, letting Truth know she didn't like being ignored and needed a pit-stop.

Larry came in and bought a carton of worms. "Thought I'd try my luck on the boat launch dock after dark," he informed her, his attitude seeming almost defiant.

Shocked Fran hadn't persuaded him to leave, it occurred to Truth that his wife's nagging had made him dig in his heels to stay. Unless he was afraid he couldn't hitch onto the trailer and successfully get it out to the road, a distinct possibility. The notion drew a small smile from her as she greeted him.

"Your hired girl been found yet?" he asked gruffly as he handed over money for the dozen worms.

"No word."

"And the old lady? They caught her killer?"

Truth blanched. "I don't think so."

Larry harrumphed. "A real shame. She was a nice old gal, what I saw of her. Why would anybody do such an awful thing? Beat her head in, I heard. She didn't look like she had anything worth stealing, let alone killing her for."

Seriously? Did Larry think Mrs. Thompson had been killed during a robbery? After all that had gone on here at the Golden West with the girl with the amputated hand? But that brought up another question. Why *had* Mrs. Thompson been murdered? Had she seen something or someone she shouldn't have?

Truth made change, the questions whirling through her mind. Was Larry being disingenuous, trying to divert suspicion? She didn't know what to think. Nah, she decided a minute later. This all started before he showed up at the Golden West, even though his arrival precipitated the resort's involvement.

"Take care," she told him as he left, meaning it with all her heart.

He waved a nonchalant reply over his shoulder, the outline of a rather large automatic pistol showing at his back. Another man figuring, he could take care of himself.

Rory, a trained FBI agent, had no doubt thought so too.

She touched her own small automatic hidden under her apron and had doubts.

On the heels of children shedding ice cream wrappers as they went, she got the door locked and the 'closed' sign out before any other customers could get in, although someone knocked just as she reached the landing at the top of the stairs. She didn't turn back to see who it was. She didn't care.

CHAPTER 27

ACCORDING TO HER IMPERIOUS BARKING, RAZZ'D HAD ENOUGH of confinement upstairs. A sense of caution urged Truth to put the little dog on a leash before they went outside. Razz gave her mistress *such* a look. Probably afraid of a trip to the vet, Truth thought, since that was generally the only time she resorted to such restrictions. Razz had an uncanny ability to sense when check-ups were due.

But this wasn't a day to indulge the dog. Who knew what kind of monster was on the loose. Certainly, one who didn't balk at chopping off a young girl's hand or bludgeoning a harmless old lady to death. What might he do to a little pooch like Razz?

Locking the door as they left, Truth allowed Razz to take the lead. Unobtrusively, she urged the Pomeranian toward Digbee's RV where she hoped to find Pratt. But even before she got to the Madden's space, she could see his pickup was not in its regular parking spot.

And neither, she discovered, was Digbee's big Ram.

"Blast!"

The exclamation, though spoken quietly, caused Razz to look up her and give a questioning "Woof."

"Do you think I should go ahead and leave Pratt a note?"

Razz shook herself and curled her tail tightly over her back.

"No. I don't think so either. What if—" Yeah. What if someone was watching and got to the note before Pratt or Digbee? She had a skin-crawling sensation of being under observation at this very moment and had ever since she'd gone down to the beach on clean-up duty.

And then Hunter showed up. And Mandi, acting— Weird didn't seem a strong enough word.

Trying to shake the unease aside, Truth took a meandering path as they trudged back to the resort. Her every cell urged speed each time Razz stopped to sniff or mark territory. Each time she resisted.

"Feel better, girl, after a nice walkie?" she said loudly, hoping the comment would reassure anyone who questioned the direction they'd taken. Losing no time once they were inside, she repeated the security routine instituted earlier. Then, a trace of paranoia urging even more caution, she went around checking the locks on all the windows and doors a second time before they went upstairs.

Her impatience and sense of urgency grew as she waited for Pratt to return. She needed him. Why wasn't he here? Where had he gone? What was he doing?

All senses alert, she opened a can of chili beans for her dinner, heating them in the microwave and carrying the bowl and a stack of soda crackers over to the window where she could watch for Pratt's return.

Just at dark, Digbee drove in, Sam in the passenger seat. They went past the resort without stopping. The car park was deserted by then, the playground swings empty, all her rental boats at anchor. Smoke from a few campfires and barbeques wafted through the trees, fewer of them now than at any time since summer began.

The Golden West felt almost abandoned compared to previous days.

"What do you think, Razz?" she asked the dog. "Should we try walking over to Digbee's place again?"

Razz cocked her head and remained silent.

No, Truth decided, an involuntary shudder wracking her. She'd wait until she knew Pratt had returned. Besides, it was already dark under the trees. Call her a coward, but she swore she heard voices in her head urging her to stay inside and be safe.

As if she weren't already scared enough! Sweat dampened her skin, a reaction not only to tension, but the heat gathered under the old roof. She opened the window in her bedroom, grateful to live on the second story, unreachable unless someone had a very long ladder.

Don't even think about it.

At eleven o'clock she gave up on waiting for Pratt and went to bed.

At midnight she awoke, eyes wide, ears straining to hear . . . what? Utter stillness outside. No crickets. No wind. Just Lost Girl Lake, lapping gently at the shore.

Razz stood on her chest, pawing at her chin and growling low in her throat.

A repeat of last night, before she'd found Mrs. Thompson.

Despair touched her. *Dear God, who is dead now?*

Becca? Please no.

"Shhh." Even trying to shush Razz sounded loud, but not so loud as to cover the clatter as the screen door to the patio banged three or four times.

Her breath caught. Held.

A moment later, footsteps came her way, hesitating under her window before retreating down the path.

Gasping air, Truth rolled off the bed. She made it to the window in time to see the dark form of a man leap over her garden gate. Down on the dock, another man waited. As she watched, the pair strode quickly and without hesitation to a boat slip—Truth counted, three, four, five spaces—to where Ken Henning habitually moored his twenty-one-foot Lund fishing boat. The men climbed aboard and let go the lines. One of them pushed the boat out into the water by kicking off strongly with his foot from the dock.

Although a dark night, enough ambient light reflected from the water for her to tell the other guy had a long aluminum pole. Thrusting it into the shallow lake bottom, he propelled the boat forward in silence. Not until they were about a hundred yards from shore did he collapse the pole and start the electric trolling motor.

She bet she was the only one watching. The only one to see or hear them go.

Had one of the men been Ken? Or someone stealing his boat? What had the man wanted, trying the locks on her doors?

Did he want her? But why? Where the police when she needed them? Where was the FBI? To be specific, where in the world was Pratt Madden?

Her mind stuttered from all the questions whirling through her brain.

It came as a shock to realize she'd even welcome the snap of Gunderson's fingers right now.

PRATT'S PHONE VIBRATED. He handed a twenty-dollar bill to the restaurant cashier, a bosomy thirty-something woman too scantily clad considering the blast of the air conditioner and plucked the phone from his pocket.

"Yeah?"

Ernhardt's voice answered. "We caught a break," he said without preamble. "You can thank Deputy Ortiz for this. Looks like the two of you have been thinking along the same lines."

"We've discussed a few possibilities and what-ifs," Pratt said. "Talked to a few people."

Ernhardt was almost chortling. "Excellent. Apparently, your cooperation is working out. Ortiz caught a delivery truck on the road above the resort late this afternoon, in a place it had no business to be. It looked odd to him, so Ortiz got Gunderson to authorize bringing the driver in for questioning on suspicion, and guess what?"

Pratt shifted the phone to his other ear and took his change, the cashier sending him an inviting smile. Automatically, he smiled back. "What?"

She seemed disappointed the question wasn't for her.

"The driver's name is Kravtzov, too. Anatoly Kravtzov." Ernhardt sounded pleased.

Elation lit in Pratt. "Are they brothers?"

"This one is older. I'm guessing he's an uncle, or maybe a cousin. We're checking."

Pratt heard the cashier's thank you and cooed, "Do come again," without it registering. Turning away and stuffing the coins and bills in his Wrangler's pocket, he headed for his pickup. "Is he talking?" he asked.

"No, but he's sweating. I thought you might like to take a shot at him."

Anger made Pratt's reply grim. "I'd take a shot, all right."

Ernhardt chuckled. "I'll bet you would. Let me rephrase

that. I thought you might like the first crack at questioning him."

"I like your other idea better."

"Sorry, not tonight. Tonight, if you get over to County right away, you can get to him before Gunderson screws everything up." Ernhardt paused. "The detective thought any questioning could wait until morning. Said he was too tired tonight."

Pratt made a sound of disgust. "That's typical Gunderson, all right."

"Fortunately for us, Deputy Ortiz is cut from different cloth. Which means tonight Mr. Kravtzov is all yours." Ernhardt sounded downright cheery about the prospect.

Pratt was cheered, too, at what he hoped would be real progress. But he couldn't help dwelling on the other things on his plate right now—like keeping an eye on Truth and his granddad. With Rory out of commission, no one was at the resort to provide security. But if he got anything out of Kravtzov, chances were they had an opportunity to find Becca before she disappeared. *Dead or alive?* He figured alive.

So far.

He burned rubber, getting out of the parking lot.

At the county jail, he discovered Ernhardt already there. The supervisory agent had taken control, arranging for him to meet with the driver. Ortiz was on the scene, too, working overtime and waiting to fill him in on how he'd come to stop Kravtzov. Together, he and Ortiz entered an interview room where Pratt found an older edition of the man he knew from the resort.

Ortiz looked at him and grinned. He knew he'd done good. Credit where credit was due.

This Kravtzov wore a jacket with a *Supreme Bakery Serving the Northwest* logo stitched on a breast pocket. His glacial blue eyes glared at Pratt and Ortiz across a scratched and scarred metal table. Stocky shoulders were set in stubborn lines.

A tough nut, Pratt surmised. But would he be so tough when threatened with deportation? Anatoly Kravtzov hadn't been in the United States long enough to qualify for citizenship. Something he would never attain if proven guilty and thank God for that.

Pulling up a chair, Pratt straddled the seat. Ortiz remained standing behind him. Pratt leaned forward and studied the man without speaking. Ernhardt had been right. Kravtzov sweat like a racehorse as he fidgeted in his chair.

After a few moments of silent contemplation, Pratt fired off his first question. "*Supreme Bakery*, huh? Serving the Northwest? Just how much territory does that encompass?"

A shrug of those thick shoulders replied.

"I checked. Tri-cities and into British Columbia." Ortiz had the answer.

"Convenient." Pratt nodded, then, staring hard at Kravtzov, said, "Since when do you make deliveries at night?"

Kravtzov met his eyes, scowling. "Emergency. Special order." He had a strong accent.

"Special order? Who placed this order? Where were you taking it?"

A bead of sweat trickled down the side of the man's face. "Do not know."

"You don't know where you were going?"

"I only drive. Go where I am told."

"Who tells you? Where did he tell you to go?"

Ortiz's quiet explanation came from over Pratt's shoulder. "I caught him turning onto that little overgrown road a half mile past the Golden West's turn-off. It leads down to a cove. The water is deep there with a rocky bottom. No diving or swimming there. It's not safe. That's why Truth has it blocked off."

Pratt nodded. "I know it." He faced back to the prisoner. "Blocked by no trespassing signs with a heavy chain."

"Got lost. Turning around." Kravtzov crossed his arms over his chest.

"He was out of the truck, Agent Madden," Ortiz said, sounding almost happy. "Had heavy duty bolt cutters on him."

More sweat rolled down Kravtzov's face.

Pratt allowed a phony grin to curl one side of his mouth. "Lost? Funny. I've seen the Supreme Bakery truck making deliveries to the Golden West before. Every week, in fact. I figure any driver has to know his way around the area pretty well. Nope, you weren't lost. Where were you going, sneaking around after hours with bolt cutters in your possession?"

Kravtzov remained silent.

"Funniest thing," Ortiz said, off-hand. "The truck was empty, except for some rolled up blankets."

Pratt smashed his fist onto the metal table, making the prisoner flinch. "Who were you supposed to meet, Kravtzov?"

Silence.

"Why meet at that particular cove?"

A longer silence.

Pratt was sweating, too.

"Boats can come right up to the bank there," Ortiz said. "Don't need a dock. A person can step right off the boat onto dry land."

"Convenient," Pratt said.

Kravtzov sent Ortiz a baleful glance.

"Is that it?" Pratt demanded. "This the night you planned on moving those girls out?" *Including Becca Keene?* "Where've you been keeping the girls after you moved them out of the old barn at the Golden West? Where'd you plan on taking them?"

Kravtzov paled, but held his silence, even as Pratt, then Ortiz, then Pratt again hammered at him. "Where did Marko Kravtzov tell you to take the girls?"

An hour passed.

Pratt reached the breaking point first—or so he let Kratzov believe. He stood, sending his chair sprawling. The prisoner shrank backwards as Pratt grabbed his shirt collar, and with one powerful flex of muscle yanked the man out of his chair.

Face turning puce, Kravtzov flailed wildly at him.

"Speak up. Where are those girls?" Pratt ignored the blows, not even feeling them. He tightened his grip.

Kravtzov gagged, wholly unnecessary in Pratt's view. He wasn't choking the guy—much.

"Take it easy, Agent Madden," Ortiz said, a voice of calm reason, which Pratt ignored.

"Easy? Did he take it easy when he cut off that girl's hand?" Pratt made his real fury into a good show. "When he cut her throat and she bled out?"

"No!" Kravtzov's eyes bugged. "Not me. I did not cut off girl's hand. Did not cut throat. Not me."

"Who did?" Pratt demanded.

Kravtzov went silent again.

"Who?"

Silence.

"Then I guess you're willing to take the murder rap," Pratt said. "Serve a life sentence for murder and human trafficking as well as violating the laws of the United States. Double life sentence, would be my guess."

"Probably get the death penalty," Ortiz amended. "Judges and juries in this neck of the woods don't go easy on people, especially foreigners, who torture girls."

"Right." Pratt put on a happy face. "They still hang them in this state, don't they?"

"Sure do," Ortiz agreed. "Tried and true method of execution, as long as the hangman knows his stuff."

Pratt nodded thoughtfully. "Has the hangman had much practice lately?"

"Afraid not. Hope he's a good mathematician, gets the weight and height of the prisoner right. I hear he screwed up and the last one got his whole head popped off. Just like a cork coming out of a bottle."

"Gruesome," Pratt said. "About as bad putting a girl's arm over a chopping block and whacking off her hand."

Kravtzov broke.

CHAPTER 28

ANY INCLINATION TO GO BACK TO BED ELUDED TRUTH AS SHE crouched by her window, watching and waiting. Her eyes felt gritty from lack of sleep and the strain of trying to see through the dark.

She considered a few thumps to her own head until good sense made a comeback. What an idiot to put herself under so much stress when she didn't even know who she was watching or waiting for.

Well, yes, she did. Watching for Pratt and waiting for the two men in Ken's boat to return. Unless the boater wasn't Ken, but someone who had stolen the craft. Unlikely, she admitted.

And what would she do when, or if, they did come back? All she knew for sure is that the hair on the nape of her neck stood on end, roused by the tension thrumming through her entire body.

At some point, she stepped away from the window long enough to dress. Black jeans, black long-sleeved T-shirt, black sneakers. Most importantly, a black knitted cap over her all too bright platinum hair. She had to be ready.

For what?

She had to laugh at herself. Imagine. Truth Diamond, hard-working resort owner, dressed up like a spy on a clandestine mission. Who did she think she was fooling? And yet her pistol rested on the nightstand next to her as she kept watch, and every once in a while, she picked it up and ran her fingers over the cool steel barrel. Reassurance of a sort.

She'd been at the window an hour when she caught the sound of a boat out on the lake. The motor rumbled low, slowing as it powered down. It seemed to come from the southern end of the lake, headed toward the Golden West. Ken's boat? She figured yes.

Her heart gave an extra thump. Her nape hair, which had finally settled down, rose again. *The southern end?* Why? There was nothing over there except the ruins of an old homestead. For some reason, even the fishing had never been good.

The folks who'd settled the southernmost quarter section of land at the beginning of the previous century had sold out to her family in the 1930s. The buildings had collapsed many years ago. They'd perched on a bluff above the lake and, as she remembered, there'd never been any kind of beach on the property. No real access except a steep, stony hike down to the water.

Even she had only observed the place from a boat on her annual spring excursions around the lake. She'd been too busy in recent years to go by road and do a real inspection any time since her parents died. The Golden West owned her, all her resources, and all her time.

But one feature of the old Heckler homestead had always intrigued her, and as a little kid, fed her sense of adventure. About halfway up the bluff, a cave's dark opening helped a child with a vivid imagination dream of adventure. Before the age of ten, she believed the cave an old pirate hideaway. As a teenager, her dad had told her the story of Lost Girl Lake's most famous bootlegger. According to him, Heckler had used the cave as a way station for hooch smuggled down out of Canada. Bushes clinging to the rock bluff had made the opening almost invisible, helping hide it from revenuers.

Exciting stuff. Unless—

Was the cave being used once again as a way station, only for human trafficking this time? Right under her stupid, oblivious nose? Right under the equally stupid and oblivious nose of FBI agent Pratt Madden?

Truth snorted, disgusted and incredulous.

Out on the lake, the boat motor revved a single time, then died.

"What the—" Where had it landed? It certainly hadn't entered the Golden West's cove.

Truth got up, keeping to the side of her window, and peered through the glass. The yard, the docks, the beach, and farther out, the lake. Nothing. No sign of Ken's boat returning to his normal slip. No, but she had a hunch where it was right now.

Her hunch didn't stop with where. How about why and who? Was Becca as close as Ken Henning's boat?

Turning away from the window, she picked up her Ruger and left the bedroom, sneaking, so not to awaken Razz who slept curled in a tiny pale lump. She slipped from the room into the hall, closing the door with a quiet snick, and made her way down the stairs without turning on any lights. She'd lived here all her life. Two or three squeaky steps held no mystery for her and she easily avoided stepping on them, even as she tried to laugh at herself. Who was there to hear if the steps squeaked or not?

In the kitchen, she crossed to the wall phone, picked up the receiver, and punched in 911 by feel. A half-dozen heartbeats later she realized nothing was happening. No dial tone, no busy signal, *no answer*. Nothing.

Goosebumps rose on her skin. Her pulse beat in her ears. She felt a little dizzy.

Face it, woman. You're in trouble.

Truth didn't try to kid herself. She was scared. She'd be crazy if she weren't.

HEADLIGHTS DARK, the caravan of vehicles pulled off Highway 195 and parked on the shoulder of a gravel secondary road. Two sheriff's department cruisers led the way, followed by a black SUV belonging to the FBI, senior agent Frank Ernhardt's Buick, a van marked SWAT, and Pratt Madden's pickup, the rigs in a line like links in a chain. One of the cruisers took a position in a long, cobblestone driveway, blocking the exit. Men, along with a couple women officers, piled out of the cars. Doors closed softly. No lights showed.

The fancy driveway led into a fulsomely treed property where a large, two-story house loomed. The house sat in the center of a brown and crispy lawn, a definite oddity in the upscale neighborhood where spacious green lawns were the norm.

Pratt guessed traffickers had more to think about than watering the grass or whether their automatic sprinkler system was correctly programmed. A faint gleam, muted by heavy drapes drawn over the many windows, indicated someone at home and awake.

Deputy Joseph Ortiz, driver of the cruiser blocking the driveway, met Pratt as he stepped out of his truck.

"Must be a lot of money in buying and selling girls," Ortiz said. "Look at this place. I figure it set them back at least 500K."

Pratt nodded. "Looks to me like they could use a yard service." He shrugged into his bulletproof vest and layered on a jacket with the FBI logo on the back. He hadn't worn official garb in so long it felt foreign. "Convenient site for the operation. Handy to town, yet no close neighbors."

Ortiz stared at the building. "I can't figure out why they brought the girls in through the Golden West. Why not just bring them here to begin with? It doesn't figure."

A half dozen men wearing SWAT gear jogged toward the house to take up position surrounding it. They trod on the lawn and, except for the crunch of dry grass underfoot, moved silently and almost invisibly in their dark clothing. Leaving nothing to chance, they carried sniper rifles and drawn automatics. Pratt approved.

He turned back to Ortiz. "I'd say they kept this place separate for their customers, a way to showcase the girls before shipping them out or sending them off to their buyers. Meanwhile, they break their victims in at some out-of-the-way spot. Terrorize them, get 'em hooked on drugs, do what's necessary to break their spirit. Not so easy for a girl to escape when she's lost and faced with a lot of barren land. Some of them might not even know what country they're in."

Gravel crunched beside them. Gunderson, careless of noise, had arrived to stick in his oar. "Girls probably aren't too bright to begin with," he said, adding as he took note of Ortiz's expression, "Well, they got swept up in this, didn't they? Must've been somewhere they shouldn't've been."

Pratt drew a breath, trying to shake off the crawly feeling he got every time he was in Gunderson's vicinity and had to listen to him spout off. "Are you including Becca Keene in that opinion?" One of his eyebrows lifted.

"Special case," Gunderson said.

Frank Ernhardt stopped beside them in time to hear this

exchange. He put his hand on Pratt's arm and shook his head in warning. "At any rate, I doubt any of these girls tried to escape after seeing one of them get her hand lopped off with an axe. Lesson learned."

Ortiz scowled. "You think that's what it was? An object lesson."

"I do. Probably. Although I've heard some people are intrigued by mutilations."

"Could've been a special order that went wrong." Gunderson didn't appear bothered by the thought. His fingers snapped.

"We'll inquire when we've got the gang in custody," Ernhardt said mildly.

Ortiz rolled his shoulders and shifted his feet. Poised for action, ready to roll. "You think we'll find Becca Keene here?"

Pratt shared a glance with Ernhardt. "Let's hope so," he said.

The SWAT captain's voice came over the earbud, muted almost to a whisper. "We're in position. Ready to move at your word."

Tired of talk, Pratt welcomed the interruption. He wanted this operation finished, with a clean takedown. However many girls were in the house, no matter whether local or another country of origin, they'd all been through enough.

Ernhardt, done with waiting, ordered the operation. He started forward. "Let's go. Quiet now. We want to keep this quick, clean—and quiet."

The four of them jogged toward the house, taking a page out of SWAT's book and staying on the road's verge, making as little noise as possible.

Gunderson breathed heavily, spoiling the silence request, gasping as they ran.

Without a moon to help light the way, Pratt depended on his night vision, by now fairly well attuned to the dark. Even so, he missed an obstacle lying in his path. His foot slammed into whatever it was, kicking the heavy object forward. Caught, he fell to his knees, his hand coming down on something warm and resilient—and unmoving.

"Who?"

Not who. A dog. A large one, erect ears, slick of hair, perhaps a Doberman, tongue dry and lolling out of its mouth. It didn't move and regret for the animal's death swept over him. Another innocent victim. Then he felt the dog's side move and realized one of the SWAT team must've darted it. Good men, prepared for all exigencies.

"You all right?" Ernhardt stopped beside him.

"Fine." Except for the knee wounded in Afghanistan that'd come down on a sharp rock. Pratt picked himself up. Limping, he went on.

They reached the house. The county SWAT team was taking the lead. A member waited for them at the wide concrete steps. With arm gestures, he instructed the rest of them to spread out. Pratt took a position beside the big front window. Unsnapping his hip holster, he drew his Glock 23, its butt smooth and familiar in his hand.

After a pause in which it seemed none of them drew breath, they heard a crash and commotion from the rear of the house, then Benson, the team leader, yelled over the mic, "Inside. Now."

At the first sound, their man put his shoulder to the heavy wooden front door. The door bounced. Held. Ortiz took a position beside him. They hit the door together. With a sharp 'snap,' the latch came free. The door swung open. Brilliant light spilled out. The SWAT guy rushed in first, his pistol out in front. Second in was Ortiz, Pratt on his heels as he shoved in ahead of time.

They entered a large foyer with elegant, carpeted stairs

leading to the upper story. A chandelier dangling hundreds of lighted crystal pendants swung from the thirty-foot ceiling.

Momentarily blinded, Pratt blinked in the brightness. Footsteps thudded overhead. He heard music wailing in the background, stuff with a distinctive Eastern European sound. Over it, a girl screamed.

Apparently, they were in the right place.

Two SWAT team officers ran into the living room. Another two dashed from room to room, inspecting the downstairs.

"Clear," one said from the kitchen. "Clear," from the dining room, the utility room, the three-car garage, filled to capacity with a couple big BMW SUVs and a Corvette convertible. The basement proved empty—of humans. From the expressions of those chosen for the inspection, it held other items of interest.

There remained only one direction to go. Up, the stair climbers sitting ducks to fire from above.

Overhead, the music stopped—a blessing. A girl, maybe more than one, sobbed hysterically. A man's voice commanded silence. He was almost, not quite, obeyed.

The chandelier flickered and went dark. A single bulb on the upper floor provided the only light, a faint glow.

With a collective intake of breath more sensed than seen, and a softly spoken command, SWAT officers raised their shields. They went up in pairs, shoes thudding, swarming the wide staircase. Less heavily armed and shielded, Gunderson, Ernhardt and Pratt remained below to guard the rear—and to wait.

A gunshot ripped through the house, then another two or three sharp pops of a pistol. A shotgun roared. Men yelled. Women screamed.

The slap of a rope ladder as it hit the side of the building jerked Pratt's head around. Not that he knew it was a rope ladder at the time, but he recognized the noise as something out of place. Touching Ernhardt's arm, he nodded toward the house's open front door.

"I heard a noise out there," he said. "I'm going to see what's what."

Ernhardt nodded. "Be careful. We might've missed one."

"Yep."

Stepping onto the porch, Pratt scanned back and forth across the driveway and the front yard. He never thought to look up and wasn't expecting a heavy body to jump on him from above.

They went down, Pratt at the bottom of the pile with a knee in his chest. He struggled for breath even as he fought to keep his assailant from grabbing the Glock out of his hand. They rolled off the porch onto the ground, slugging at each other. He took a fist to the cheekbone. His opponent a knock just below the ribcage. Air gushed out of the man, who reeked of sausage and sweat.

Vaguely, Pratt was aware of another body descending the ladder.

There was the meaty thud of flesh colliding and a sharp yelp. Ortiz shouted, "Freeze. Drop your weapon or I'll shoot." Or something along those lines. Pratt, busy himself, didn't care to repeat the deputy's exact words.

So much for a quiet takedown. He avoided the fist aimed at his jaw and fired a shot into the ground, barely missing his opponent's left ear. The man went as still as though Pratt had shot him through the heart.

"Not today, buddy boy," Pratt said.

CHAPTER 29

FEELING AS IF SHE'D GONE BLIND AND DEAF, TRUTH STOOD IN the dark café kitchen with the dead phone receiver dangling from nerveless fingers. She was unsure of what to do next. Someone had been using *her* land and *her* place of business. Using it as a murder site. As a place to terrorize, to mutilate, to *sell* young girls. This person had also done his best to ruin *her* reputation and the reputation of her resort, and he had taken— kidnapped—*her* employee.

And now he'd cut her doggone phone line to render her helpless. Pure rage surged through her, almost, if not quite, supplanting a healthy dose of fear.

Was she going to stand for it? Let this thug or group of thugs continue their so-called business with impunity?

She snorted into the silence until cooler reason took over. Did she have a choice?

And yet, what could it hurt if she slipped from the building and carefully, oh so carefully, scouted around? What if, provided she found the way clear, she hiked to the top of the hill to where her cell phone got service.

Thinking of Becca, she didn't believe she had a choice. What kind of person would she be if she went back to bed and pretended nothing was happening here tonight?

A clear answer came to her. Not much of one.

Truth felt for the pistol she'd jammed into her back pocket. "Just don't shoot your behind off," she muttered.

As an afterthought, she got her trusty multi-purpose tool from a kitchen drawer and stuck it a front jeans pocket, as satisfied as she could be about her protection. The element of surprise worked for her. No one would be expecting her to stir beyond the safety of the resort. Not until dawn, at least. Especially not after finding Mrs. Thompson dead on the beach less than twenty-four hours ago.

She went out the pantry door instead of the regular kitchen door, or the one leading to her patio where someone had already tried to enter. The pantry exited into a small utility area where garbage cans were kept out of sight and smell of the patrons. No one, except the hired help, knew this way out even existed. If anyone was watching the building, he'd be thwarted.

Truth crept around the privacy fence and darted to the shelter of the trees, seeking the darkest shadows. The night breathed with her, an eerie sensation, but now she had no sense of being overlooked. She stood stock still, listening with every sense tuned. When nothing stirred, she felt confident enough to slip down to the lakeshore and cross an open area of beach, finally hitting the path that took her to the Madden's RV. Pratt hadn't come home, but perhaps she could enlist Digbee.

Enlist Digbee to do what? She stopped and pressed against the trunk of a hundred-year-old Douglas fir, its bark rough against her shoulders. All seemed well around the resort. For the moment, anyway. All she had were suspicions and feelings.

Along with a phone that didn't work, she reminded herself. And a boat was taken in stealth from its slip, and now, sounds coming from the middle of the lake where no sounds should be.

What should she do? Truth, hating herself for it, stood still and dithered.

A scream echoed starkly across the dark water. Not overly loud, but distinct. Her heart seemed to stop as a second scream choked off in mid-cry.

Truth tried to convince herself what she heard was a startled night bird. A loon, perhaps. They were notorious for their awful disturbing calls.

The denial didn't work. She quickly discarded the idea when another cry followed the others. Not a bird. Not with that raw sound of terror. Of pain. She was pretty sure she'd heard "help" mixed up in it.

She gritted her teeth. Someone out there had forgotten how sound carried over water, especially at night. And someone else had not.

Becca?

The phone, she reminded herself. 911. She had to go for help. There was no one else, no other choice. And no more time.

Moving as silently as she knew how, Truth broke into a jog, up the bank to the deserted car park, slowing as she sneaked past the scattered occupied campsites. She avoided the security light as she crossed to the gravel road. Once there, she turned left and kept on going, running now. Most people didn't know going left was a shortcut to the top when on foot and if you cut across the switchback.

Moments later, sweating and breathless, she punched in 911. Reported her emergency, gave her address, begged for speed from the calm-voiced operator.

"Tell Detective Gunderson." She heard a hint of hysteria in her plea. "He'll know. And Deputy Joseph Ortiz. And the FBI. They know about this too."

The dispatcher was remarkably unshaken. "Stay inside and on the line," the woman told her. "Someone will be with you shortly."

Inside. Right. And shortly. What did that even mean? The operator had taken the report, but did she even believe in the emergency?

Truth hit the phone's off button.

Time. Time. How long did it take to kill someone? Or to waft them away, never to be heard from again? Well, it wasn't going to happen to Becca. Nor to any other girl, if she had anything to say about it.

She put on another burst of speed, breathing hard now, unaccustomed to the strenuous exercise as she retraced her footsteps.

Truth, who'd lived on this lake all her life, who had explored every inch of it back in the day when she was a care-free child, before inherited responsibilities had taken all her time and energy, knew precisely where she had to go. The only question? What was she going to do when she got there?

Before she might have wished, certainly before she'd planned of approach, the turn-off she was looking for opened to her right. Even in the dark, she noticed something odd and disquieting in the trail leading down to the lake. Beaten down grass and bushes. Tire tracks that hadn't been here a week ago, the last time she'd passed this way to use her cell, and they shouldn't be here now.

She stopped. Barely breathed. Listened.

Was that the murmur of voices she heard? Yes, and they were coming her way.

Had they heard her make the call?

"Something's happened. He isn't going to show," a man's voice said, close enough now for his words to carry clearly.

Truth, eyes widening, peered down the dark tunnel of road.

A cigarette lighter flared, showing two men stopped in the middle of the trail. She caught a brief glimpse of a face as he lit a cigarette.

All life seemed to stop. *Oh, no. No.* She put a hand over her mouth to keep from speaking out loud.

"We'll wait a little longer," the smoker replied. "He'll be here. Maybe he had a hard time finding the turn-off in the dark."

"The arrangement was for him to meet us at the old farm at noon. Missing that window put everything out of kilter."

"Yes, but our standing procedure is to meet twelve hours later. Right about now, in fact."

"So, where is he?"

The smoker's voice hardened. "He'll be here, I tell you. Manya is watching at the resort. If anything goes wrong there, she'll warn us."

"Moving the merchandise here makes it twice as dangerous," the first man said.

The smoker drew on his cigarette, the end glowing brighter, then fading. When he spoke, he sounded angry. "You can see we have to get rid of the Keene girl, can't you? If any of these girls are trouble to us, it's her."

"But the most potential for profit. The buyer is anxious to get his hands on her." The other guy sounded a little anxious, a little defensive.

Now the smoker sounded worried, too. "I can't figure what's happened to delay Anatoly. He's usually the most reliable of our drivers."

"He's your cousin," the first man said. "You always cover for him, you and Manya both." He paused. "I'll walk up to the road.

See what I can see. If he's not there, we'll have to take the girls back to the farm."

"No." The cigarette end glowed before the smoker tossed it to the ground and stomped on it. "If he's not there, get your truck and bring it here. Something must've gone wrong. We've been at the farm too long already. It's too close with the FBI nosing around. We'll find somewhere else."

A snort. "Where?"

"You tell me. This is your territory."

The figures separated, one going toward the lake again, the other walking swiftly toward her.

With no time to retreat, Truth stepped to the side of the trail and slithered behind a towering fir, hoping its trunk would hide her. She pressed against the rough bark as the man drew abreast, grateful for her dark clothing and the knit hat jammed over her head and ears.

Truth closed her eyes, afraid the whites would show, afraid if she looked at him straight on he would sense her presence. She was afraid of many things, at the moment. Especially the one finally confirming what she'd suspected since this afternoon. Talk about setting a fox to help a hen!

Hunter Blaine, still in his Washington State Fish and Wildlife uniform, went past her without stopping. No shout of "Gotcha"; no bullet to the head.

Not that she breathed any easier. Heart hammering until she thought she'd be sick, Truth waited until he'd had time to reach the road before she moved, extricating herself from dew-damp weeds that clung like chains to her feet. A few minutes, then, that's all she had, when there'd be only one man to face.

Right. Only one man.

Now what? How could she stop them before they took Becca away, possibly to disappear forever?

Swallowing hard, Truth went on, walking as softly as she knew how. In a couple hundred more yards she'd reach the lakeshore. She hadn't the least idea what she was going to do when she got there.

~

PRATT JERKED his prisoner to his feet. He twisted the man's hands behind his back and clipped a plastic tie around thick wrists. "What's your name?" he asked roughly.

The man turned his face away. He didn't answer.

A quarter mile down the road, at the next house, a dog began barking. Men inside their target house shouted orders. A girl squealed. No words, just a squeal. One of the female deputies came outside, spoke to Ernhardt, and dashed back in.

Chaos. Not particularly organized. The usual at a bust of this kind.

Pratt eyed his prisoner and shrugged. "Doesn't matter who you are at this point. All you need to know is you're under arrest." Ortiz sped through the Miranda statement, loudly enough a couple uniformed cops could verify he'd followed procedure. No getting out on a technicality.

Sheriff's deputies herded a group of prisoners from the house. One prisoner wore what Pratt figured for an Armani suit, and a diamond the size of a bird egg on his finger. A potential buyer of human flesh, he supposed. The one who belonged to the sporty black Jaguar sitting at the side of the house. Pratt heard him asking for an attorney.

Two other men and a woman, sporting matching cuffs and scowls, stood in a separate group. Pratt gave his own prisoner a shove, indicating he join them. Sullenly, the man went.

"Sergei," the woman said to him. "I thought you got away." She spoke with a distinct accent.

The aforenamed Sergei shook his head and glared at Pratt. He grinned.

But then a quartet of girls under the protection of a female deputy, came through the door and his moment of relief passed.

"Is this everyone in the house?" Pratt asked the SWAT team member guarding the prisoners.

He nodded. "Yes, sir. This is everyone. We got them all."

Pratt sucked in a breath, feeling sick. "You're sure?"

The officer sent him a questioning look. "Yes, sir. We've been through the attic, every floor, the basement and the garage. You don't want to know about the basement." He paused, an eyebrow rose. "Or maybe you do. Anyway, this is it."

Pratt let loose with an expletive.

Ernhardt joined him in time to hear. "You don't look happy, Madden. I'd call this bust a success, if you were to ask me."

Pratt's teeth ground together. "As far as it goes."

"What do you mean?"

Unnoticed until he spoke, Joe Ortiz had joined them. "He means we're missing half the gang."

Pratt grunted. "And Becca Keene isn't one of these girls."

Gunderson, snaggle teeth showing a broad smile, took a break from ordering the SWAT force around in time to stick his nose into the discussion. "Told you the girl ran off."

Pratt turned on him, his face fierce. "She didn't run off."

"Don't get all het up." Gunderson stepped back. "I don't know why you're so certain she isn't a runaway. She isn't here, is she?"

"No, she's not." Pratt surveyed the line of prisoners, his gaze lighting on one. "Neither is Manya and Mark Kravtzov, nor Sorenko."

"Who?"

"You might know them better by other names," Ernhardt

said as Pratt stalked toward the prisoner who'd drawn his attention.

Gunderson's fingers snapped a question.

Ernhardt complied. "Mandi and Ken Hennings, and our fellow law enforcement officer, Hunter Blaine."

Gunderson's jaw dropped. "Huh?" His breath gusted stale coffee. "Well! I didn't see that one coming."

CHAPTER 30

TRUTH CREPT DOWN THE TRAIL BEHIND THE MAN SHE KNEW AS Ken Henning. Her always helpful friend, Ken Henning. A vision of him helping park Larry and Fran's trailer the morning this all started, at least for her, popped into her mind.

One curve remained before the path broke into a clearing where twenty years ago there'd been a dock. Picnickers had come here by boat then, before they started leaving too much trash strewn about and her dad put the place off limits. The unsafe diving area had raised the potential for lawsuits, as well. Not worth the risk.

"We'll corral everybody at the Golden West and keep their mess in one place," he'd said. "It's easier when you can keep your eye on troublemakers."

Truth held the same reasoning today. She guessed it worked. Sort of.

Anyway, she was surprised anyone still knew about Sun Rise Landing where people could step right off a boat onto shore. The last time the road had been used—until now—was more than a year ago when she'd allowed a logging company to thin out some of the too-thick timber.

But Hunter had been around then, and he'd been friendly with the loggers.

Her gorge rose, rage burned bright. How long had this been going on, anyway, using her resort as a waystation for human trafficking?

Placing her feet with care to prevent any noise, she rounded the curve and stopped. Ahead of her, the clearing lay open beneath an ink-dark sky. An all too familiar boat bobbed just offshore, secured by a line tethered to a downed tree leaning out over the water. A battery-powered camp lantern sat on one of the seats.

Two girls were perched on the shoreward part of the tree, the roots of which were still anchored in the ground.

Truth squinted, wishing for better night vision. Something about their position struck her as weird. Were they really sitting back-to-back, knees practically bumping up against their chins?

Another couple steps forward allowed her eyes to focus. Yes, they were indeed back-to-back, arms bound together and stiff at their sides, unable to move. One of the girls was crying and trying to wipe her nose on her shoulder. From the way her head bobbed, she couldn't quite reach.

A third girl sat in the boat.

Becca! Although the girl was at the farthest end of the boat from shore, Truth would know her employee's profile anywhere. Much like the other girls, her arms were stiff at her sides. Her shoulders slumped. A band of white showed where her mouth should be.

So, it must've been Becca's screams she'd heard, and these dirty—she couldn't think of a word bad enough to describe the men she'd thought of as friends—had taped her mouth shut to keep her quiet.

It was Ken, she remembered, who'd said they should get rid of the girl. And it was Ken climbing into the boat right now.

Cold sweat oozed down Truth's sides. Her heart galloped.

She had to do something. Immediately, before Hunter returned with his truck. She had no idea where he'd parked it. Out of sight somewhere, because it hadn't been visible from the road. So she had no time to wait for the police. For Pratt.

No time.

She fumbled for her pistol. Could she bring herself to shoot Ken, a man familiar to and once trusted by her? What if she missed? Becca was so close to him in the boat, even a couple inches off could spell disaster. The uncertain light—

Yeah. Uncertain light, uncertain Truth.

The weight of the multi-purpose tool in her pocket served as a reminder. Deciding against the Ruger, she switched to the multi-tool, opened the knife blade and stepped from the trees.

The girl facing her, the one with the drippy nose, saw her first.

"Mmmm," the girl cried, sort of bouncing on the log and jarring the other girl into "mmmming" too.

Truth put her finger to her lips. What on earth was this stupid girl trying to do? Tip Ken off that he had a visitor? Thank goodness the bad guys had the foresight to stick a gag in these girls' mouths as well as in Becca's.

Ken didn't even turn his head toward them. "Shut up," he commanded in a muted roar.

The girls obeyed. Well-trained, and right now, for their own sakes, that was a good thing.

"Now, then," he said to Becca. "What am I going to do with you? Grigory—that's Hunter, to you—says you're worth a lot of money to us. I say you're too dangerous to keep around."

"Mmmm mmmmm!" Becca said, straightening her shoulders and raising her head.

"And, I may point out, I'm here and Grigory isn't. Looks like I'm the one who decides." He sounded amused. "And I'm right on the verge of deciding you're not worth the risk, even if the deal is for twenty-five thousand. Bet you never thought anyone would be willing to pay that much money for you, right?"

Truth took another step, and another until she was committed to forward momentum. No chance to dodge and hide even if Ken turned around. She knew when Becca noticed her because the girl's face pointed right at her. But now a little noise served a purpose. And Becca performed great, her "mmmmms" rising to a screaming pitch even as Ken continued his awful chatter.

"How do you want it, Becca, huh? A nice bullet in the head? Or maybe the separation of one of your appendages from your body? That's a bit messy, as you might be aware. Kind of a slow way to go, with too much evidence left in my boat." He smirked. "The boat some crook stole during the night. I'll be sure to report its theft to our friend Ortiz in the morning. So how does a sink or swim sort of affair sound to you? Slower, but much cleaner, I'm here to tell you. It's pretty hard to swim with a fifty-pound chunk of concrete tied to your feet." He laughed.

"Mmmm, mm mmmmmm!" Becca forced quite a lot volume through the gag. And, bless her, she kept it up as Truth crept closer.

Ken's hands were busy as he crouched on the bottom of the boat. As Truth got to within ten feet, she realized he was threading some stiff rope through the openings of several concrete blocks and attaching them to Becca's legs. More blocks from her own store in the barn, she felt sure.

She believed his attention was completely involved with his task, but as she reached the edge of the bank, he looked up at her and grinned.

"Well, well, imagine meeting you here, Truth Diamond. Just the lady I wanted to see. We tried earlier, but Grigory said he couldn't get into your building. But here you are now, right on time."

He reached for her, meaning to grab a leg and drag her into the boat. Which is when Becca, with a gigantic effort, lunged forward. The boat rocked, throwing her down on top of Ken. Knocked off balance, he toppled sideways, between the seats.

Truth jumped for the boat. With the added height of being on shore, she had impetus on her side, as well as the multi-tool in her hand. The blade—too bad it was a mere two and a half-inches long—pierced his cheek. In an instant she'd pulled it out and stabbed for his eye, slicing off a part of his nose as she missed.

His outraged howl rocked the trees around them, echoing off the lake. A bird flapped its wings as it rose into the sky.

And then she was pounding at him with the steel shaft, again and again, her rage lending strength, lending quickness.

Ken sank beneath her blows. Becca kicked loose from the rope and added what force she could muster. She kept on kicking even after he quit moving. Dark blood flowed from his face, his head.

Success! Truth finally paused for breath. Euphoria flooded through her. Until Becca suddenly froze, and the business end of a gun poked into Truth's back.

"You're a dead woman, Truth Diamond," Mandi Henning snarled.

~

PRATT APPROACHED the youngest of the men in the group of prisoners and pointed at him. Not much more than a kid—maybe in his late teens—he looked Hispanic, and stood a little apart, not one of the Eastern European bunch. He also looked scared.

Some people might have chosen the woman to question, but Pratt figured her for the toughest nut on the tree. She watched everyone, saying nothing until he drew the Hispanic kid some distance away from the others.

"Lawyer." Her voice rose in an obvious warning to the others. "No talking without our lawyer present. Caesar, you hear me?"

Pratt kept his grip on the man's arm. "Wouldn't dream of asking this fine gentleman to incriminate himself," he told her, smiling blandly.

So, she was the boss of the outfit. By good fortune, Ernhardt caught the small by-play. Even as Pratt situated Caesar, so the woman couldn't overhear what they said, his own boss hustled her over to a sheriff's department cruiser.

Pratt folded his arms, the stance aggressive, and gave the kid the evil eye, which, if he said so himself, had proved satisfactorily intimidating in previous cases. "Your name is Caesar. Caesar what?"

The kid's gaze drifted toward the woman. Silence.

"Are you an illegal?" Pratt's left eyebrow lifted. "That why you won't tell me?"

"Nah." The question irked an answer from the kid. "Born here, dude, same as you."

Aha. Progress. Pratt felt a surge of optimism. Get'em talking and one word leads to another. Just hope he's got something real to say.

"You know Marko Kravtzov? Or Grigory Sorenko?"

The kid stared at him, black eyes dull.

"No? Funny. I'm betting you do. Maybe you know them by other names. How about Ken Henning or Hunter Blaine?"

A flicker in the kid's eyes indicated recognition.

Pratt threw another name at him. "Mandi Henning, I'll bet you know her, too."

The kid shook his head in denial, but Pratt saw a telltale tic jump in his cheek.

"So, you do know her. Where are they, Ken and Hunter and Mandi? Why aren't they here tonight?"

Caesar's gaze drifted toward the woman. She was seated in the cruiser now, Ernhardt standing in front of her, blocking her view and holding her attention.

"I guarantee that one's got her own problems," Pratt said. "Big time. She's got more to worry about than you answering a few questions. The FBI will get the truth out of her."

FBI? Caesar's mouth formed the letters.

"Yeah. We're federal, bud, not the local cops making some massage parlor bust. The charge here is human trafficking. And human trafficking, Caesar, is a serious crime. A federal crime when it involves kidnapped girls and girls from foreign countries. Breaks just about every law you can think of. We crack down hard on offenders like you." Sincerity oozed from Pratt's quiet voice. "We'd prefer to get the people in charge. Get them, we go easier on the little people."

Pratt allowed a few seconds for the words to sink in. "You are one of the 'little people,' aren't you?"

Caesar nodded eager agreement.

"But you know things, right? Things that might make us go easier on a man who helps catch the real bad guys?"

Sweat started on Caesar's forehead.

Fear sweat, Pratt figured, because the night had cooled at

least twenty degrees from the day. He, himself, wasn't hot. He was cold. Stone cold.

Noise from the operation finally dropped to a dull roar. In the background, he heard the female deputy asking Gunderson to call for a Ukrainian interpreter. The girls apparently didn't speak English, or not enough to tell their stories. Crime scene investigators were swarming into the house. The chaos was controlled now, indicating a successful bust and a scene finally under control.

He concentrated on the kid. "Where are the Hennings and Hunter Blaine? Where are they right now, because I don't have a whole lot more patience in me. Speak up and I'll put a word in for you."

Caesar's eyelids flicked from side-to-side. "I don't know, man. Not an address or nothing. But Raisa said something earlier about three more girls—maybe even four—coming in tonight. She was laughing. She said one was ordered up special and Hunter knew just the one, even if she was a . . . uh . . . dangerous commodity. He said there might even be a two-fer-one there."

Becca. And Truth. Were they talking about Truth? Pratt's stomach knotted. He wanted to shake the kid. "Where, man, where?"

"From that place." Caesar shrugged. "Where they been holding the other ones. Raisa laughed, I tell you. She said . . . she said right under the cops' noses."

Done with him, Pratt gave the kid a shove toward the other prisoners and hurried toward Ernhardt.

"Leave her," he said. "I got what we need."

Ernhardt straightened. "Yeah?" He didn't miss the woman's narrowed glare toward Caesar.

"We need a couple men for back-up." Pratt was already taking long strides back toward the road where they'd left the vehicles. "Get Ortiz," he yelled, leaving cross jurisdiction niceties to Ernhardt.

"Where are we going?" Ernhardt called.

"The Golden West."

But Pratt wasn't waiting.

CHAPTER 31

TRUTH FLINCHED AT THE VENOM OOZING FROM MANDI'S VOICE as much as the pistol jabbing painfully into her backbone.

"You two deserve an Academy Award, you know that?" Truth said. "You and Ken. And Hunter, too. Always so helpful and caring. You fooled everyone. Took them all in."

"Of course. Easy as pie. People are such dopes."

"I think you mean dupes," she said.

"Shut up."

In response to another prod of Mandi's gun, she slowly turned to face her friend . . . former friend . . . never her friend. Always an enemy, even when unknown. Bile rose in her throat.

"Step back," Mandi snapped, poking at her again.

Careful where she placed her feet, Truth avoided Ken who was writhing like a snake in the bottom of the boat, moaning and cursing. Becca used what little slack she had in her bindings to scoot out of the way of his flailing legs.

Mandi stared down at her husband—or whatever he was to her—with something approaching horror on her face.

Her attack hadn't done his looks any good, Truth had to

admit. From where she stood, she could see his nose already swollen into a shapeless blob, and blood pouring from the gashes the multi-tool had opened on his head. His right temple showed an ominous dent. One of his eyes, the one with a violently broken vessel turning the sclera an unbecoming red, had a funny cast. Concussion, maybe. She hoped so.

"Ken . . . Ken." Mandi's horrified gaze switched back to her. "What have you done?"

"Prevented another murder," Truth said, her voice shaking only a little.

"Drop the knife."

Stubbornly, Truth retained her grip. Adrenaline still coursed through her body. She felt strong enough for anything. Strong enough to take on a woman with a gun.

"Why should I?" she demanded. "You already said I'm a dead woman. What makes you think I'll make it easy for you?"

"Oh, you want to watch this one die first?" Mandi shifted the pistol's aim to point at Becca. "Okay with me. But it'll be your fault."

"Mmmm." Becca strained to speak through the gag. Tears glistened on her cheeks.

"No!" Truth cried. "Wait. Look. I'm putting it down." What choice did she have? She couldn't take the chance of Mandi shooting Becca. Flicking her eyes at the girl, she started to place the tool on the motor cowling, where she might have a chance to get at it later. Or maybe Becca—

"Not there," Mandi snapped. "Drop it in the water."

Truth hesitated, unwilling.

"Do it!"

Seething, Truth took a half-step sideways, trying to nerve herself to use the same tactic on Mandi that she had on Ken. Her muscles tensed, ready to spring. Was she fast enough?

Mandi, probably reading the intention on her face, inched

backward, until she reached the gunwale. She gripped the side and made an impatient motion with the gun.

The muted roar of a truck motor blasting down the road above reached them both at the same time.

"Grigory," Mandi said, as though relieved.

"Not Hunter. Pratt." Truth contradicted the other woman. "The FBI is on its way." In her dreams. But surely only Pratt's old pick-up had that distinctive, deep-throated V-8 rumble.

"No." Mandi's denial lacked force. She'd heard Pratt's truck often enough to recognize the sound, too. "Marko?" she said, urgency in her tone. For a moment, Truth didn't know who she meant.

Oh, right. Ken.

"Marko." Mandi spoke louder. She reached down and shook his shoulder. "Pull yourself together. We've got to get out of here. Can you run the boat?"

A groan answered.

Mandi eased around Truth and knelt beside her husband. She lightly touched the dent in his temple with a finger and caught her breath.

Hope leapt into Truth's heart. Now. Starting forward, she checked all movement as the gun in Mandi's hand came back to her.

"Marko. Get up. I need you." Mandi gripped his arm and gave it a shake. Groggy with pain, he tried, responding enough to pull himself into a sitting position against the side of the boat. Even so, he immediately sagged again. His eyes closed.

It was just enough distraction to allow Truth to push the multi-tool under Becca's leg with her foot.

Becca's eyes rolled toward her. Acknowledgement.

Up on the road, a second vehicle joined the first. A door slammed. A few seconds passed, then a gunshot cracked, splitting the quiet night with a sharp pop, followed by another and another.

Whose gun? Whose?

Mandi lurched to her feet. The bore of her pistol centered on Truth again. "Start the engine, Truth. You're going to drive this boat."

Truth squared her shoulders and lifted her chin. "Do it yourself." Mandi never drove the boat when she and Ken took it out, she remembered. Chances were, she didn't know how.

Mandi sighed. "Are you really going to force me to shoot Becca first? I will, you know. I've got nothing to lose."

Before Truth could move or speak, comply or not comply, the other woman shifted aim and pulled the trigger.

Becca, behind the gag, cried out in a low, sustained shriek. The two girls on shore, nearly forgotten in the drama of the moment, also made a noise. Mandi ignored them all.

Truth, for a moment, stood paralyzed, eyes stretched wide with shock. Finally, as Becca neither squirted blood nor toppled over, she realized Mandi had missed—and not by accident.

"A teaching moment," Mandi said.

Lesson learned, Truth moved where Mandi directed. Her insides quivered so much her legs barely supported her as she sagged onto the seat behind the steering wheel.

"That's better," Mandi said in satisfaction. "Now get this boat started. Hurry up."

Fingers hovering over the keys still dangling from the ignition, it crossed Truth's mind to fudge a bit, to delay, and trust help would soon arrive. But whose gunfire had won the battle up on the road, Pratt's or Hunter/Grigori's? She couldn't take the chance. If the Fish and Wildlife officer—

No. No. Pratt had to have won. *Had to.*

The roar of the engine as it took hold drowned out her pained gasp.

~

On the road above the cut-off, Pratt holstered his automatic, hearing yet the echo of female screams, muffled in the distance.

That gunshot—why a gunshot? A signal?

Or was somebody else dead? Maybe not, because he heard the boat retreating down the lake, slowly at first, then accelerating.

"Sounds like your partner is taking off without you." Still surprised at how easy it'd been to subdue Hunter Blaine, he jerked the Russian to his feet and yanked his arms backward, binding his wrists with a plastic tie.

Blaine yowled like a cat in heat. Blood dripped from the gash in his upper arm, marking the path of Pratt's well-aimed bullet.

"Who's driving the boat, Blaine?"

Blaine replied with a smattering of Russian, which Pratt understood perfectly well. Huh, was that the best insult Blaine could come up with?

"Shut up." Pratt frisked Blaine, removing a small folding knife, a hunting knife and a pocket pistol he found affixed to Blaine's ankle. Grabbing his prisoner by the shirt collar, Pratt marched him over to the State rig and used another tie to attach the makeshift manacles to the SUV's door handle. "I expect it's our friends Ken and Mandi. Have they got Becca with them?"

A wild gyration as Blaine struggled against his bonds hinted at the answer.

"Where are they taking her?"

Blaine glared. "I want a doctor."

"For that little cut?" Pratt's snicker held a wealth of scorn. "Who was it chopped off that girl's hand? You? Funny how blood strikes you as different when it's your own."

"I want a doctor!" Blaine yelled.

Not an answer, Pratt reflected. "You ever hear that old saying about people in hell and ice water?" He laughed, forcing back the urge to beat Blaine's handsome face to a pulp. To tear open the wound in his arm until blood sprayed wide with every pump of his heart. Just like he or Ken or one of those other louts they'd caught tonight had done to Yudif Maruseva.

And what about Truth?

The smooth rumble of the boat's four-stroke motor faded in the distance. The sound is deceptive on the water, but Pratt judged the heading as toward the resort.

Fast, too. It wouldn't take whoever was driving long to reach the Golden West. Truth was bound to hear the engine. What would she do? Stay inside and be safe or go out and try to protect her property.

Pratt hated the guess he took about that.

Abandoning Blaine as soon as he was secured, Pratt sped to his pickup, finding the satellite phone he'd been issued for the bust tonight tossed on the passenger seat. He keyed up Ernhardt even as he was turning his rig around.

"Go," Ernhardt answered.

"I've got Blaine." He told Ernhardt where. "I'm leaving him here for the deputies. A boat took off from the landing as I drove up. I heard a gunshot before the boat headed for the resort. I'll try to catch the rest of them there."

"Be careful," Ernhardt said. "Our ETA is twenty."

"Make it fifteen." Pratt heard Ernhardt issuing new orders even as he flung the phone aside and put the pedal down.

THE THRUST as she goosed the boat's throttle pressed Truth against the seat cushion. A stab in the small of her back was a sharp reminder of the little Ruger LCR stuck in her jeans back pocket. She'd almost forgotten about the pistol, and Mandi, praise be, hadn't thought to search her.

No doubt Mandi was accustomed to a more docile type of girl than Truth and hadn't realized the need.

She took comfort in that—but not too much. Not with Mandi standing behind her, hanging onto the seat back with a one-handed death grip and rocking to the motion of the boat. Her other hand alternated waving her gun between Truth and Becca.

"Watch where you're going," Mandi snapped as Truth glanced up at her. She gave Truth's shoulder bone a sharp smack with the gun barrel.

"Ouch!" The boat swerved, throwing Mandi to the side as Truth's whole arm went numb. Mandi glared, striking at Truth a second time and only missing because she was off balance. The lantern, which had been sitting on the passenger seat, turned over, it's beam pointing toward Ken. He, too, was a victim of the swerve, and lay on his side, moaning. He still hadn't extricated himself from between the seats, and Mandi had done little to help him.

Becca, Truth was glad to see, had braced her legs against one of the rear seat stands and seemed safe for the moment. The girl stared back at her, eyes wide and terrified. Truth's multi-tool had disappeared.

"Stop that," Mandi screamed as Truth yanked the wheel to bring them back on course.

"Then stop hitting me," Truth retorted. A modicum of hope lifted her spirits. Mandi had the gun, but Truth had the boat.

She always knew the other woman eschewed anything to do with Ken's boat except for riding shotgun. But she hadn't known Mandi was downright afraid of the vessel. Unless it was the lake she feared. Thinking back, she'd never seen the woman swimming, either. Maybe she'd heard the legend of Lost Girl Lake. And that might give Truth an edge.

If only she got a chance to use it.

"How about," she said to Mandi over her shoulder, "you tell me about the dead girl."

"You don't need to know." Mandi's voice dripped ice water.

"C'mon. For old times' sake? What did she do? How did her hand get burned? Or lost? Because I'm sure you didn't mean for it to show up at the campsite."

"You're right; we didn't." Mandi chuckled with what struck Truth as a totally evil sound. "What a farce. Funny as hell. Okay. I'll tell you."

Funny? She said funny?

"Yudif was a troublemaker. Agitating the other girls, always trying to escape. Then one night she nearly succeeded. She'd gotten the other girls almost all the way to the Golden West when Ken and I finally caught up with her and those two Hunter is taking to . . . well, you don't need to hear that part.

"Anyway, we got them all into the old barn and had the first two tied up and gagged, but while Ken was tying Yudif's hands, she managed to kick him in the you know whats."

Truth turned and looked at her. Mandi was smiling, staring ahead into the dark night.

"As you can imagine, Ken was fed up by this time. He was so mad he lopped off her hand, made a fire right there in the center of the barn and burned it. Then he hung it up over the other two girls' heads. You should've seen their faces! Believe me, after that we had no more trouble with them. All any of us had to do was look at them. Especially after we had to get rid of Yudif."

Oh, yeah, Truth's imagination worked on the scenario, all right.

"How did the hand get to the campsite?" she ventured finally.

"No idea. I expect Dottie had it right and a coyote got hold of it. Hunter was supposed to have buried it when it started stinking, but he's always been a little squeamish. Probably didn't dig a deep enough hole." Mandi went silent then, until, as they cut through the dark water of Lost Girl Lake toward the resort, Truth cranked the wheel again.

Mandi swayed, almost losing her feet. "I told you to watch it," she cried through clenched teeth. "Or I'll shoot you right this minute. I swear I will. Or maybe I'll cut off *your* hand. Give you first hand—hah, hah—knowledge."

"Sorry," Truth lied, surprised by how calm she sounded. "Hit some chop."

Mandi's hand clutched her hair. Yanked hard. "Sorry, smorry. I know when you do something deliberate. But you'll think sorry when you're sold to a certain Saudi who has a taste for blondes. He's our very best customer."

Truth squeaked as Mandi's hand tightened in her hair.

"*Best customer*," Mandi repeated, her voice low and vicious, "because he goes through blonde's like you at the rate of six a year. Got that? If you please him, maybe you'll last a whole two months."

"Not gonna happen," she said, jerking her head away and leaving a few strands of hair in Mandi's fist. Still, quite unintentionally, the boat skewed sideways again as she lost control. The swerve sent Ken sliding. A quick glance over her shoulder showed him now lying curled in a fetal position wrapped around one of the seats.

"Hadn't you better take a look at your husband? He doesn't seem to feel well." *And she wasn't one bit sorry.*

"Because of you." Mandi bit her lip. "There's nothing I can do for him now. But you're going to pay, lady, I can tell you that."

There went her plan to distract Mandi long enough to sneak her own gun from its hiding place. Another hope crushed as Mandi faced front and watched every move Truth made. The only good thing was an opportunity for Becca, with Mandi's attention elsewhere, to work at freeing herself.

Maybe. If the multi-tool hadn't slid away and the girl had managed to grasp hold of it.

All too soon they neared the opening into the Golden West's bay. Truth cut back the engine. The boat idled through the dark water, dead slow and almost soundless, as she steered for the dock and Ken's regular slip. Headlights gleamed up on the road coming into the resort. A brief flash quickly extinguished.

Hunter or Pratt? Please, please, let it be Pratt.

Mandi didn't seem to notice the lights, or if she did, assumed it was Hunter, catching up with them.

Grigory, rather. Ken had said Hunter's real name was Grigory.

Assume it's him, just in case.

In what was not the smoothest docking of Truth's experience, they bumped into the slip, scraping paint. She killed the engine and grabbed onto a dock cleat, pulling the boat in close.

"You should put out bumpers," she told Mandi.

Mandi ignored the advice. "Tie the boat. Now. And hurry."

Furious, heartsick, Truth took the line, moving as slowly as she dared. "You won't get away, you know. Pratt will be here soon."

"Shut up." Mandi moved to the back of the boat, where her

husband lay in a heap. She used her gun to prod Truth in the ribs. "Come here. I need your help with Ken."

She seemed to have given up on calling him Marko. Truth wondered if the life they'd been living confused her, too. Wincing, she obeyed the other woman, sparing a quick glance at Becca as she knelt beside Ken. Her breath caught as Becca dipped her head in a nod. At least she hoped it was a nod. She lived on hope. Hope that the slack in the ropes securing Becca's bound arms to her legs meant they were no longer fully attached. That a sudden sharp move would make all the ropes fall away. Most of all, she hoped Mandi wouldn't notice too soon.

Mandi on one side of Ken, Truth on the other, the two women hoisted him semi-upright.

"Get on the dock," Mandi said. "You pull, I'll push. And don't you dare drop him. If he falls, I'll kill you. Customer waiting or not." Her pretty face, in days past so calm and friendly, glowered like an evil gargoyle in the weak lantern light.

It wouldn't, Truth believed, look any better in the daytime than right now. How could she have been so fooled by her? By all the people involved?

Releasing Ken, in the awkwardness of refusing to turn her back on Mandi, she crawled from of the boat onto the dock, scraping a knee and feeling the blood start. She reached for Ken's wrists, holding him steady and breathing hard with the effort as the other woman got behind him to push.

When they were all on the dock. That's when she'd make her move. She'd hustle to Ken's right and while Mandi was busy helping her husband—

All plans flew from her head as Mandi, with a casual gesture sure to give Truth nightmares for the rest of her life, gave Becca a shove in passing.

Struck hard, Becca tumbled head over heels off the end of the boat. Water gysered as she went under.

"Becca!" Truth, bearing all Ken's weight, let go his wrists, intending to plunge into the lake after the girl.

"Nuh, uh," Mandi's eyes glittered. She didn't even bother to watch Becca fall. "Don't even think about it. I said I'd kill you and I will if Ken goes over." He lay half in the boat, half on the dock.

Tears streamed down Truth's cheeks although she was unaware of crying. She heard herself making an odd kind of wheezing noise.

"Grab him, I said!" Mandi shouted.

But Truth was beyond fear of the woman. She knew what Mandi had in store for her, too, the second Truth provided all the help she needed.

Definitely not going to happen. Not.

Truth held Mandi's eyes. She acted as if she were obeying, even as she reached behind her back and whipped the Ruger LCR out of hiding. In an action as smooth and fast as if she'd been practicing every day for a solid month, she fired into Mandi's chest. Once . . . twice . . . the double action worked with barely a kick.

Mandi screamed. Her pistol fell from her hand and into the water as she plummeted backward into the boat, twisting and choking. Blood gushed from her mouth.

Ignoring Ken, still hanging over the Lund's side and wriggling like a caught fish, Truth dropped her pistol on the dock, out of anyone's reach. She kicked off with a racing dive into the dark water.

"Becca," she called as she came up. "Becca?"

The girl swam like a champion. Even trussed like a chicken she might be able to float. *Might.* Where was she?

Not on the surface. She couldn't see the girl anywhere.

So she dove into water as dark and opaque as a black tar pit. She felt around with her arms spread, her feet reaching. Found the pilings, felt the slither of seaweed against her legs. Tried to think. Becca had gone off the end of the boat. Was she under it, trapped there?

Truth dove beneath the boat. *Blind.* She swam blind, a little lost. At first, she brushed away the clinging tendrils tickling under her chin, until she realized they were not more seaweed, but hair.

She grabbed. Pulled. Found up and stroked hard for air. Even pushed Becca out of the water first. Surfaced herself a fraction of a second later and ripped the tape from Becca's face, even if it did take skin along with it. Beside her, Becca gasped a harsh intake of precious air. She looked and saw the girl's eyes were open and aware.

And heard, finally . . . *finally* . . . Pratt yelling, footsteps running, and saw friendly hands reaching to grab first Becca, then her.

Triumph soared. No victims, this time. Not today, Lost Girl Lake.

CHAPTER 32

PRATT FISHED TRUTH OUT OF THE LAKE LIKE SHE WEIGHED NO more than one of the rainbow he'd spent the better part of the summer catching and releasing from this same dock. Only he didn't release her. Not right off anyway.

And, he admitted to himself, it felt good.

"You okay?" He ran his fingers through platinum hair stuck against her cheeks as though glued there. A string of slimy green algae mixed with the blonde. He pulled the algae away, lips curling in a smile.

"I think so." She sounded breathless, and no wonder. She pulled out of his arms and reached out to Becca, who lay on the dock gasping and coughing. Her arms were still bound, although her legs were free. The ability to kick had probably saved her life. "Becca?"

"Cut . . . me . . . loose. Please, Truth." The girl's voice rose in a thin scream. "Please."

"Let me." Pratt flicked open his pocket knife, so razor sharp it sliced through the ropes like they were made of thread.

"I thought I was going to die!" Freed, Becca threw herself into Truth's arms.

Patting the girl's back, Truth met Pratt's dark eyes. "I know the feeling," she said. "But you didn't."

Becca drew back. "Hunter . . . he took me. I thought he . . . but all he wanted was to *sell* me. Sell me," she repeated. "To somebody. For sex." She shuddered. "I thought he *liked* me."

"We all thought he was a good guy, honey," Truth soothed her. "None of us guessed he's rotten to the core."

Pratt cleared his throat. "Not quite everyone."

Up on the road, headlights flashed as a vehicle passed the turn-off into the resort and continued up the road to where Pratt had left Hunter manacled to his own Fish and Wildlife SUV. The following car pulled in. Leaving the headlights on and pointed toward the dock, two men, one in uniform, got out.

"FBI," Ernhardt called out. "Madden, you here?"

"I'm here," Pratt yelled back. "The situation is under control, but you'd better call an ambulance." He studied Becca a moment. "Make that two. And call Mrs. Keene. Tell her Becca is safe."

THE SKY over the eastern bluff turned a soft milky color as dawn neared. The three of them, wet from their drenching in Lost Girl Lake, had moved from the dock to Truth's patio while they waited for the ambulance. Pratt had carried Becca. Ernhardt joined them, while the deputy remained on the dock, keeping an eye on the Henning couple. Mandi clung to life, while Ken lay on his back staring vacantly up at the dark sky and occasionally twitching.

Truth had rummaged blankets for both she and Becca and

even bundled and semi dry, they both still shivered. Reaction, she supposed. She'd also brought Razz down and the Pomeranian, sensing her mistress's distress, sat on her lap, every once in a while, licking her hand or reaching up to her chin as Truth repeated everything Mandi had told her.

Ernhardt reached over and tucked the blanket around Becca's bare feet. "Can you tell us how Blaine managed your abduction, Becca? We've been a little puzzled over that. Your mother couldn't find anything out of place at your home."

Even in the poor light they saw the girl's flush. "After Hunter dropped me off, I went upstairs and painted my nails and watched a movie. Mom and Jason had already gone to bed." She stopped and swallowed. "Then I heard a pitter patter on my window, and when I looked out, Hunter was outside. He'd thrown some dirt clods at it. So, I went down."

"Becca," Ernhardt said gently, "did you go with him of your own free will?"

Becca shook her head. "No, sir. I sure didn't. Yeah, I'd been flirting with him . . ." A defiant look crossed her face. ". . . and he'd been flirting with me, but . . . I don't know. When I got downstairs, he seemed funny, nervous, and not at all like usual. He acted like I was some stranger, not me, Becca. Sort of looking through me instead of at me, if you know what I mean."

Truth did. She'd experienced the same feeling from him a time or two herself, as if Hunter's interaction was by rote.

"What did he do then?" Ernhardt asked.

"I—" One of Becca's hands emerged from the blanket cocoon and touched her neck. She blinked. Her eyes opened wide. "Did he do a Vulcan nerve pinch on me?"

Ernhardt's gaze swiveled to Pratt whose lips twitched.

"Pressure on the carotid artery," Truth translated. Well

acquainted with the Keene kids, she knew they were fans of all things Star Trek.

"Oh." Ernhardt coughed. "I guess you'll have to tell us whether he did or not."

Becca flounced, an action Truth welcomed as a sign the girl was recovering her spirits.

"Well, he did," Becca said. "I don't know how long I was out. He drugged me, you see, it could've been days, for all I know. I woke up when he was taking me out of the car. I tried to fight him off, but he tied me up. He carried me down to the beach. That's when I saw—" She stopped, her eyes rounding. "Oh, no. She . . . he—"

"You saw Mrs. Thompson killed, didn't you?" Ernhardt made the question cool.

Becca bent over her knees, tears streaming yet again. "Yes. Ken and Mandi together. But mostly Mandi . . . blood splashed all over her . . . in her hair."

The girl reached out for Truth, gripping her hand so hard Truth's fingers went numb.

Not strawberry jam. No, Truth figured, but probably the reason they were gone when she got down to the beach and found the old lady. Mandi wouldn't have wanted to have anyone spy bloodstains on her. And then she'd missed that one clump in her hair.

"Mrs. Thompson was sitting outside her motorhome and saw Hunter and me," Becca went on after a moment. "So, she followed us, asking what did Hunter think he was doing. Ken knocked her down, but Mandi hit her in the head with a rock. Hard. So hard."

Becca wiped her eyes without noticeably stemming the flow before continuing. "Anyway, I wiggled my bracelet off my hand and dropped it on the path when they took me to the boat. I was hoping somebody would find it and guess Hunter and the others had kidnapped me. But he noticed the bracelet was gone and he slapped me when I said I didn't know where I'd lost it." She touched her cheekbone where a purple bruise bloomed on her fair skin. "Ken wanted to kill me right then and there. Mandi said no, that I was too valuable. And Hunter agreed. But he was really mad."

Truth didn't think Becca knew how close she'd been to death at Sun Rise Landing, her body sunk to the bottom of Lost Girl Lake. If she, herself, hadn't shown up at just that time—

"I found your bracelet," she said, "when I got clearance to clean up the beach. I palmed it when Hunter appeared. At first, he didn't notice me. He was concentrating so hard looking for something in the bushes around the path, and I . . . I don't know. When he did spot me, something about the way he acted struck me as odd. So, I didn't tell him about it."

Pratt eyed her. "You should've told me."

"I wanted to. Believe me, I wanted to in the worst way, but you weren't around. I waited and waited for you to get back to the resort. That's one reason I heard Hunter trying to break into my house. How was I to know you were making a bust?"

Blaring lights and a screaming siren announced the ambulance's arrival at that point, although Becca denied she needed to go to the hospital, bruises notwithstanding. She told them she just wanted to go home and see her mother.

Truth smiled a little. Sandy was apt to be shocked by the news. And pleased, too.

"I'll bet those other poor girls would like to see their mothers." She ran her fingers through her hair, trying to raise spikes, without much success.

"Yes." Becca started crying again. "They don't even know how to speak English. They were so scared the whole time we were tied up in that cave. And everyone, Mandi and Ken and

Hunter were so cruel to them. Even worse than they were to me. It was awful."

"What other girls?" Pratt jerked erect, his question beating Ernhardt's by a nano-second.

"The girls tied to the log at Sun Rise Landing." Truth frowned. "Didn't you find them? Hunter didn't have a chance to do anything awful to them, did he?"

Pratt jumped from his chair so fast Razz barked. "I'll radio Ortiz."

CLUNKING his tackle box into the bed of his GMC, Pratt glanced down at the woman standing beside him.

"So," Truth said, digging a little hole in the parking lot's gravel with the toe of her sandal, "you're leaving."

"I am. I expect you're glad to see the last of me." Oddly enough, the last part of that came out of his mouth sounding like a question. "Now the case is cleared up and the bad guys in jail," he hastened to add.

Sunshine made a halo of her platinum hair as she tilted her face up to him at his remark. "Not necessarily," she said. "Although I'm glad my resort is safe." She looked down again.

Not necessarily? What did she mean by that?

He'd been in town the last couple days, clearing the details of his undercover trafficking investigation. Turned out Ernhardt had taken a post in D.C. and Pratt, if he wanted it, was in line for Ernhardt's old job as the supervisory senior resident agent in the Spokane area. He was still trying to decide if he wanted to take it on.

One thing for certain, he was finished here. The only thing left to do at the Golden West was to clear his things from his granddad's fifth-wheel.

A few minutes ago, on the verge of stepping into his pickup, Truth, Razz at her heels, had emerged from the campground shower room and this meeting became unavoidable. He didn't want this to be a final goodbye; she probably couldn't wait to see him drive away.

Who was it had told him she and Hunter Blaine had something going? He couldn't remember, but she must be feeling pretty let down.

To his surprise, she seemed to feel as awkward as he did. Truth refused to meet his eyes, keeping her gaze fixed on the ground.

He hardly knew what to say to her. Now he was leaving. That he'd be back? But only if she agreed. After what had happened here, she might never want to see him again, a reminder of this summer's . . . he guessed he couldn't call the operation an adventure. Not where Truth could hear him. Try successful mission.

At least Digbee, considering the Golden West home to his favorite fishing hole, wasn't going anywhere. His granddad provided a link to her.

He leaned against his rig, inadvertently rubbing a clean spot in the dusty fender. "They planned to take you, too, Truth. Blaine is telling us the only reason they didn't is because Digbee or Sam or somebody was always with you and because you have locks on your building he didn't have the time or equipment to break through."

Her hair gleamed almost white in the sunlight, perky with spikes. In contrast, her expression was subdued, tired. "I guess being armed didn't hurt anything, either." She hesitated. "Is Mandi going to live?"

"Manya . . ." he deliberately used the woman's Russian name, ". . . will be fine by the time her trial starts."

"Good. I'm glad I didn't kill anyone. Even Ken." She still

wasn't looking at him, too busy surveying the almost deserted parking lot. Razz was off to the side, checking out an empty campsite, of which there were several. Too many.

His expression hardened. "Mandi and Ken both deserved their wounds. Look at it this way; you helped shut down a major trafficking ring and rescue several scared girls who are a long way from home. The girls are very grateful, by the way. They asked me to give you their thanks."

"Sweet. Tell them they're welcome." She sighed and at last raised her gaze, meeting his eyes.

Gulls soared overhead. Lost Girl Lake lapped at the shoreline. The farthest dock, the one he'd so often claimed as his territory, rocked gently on the sparkling water. It all smelled delightful—and so did the woman standing next to him.

He found himself disinclined to step into the pickup and leave. The Golden West had begun to feel like home.

"Anyway, I'm happy to have helped." She sounded like maybe she was trying to cheer herself up. "I can't imagine how frightened they were. And probably still are. By the way, did you ever find out who Bill Billous represents . . . represented? Is he involved in this, too?"

Pratt dredged up a chuckle. "Yes and no. Yes, the offer to buy the resort came from the trafficking consortium, but no, he isn't part of the ring. He's just an unscrupulous shyster out to make all the money he can. I'm afraid greed isn't against the law."

"Yeah, money. Tell me about it. This affair has been terrible for business. Look at all the empty spaces." Truth made a wide gesture, but even as she spoke, a mammoth Ford F-350 hauling an equally large fifth-wheel turned into the parking lot and stopped. Her expression brightened.

"Hope he isn't lost," she muttered as Razz, tongue curled, ran to join her.

The pickup's two front doors opened, disgorging a man, a woman, and, a minute later, two small boys. The woman reached into the cab again and deposited a sparkling white and black and brown Pomeranian onto the ground at her feet.

"Looks promising," Pratt murmured close to Truth's ear.

Razz stiffened. Her little ears pricked.

The woman stretched her arms over her head and inhaled a deep breath. "Ummm. Gosh, Ben," she said to her husband, "have you ever smelled anything any better than these trees and the lake? I'm sure I smell roses, too! What a peaceful little place, rustic and fun. Perfect for Parker and Mikey and Little Doggie. They'll love it here." She waved cheerily at Truth from across the way.

The kids, spotting the playground, were off and running, gleeful shouts echoing across the park. The particolored Pom followed, barking. Razz made a low sound in her throat and took a couple steps toward them.

"Razz, stay," Truth warned her pooch. "Don't you start a fight and frighten off any customers. We need everyone we can get. You'll just have to share the territory."

Pratt chuckled. "Think it'll take more than Razz to scare this family off." As he'd been stuffing dirty clothes in his duffle bag, Digbee had mentioned she'd been dragging around these last two days like a lost soul, but she sounded perkier now, more like herself.

She whirled to face him, mouth set in a firm line. "You're not scared off, are you?"

He blinked, taken off guard. Was she issuing a challenge? Or was it an invitation, in a typically Truth sort of way?

Pratt smiled. Challenge or invitation, he was ready for it.

"I don't scare easily," he said.

ALSO BY C.K. CRIGGER

China Bohannon Series

One Foot On The Edge

Three Seconds To Thunder

Three Feet Below

ABOUT THE AUTHOR

C.K. Crigger was born and raised in North Idaho on the Coeur d'Alene Indian Reservation, and currently lives with her three feisty little dogs and an uppity Persian cat in Spokane Valley, Washington.

Imbued with an abiding love of western traditions and wide-open spaces, Crigger writes of free-spirited people who break from their standard roles.

Her short story, Aldy Neal's Ghost, was a 2007 Spur finalist. Black Crossing, won the 2008 EPIC Award in the historical/western category. Letter of the Law was a 2009 Spur finalist in the audio category.